FAREWELL APATHY

JENN HYPE

Farewell Apathy

Copyright © 2016 by Living Hype, Ltd.

ISBN-13: 978-0-692-68944-8
ISBN-10: 0-692-68944-3

Learn more about the author and access
exclusive content only at www.jennhype.com

www.livinghype.com
support@livinghype.com

First Edition March 2016

Printed in the United States of America
10 9 8 7 6 5 4 3 2 1

To the most amazing person ever -
You know who you are...

CHAPTER
ONE

Without opening my eyes, I already know I'm somewhere unfamiliar. Something wide that feels a lot like leather is currently wrapped tightly around my ankles and wrists. Why does every inch of my body ache? Even my hair hurts. My fingers twitch from the instinct every human is born with; the one that makes you want to rub your injuries in an attempt to soothe the pain. Only my hands remain strapped down, which makes that instinct turn into agony.

One eye blinks open at a time, my lashes crusted together and my corneas drier than the Sahara. If the room weren't pitch black, I know my retinas would be running for their lives, because it takes zero time for my eyes adjust to the darkness. I've been in the dark a while, it seems.

Just how long have I been strapped down like this? It feels like someone took a razor blade to my tongue and then stuffed my mouth full of cotton. I can't even pool enough saliva to swallow, so it's no surprise that when I try to call out, the only sound I make is a hoarse whisper.

Anger, fear and confusion team up with each other and throw a tantrum. I knew it was futile when I started kicking and yanking at my restraints, but just laying here helpless seems just as foolish. Of course it doesn't take long for me to wear myself out, and in a matter of min-

utes my body goes back to being limp.

Dammit. All I've accomplished is to make myself feel even more weak and dehydrated. I can think of a hundred deaths that would be less painful than this.

The light scent of cologne wafts through my nostrils, and out of the corner of my eye I make out the shape of a shadow within the depths of the darkness swallowing the room. Whoever it is could be here to save me or finish me off. Whichever one it is; I hope they do it quickly. I'm about two seconds from freaking the hell out.

Without saying a word or giving me some kind of heads up, the lights flicker on. Jesus, did someone just turn on the freaking sun? My poor corneas are fighting to not turn to ash, begging my tear ducts for help, but I'm too dehydrated to find any relief. Even with my eyes clenched shut, I can't get away from the blinding spots, yet again being reminded that my hands are strapped down.

Why are they strapped down, again? Oh yeah, that's right, I still have no freaking clue.

The saying 'splitting headache' takes on a whole new meaning thanks to the axe that's wedged into the back of my skull. At least, I think there's an axe back there. It's the only way to explain why my head feels like it's being cracked into two halves like a coconut. Slowly, so very, very slowly, I finally start peeling one eye open at a time. He's blurry, but I can tell he's a man, and he's standing right next to me. The only detail of his face I can make out is his mouth, which is formed into a placid smile.

Is he trying to be calm and reassuring, or is the jerk enjoying seeing me suffer? Either way, he looks creepy as hell.

He stands stock still while my eyes continue adjusting, and remains unmoving while I take in every detail I can about him. If I make it out of here alive, he's either getting a gift basket for saving me, or a personal sketch of his face when I book my ass to the police station and report him for cruel and unusual craziness.

He is actually pretty good looking, with blonde-ish hair that's a little too long on top, like he's missed his most recent trim. A smattering of facial hair puts a dusting of blonde scruff along his jaw and chin, giving his otherwise youthful face a much manlier feel. His dark grey eyes are strangely piercing, and though his smile is close-lipped, I don't doubt that behind those lips are perfectly white teeth.

He's not said a word this whole time, and I'm still studying his face when he speaks, scaring the crap out of me. "How are you feeling, Brailey?" He tenderly brushes a lock of my hair out of my face and pushes it behind my ear. The gesture in itself is affectionate, his expression unreadable. If he knows me or has some sort of connection to me, I don't remember him. And why the hell isn't he getting me out of here? Don't fix my hair, un-restrain me, asshat.

"Where am I?" I whisper, my voice barely audible. He lifts a cup to my face, tilting a straw towards my mouth. Could be the crazy Kool-Aid, but I'm too thirsty to give a damn. I'm pretty sure it's water, but I suck it down so fast I wouldn't have been able to taste it anyway.

"You don't know where you are?" He asks incredu-

lously, yanking his hand away from my face quickly.

"No, I don't know where I am. That's why I asked."
He scowls at my sarcastic retort. "I'm gonna take a shot in the dark though and guess I'm not staying at the Hilton." I wiggle my fingers for good measure, his eyes darting to my hands briefly before returning to my face.

"I'm sorry, you just surprised me. I wasn't expecting you to not know where you are. What is the last thing you remember?"

His calm demeanor is really starting to piss me off. I don't want to answer his questions; I want him to answer mine.

"I don't know, it's kind of hard to think when I'm strapped to a bed in a place I don't recognize. Maybe if you'd let me up and quit evading my questions then I might be more cooperative."

I'm snarling, I can feel it, but he doesn't appear put off by it. My feistiness only seems to please him, because his smile widens, revealing those beautiful teeth I knew he was hiding.

"Of course, I'm sorry. I saw you were awake and I got carried away. I'm just glad you're okay. Let me go get the guards to release you, and then we'll talk."

My body starts to relax, until I realize he said guards. Why the hell are there guards? Am I in prison? I don't care if there are sharks or lions or man-eating dragons outside of this building; I'm escaping this make-shift Alcatraz one way or another.

He returns with a man as big as a mountain, who turns an odd shaped key into the buckles of my restraints, undoing each one with quick, rough jerks of his hands, causing a sharp pain to shoot through every part of my body. Asshole. If I thought it wasn't intentional before, I'd be proven wrong by that smirk he walks away with as I rub my wrists.

Sitting up is a bitch, and dizziness hits me in waves that have my whole body rocking. My wrists and ankles are covered in wide, angry looking bruises. I don't remember it, but I had to have fought against those restraints before today; it's the only reason I would have so much bruising. Not to mention several of them are already starting to yellow, meaning they had to have happened days ago.

My fingers and toes flex, and it feels amazing and excruciating at the same time; like stretching out a sore muscle by further abusing it. All I want is to be out of this cold, sterile looking room and somewhere I recognize. A cheeseburger and fifty gallons of water also sound pretty awesome right now.

Strong arms wrap around my middle, catching me when my legs give out from underneath me. I look up into those piercing green eyes and I'm met with a warm smile. "I'm Mark. We have a lot to talk about."

Shaking myself out of the memory, I look up at Mark and realize just how much has changed in the three weeks since I woke up strapped to that bed, a stranger in my own life.

"I'm nervous." Mark's dark grey eyes look down at me with sympathy and kindness – a look he wears often around me.

"I know, but you're going to be great. You're strong, and you can do this. And you aren't doing it alone, you know that, right?"

Mark has done nothing but try and help me, and I trust him wholeheartedly, but taking on the world with no memory of who you are or where you come from is terrifying. There will be time to fake fearlessness later. This is Mark, and I don't have to pretend with him.

"You can call me anytime, day or night. You're not just a patient to me. You're my friend, and nothing is going to change that just because we won't be seeing each other every day."

Wrapping my arms tightly around his waist, I pull him in for an embrace, and after a few seconds his body relaxes and he returns my hug. I don't make it a habit of hugging him, not with our situation, but this time it doesn't feel so wrong. Mark is literally the only person I have in this world, and though my memories of him are now only few, that doesn't change how important he is to me.

As happy as I am to be leaving the cold confines of Mayford's walls, I'm not looking forward to losing the friends I've made here. Over Mark's shoulder I steal what I *hope* is one last glance of the monstrous brick building. The structure itself is actually gorgeous, having been built back in the early 1900s, the architecture reflecting the styles and themes you often see in large buildings built back then.

A large portion of the main corridor is dedicated to the history of Mayford. Apparently, the building was originally intended to be a large cathedral, but funding ran out before it was finished, and the building and the surrounding land were later purchased by Dr. John Mayford. Dr. Mayford moved to the U.S. with his wife and five kids to oversee the conversion of several local buildings being converted into Polio sanatoriums when the outbreaks started.

The doctor initially housed many Polio patients with the intent of later converting the building into a learning hospital for medical students, but over time Mayford began taking on more of the 'special' cases when other locations ran out of room. The reason is unknown, but around the mid-1900s after the Polio vaccine passed clinical trials, Dr. Mayford ultimately ended up restricting his patient base to only the ones considered clinically insane.

The name changed from Mayford Medical Institution to Mayford Mental Institution, and the hospital is now being ran by Dr. Mayford's oldest daughter.

Shaking myself out of my random reminder of Mayford's history, I put my attention back on Mark.

"I don't know how I'll ever repay you," I whisper, my voice muffled as I press my face against his chest. He's not wearing a suit like he normally wears, and I have to admit he looks good in his well-worn jeans and light grey thermal. Mark always seemed so much older than me when he was dressed up, but in his casual clothes he looks every bit his twenty-nine years. He's here on his day off to say goodbye, despite my protests, but I drew the line at him coming with me. His offer to help me get settled was genuine, but I need to do this on my own. Plus, I don't own anything, so there really isn't much to settle in the first place.

"The best way you could repay me would be to go out there and find your happiness. You deserve it, Brailey." His voice catches on my name, and I squeeze him a little tighter. I've been fighting tears all day, too stubborn to show my fear, even to myself. Crying and worrying over all the what-ifs isn't going to change the outcome of my circumstances.

"You may regret that offer to let me bug you day or night, because seeing as how you're my only friend, I'll probably be doing that a lot." I'd love to be able to stand here and pretend that I don't need anyone and that I'm capable of doing anything I set my mind to, but that would literally just be pretending, and what's the use in that?

He pulls back to look me in the eye, but doesn't pull out of my embrace entirely. My reserve crumbles just a little and a rogue tear escapes as I bite my lip to keep it from quivering. I'm way too determined to not get emotional to completely lose this battle, and the metallic taste on my tongue is a small price to pay if the only way to keep my lips from trembling is to bite down hard enough to draw blood.

"It won't be bugging me, Brailey. We've spent a lot of time together over the last couple years, and while I know you don't remember most of it, you are important to me. I know it might be hard to believe that I mean it still, but I'm saying this from a personal, not professional place. You matter to me Brailey, so trust me when I say that I won't regret telling you to call me."

He's doing that freaky mind reading trick that he does, where he figures out exactly what I'm feeling by staring into my eyes. Mark makes it pretty much impossible to put on a front around him. Well, makes it impossible for me, anyway. What he doesn't realize is how easily he gives himself away when he does it. At first I thought I was imagining what I saw, but it's real. I don't know if he'll ever come right out and say it, but he's still holding out hope that my memories come back to me.

A tidal wave full of guilt washes over me - guilt I feel towards people I don't even know - and it kicks my legs out from underneath me. My whole body threatens to crumble beneath its weight, and like he has every day for the last month, Mark is right there to catch me before I fall. Being held firmly against his chest calms my rapidly beating heart, but Mark is a safety net I'm losing after today. I can't rely on his steady embrace to hold me together, and pulling away from him, I see that realization reflected back at me in his eyes.

A horn honking alerts us that the taxi has arrived, and my heart rate picks up for an entirely different reason. The driver offers to load the taxi, but I don't own anything. Everything I once owned went up in flames, right along with my memories.

"Don't forget to take your sleeping pills, okay? It's important you get plenty of rest." I nod and steal one last hug from Mark, promising to talk soon, and then I'm sliding into the back of a taxi that smells like smoke and oriental food.

The distance between my new place and Mayford isn't much, but it is enough to feel like I've cut the last tether holding me back from truly living. Mayford is a psychiatric institution, not a five-star resort. Even though I wasn't an official patient, I still had to abide by the rules as such. Most days I wondered how in the world I was supposed to regain my sanity while surrounded by the insane.

Walking around in the same clothing everyday was almost enough to make me crazy in itself. Mayford is seriously massive, to the point where only the middle of the structure is original. Multiple wings have been added on over time, each wing dedicated to a certain set of patients. For the most part everyone gets to roam freely, but there are wings that contain patients serving out criminal sentencing. Their 'free' time is spent inside a cordoned section of the Mayford recreational area.

Like a giant scarlet letter, each 'type' of patient wears a different color clothing. Mine, the light grey set of extremely unflattering scrubs, were what the most 'normal' patients wore – their word, not mine. I would never use the word 'normal' under the circumstances, and considering taking care of those incapable of taking care of themselves is the entire purpose for Mayford, you would think they would be a little less crass and a lot more sensitive.

They aren't. Aside from a few staff members, everyone at Mayford is too busy looking down their noses to treat anyone with any kind of respect. The one thing

I'll give them credit for is that they treat each patient the same. Doesn't matter if you're wearing the bright yellow scrubs – the ones for patients who are almost totally gone – or the green ones that are for patients who are only a moderate risk to themselves or others. No matter what color your scrubs – Mayford treats you like shit.

Forcing myself to put Mayford out of my thoughts, I use the short drive to go over the list of things I need to do as soon as I'm home. *Home*. I'll have an actual home. Wow, that sounds weird in my head.

The phone clutched in my sweaty palm calls out to me, urging me to call Mark and take him up on his offer to help. Mark gave me this phone, wanting to make sure I was safe and had a way to call for help if I needed it. The glittery pink case brings to mind an image of Mark searching through girly-ass phone accessories, trying to find the one he assumes I would want. He's going to make a girl really lucky one day.

I almost refused the gift, knowing how much money it must have cost him. He would have insisted, and I didn't want to taint our goodbye with an argument, so I graciously accepted. When he smirked and said he'd already loaded credit on the iTunes account he'd set up for me so I could buy music and books, I punched him. My small fist collided with a solid chest and the result ended with the injury belonging only to me.

It's really freaking weird the types of things I remember. How can using this phone be like riding a bike, but I can't remember my middle name without someone telling me? The headphones Mark stashed in my bag when I wasn't looking make it easier to drown out my own thoughts with the music he apparently already took the liberty of loading onto my phone. Unsurprisingly, I like every song. Sometimes it feels like Mark knows me better than I'll ever know myself.

The car comes to a stop on the middle of the interstate, and I pop one earbud out to hear the driver say it's going to be a while due to a wreck. Sitting back and closing my eyes, I let myself get lost in the music. Without a lot of life experiences to reflect on thanks to the memory loss, my mind drifts to the memory of a week ago, when Mark and I first started our goodbyes.

"I'm so sorry that I don't remember, Mark," I say as I knot my fingers together, twitching nervously.

"It's not your fault, Brailey, I get it. Really, it's fine. We can just start over."

For once I kind of wish Mark would drop the good guy thing and just say what he's really feeling. Don't get me wrong, it's not that I don't appreciate that he cares enough to put my feelings first, but he does it with everyone. One of these days all those pent up emotions are going to come barreling out at once, and I worry about the long term effects for Mark.

Day in and day out, Mark spends all day talking to patients, listening to their problems, dedicating his life to helping everyone but himself. I so badly wish I could be that person for him, but I can't.

I found out today why it seemed like things were a little strained between us the past couple weeks when a nurse accidentally mentioned my relationship with Mark, which of course, I don't remember. She tried to backtrack immediately, but I wouldn't let her. Reluctantly she filled me in on what little details she knew, but it was enough. Finding out that Mark and I had been involved before my accident was a big blow. Why hadn't he told me?

I couldn't keep moving forward without knowing, which is why we're talking about it now. Or at least, I'm trying to talk about it, but Mark wants to just sweep it under the rug. I'm going to let him – for now – but only because there's not really much I can say other than I'm sorry, and I don't think that's going to do any good.

My guilt may be unwarranted, because of course my memory loss is not my own fault, but looking at his defeated and frustrated face doesn't assuage that guilt in the slightest.

Try as I might, I can't remember ever being with Mark. He's certainly attractive enough to believe it possible, but looking at him never brings back any inkling of emotions - physical or otherwise. Sometimes I catch him looking at me with what I can only describe as a focused intensity: narrow, dark eyes that make me feel like he's trying to figure out the inner workings of my brain even more than I am.

"You mean so much to me, Mark. I'm afraid of what will happen to us if I never remember. I don't want to

lose you in my life entirely." Yeah, I'm a selfish jerk. Mark is the one who is suffering – left to deal with the memories of whatever we had together while knowing I don't feel anything towards him anymore. But he's all I have, and if it makes me selfish for not wanting to lose him, then I guess I'm just a selfish person.

Mark reaches over and clasps my hand with his. It's not a romantic or sentimental gesture. Mark put on his mask the second I asked him about our past, and everything about him conveys the doctor side of him. "You'll never lose me, Brailey. I can handle it, stop worrying. I told you, it doesn't matter what was between us before, we were friends first. I'm not going to remind you of the details, because all that will do is confuse things more. Please, put this behind you and try to just focus on the present. Of all the things I'd love for you to remember, I'm the lowest on the list, because this isn't about me. It's about you."

Mark filled me in with as many details as he could over the past couple weeks, which is oddly not a whole lot considering we used to be involved, but at this point I'll take anything.

I'm twenty-six, and my brother Shaun was four years younger than me. Our parents died when we were young, and we grew up in foster care until I was eighteen when I took over guardianship.

I put myself through nursing school while being a mother to Shaun and working full time. I'd been trying to get a loan to pay for Shaun's transplant for months but couldn't get approved with all the credit card debt I'd racked up from his medical bills. That is until one *day I received a call saying an anonymous donation had been made to the hospital for Shaun's surgery. The donation was coincidentally made at the perfect time, because Shaun was called in for a transplant almost immediately thanks to a motorcycle driver riding without a helmet. After all that – the donation, the man who unknowingly sacrificed his life to give my brother a heart, then enduring the surgery – in the end, Shaun died from post-surgery infection in the hospital not long after the operation.*

The day he day of his surgery my house caught fire and that's how my memory was lost. A piece of ceiling fell on my head, knocking me out, and I still have some light scarring on my left leg and torso from the burns. Because I had no family and no memory, Mayford took me in long enough for me to get on my feet. Apparently I had woken up, freaking out and almost really hurting myself during my recovery, which is why I had been strapped to a bed.

I might know myself very well yet, but I still find it strange that I would have tried to hurt myself. No matter how scared, alone or intimidated I've felt since waking up, I've never once considered hurting myself, which leaves me wondering...

Are Mark and the staff of Mayford really being honest with me?

My eyes pop open when I hear the taxi driver clear his throat in a very loud, over-exaggerated kind of way. The car is idling next to a curb, and when my eyes meet his in the rearview mirror I see him scowling back at me. It takes all of two seconds to yank out my headphones and pay him, but his patience must have run out when I was half passed out in the backseat, because he takes off before the door is all the way closed behind me.

The key to my new home rests securely in my pocket, but I can't will my legs to move. Something about this next step feels much more monumental than any other I've taken in my life, both literal and metaphorical. Even with no memory of my previous life experiences, I can feel them influencing my every thought and decision through my subconscious. My attitude, my fears and insecurities; they come from a place that's just out of my reach. Every time I instinctually do something, I'm left wondering *where* that instinct came from, and every time I come up blank.

A lawyer - *my* lawyer - met with me at Mayford two days ago to go over my finances. He had even taken care of getting me a new license, check card and had the keys to a safety deposit box. I don't remember the guy, but if first impressions mean anything, I chose wisely when I hired him. All of my assets had been properly guarded, including the life insurance money I received from my brother's death. A brother I don't even remember having.

Every day since waking in that room, not knowing who I am or where I was, I have lived with the guilt of not remembering my own brother. I'm told he died during a medical operation, and since I was not able to take care of his funeral, he was buried in an unmarked grave, courtesy of the city, that I've yet to be able to visit.

Included in a folder full of documents given to me by my lawyer was a copy of my nursing degree. Mark of course had already informed me that prior to my accident I was employed as a nurse at Mayford, but with all the memory loss they had chosen to no longer employ me.

I could have tried to find work as a nurse, but the degree feels phony now. I don't remember school. I don't remember spending hours studying, pulling all-nighters to prepare for tests. It's possible I retained the knowledge and skill, but do I really trust myself to put someone's life in my hands when so much of my own life is still a blank?

The answer is no. It was the first decision I made without wavering or second guessing myself. No matter who I was before, I'm not someone who will take that kind of risk now. Not at someone else's expense. So in my 'new life' I'll be answering phones and running errands at a semi-successful marketing firm, and starting from the bottom feels great. I'm just happy to be doing something other than sitting around obsessing. The bare walls and limited distractions at Mayford provide the perfect environment for driving yourself batty with your own thoughts. Silence is deafening. True statement.

If Mark had gotten his way, I would be taking some time to myself before starting a job, getting acclimated and settled into my new life before adding more stress since I have enough money from the life insurance policy to live comfortably for a while. Something about living off money given to me because someone I loved died just doesn't feel right, so I'm not all too anxious to start spending it. It took some cajoling, but eventually Mark agreed to help me find a job, and he set me up with the one I'll be starting in a week, giving me just enough time to get settled in.

The sidewalk is bustling, a complete contrast to my still frozen state. I probably look like one of those living statues sans makeup and costume. The city's energy is infectious, and my toes twitch, begging my legs to move. None of the millions of things that need done before Monday are going to happen if I don't figure out how to put my body in motion.

I don't have furniture, clothes or even toiletries, and I don't think the baggy jeans and oversized hoodie I'm wearing fall under the 'business casual' dress code of my new job, so a new wardrobe is at the top of my priority list. My clothes were among the things I lost in the accident, and my current ill-fitted attire came out of the lost and found at Mayford.

By some miracle, my body catches up with my brain and starts moving. Only it's moving in the wrong direction, and my face is quickly on it's way to getting very well acquainted with the pavement.

That's weird. Why is the sidewalk squishy?

"Oh my gosh! I'm so sorry!" The squishiness is a

body, I realize, and it belongs to a woman. Even though she broke my fall and has to be in pain, she's more concerned with my well-being than her own. Soft hands push me away and then grip my arms, yanking me up to standing. It's dizzying and my eyes take a few seconds to adjust from the head rush that came with being toppled by a stranger. When my vision focuses again, I see the apologetic eyes of a pretty blonde staring back at me. She's looking me all over, like she's checking to see if I'm gushing blood anywhere, and she seems frantic.

"Are you okay? I'm so sorry! I wasn't looking. I never look. I am so clumsy. Do you have a concussion? Did you hit your head? Is anything broken? I can't believe I did that." The hyperactive stranger who came barreling out of my new apartment building keeps rambling, but I can't keep up. My thoughts wander and I watch in a daze as she apologizes over and over, making me curious as to how she can talk for so long without taking a breath. I'm not even sure she's talking to *me*, because she keeps answering her own questions before I even have a chance to respond.

It's not until she's ushering me inside the building and we're walking up a set of stairs that I realize I must have actually responded to her at *some* point, because she's holding my apartment key and my backpack, still chattering away as I follow her like a lost puppy dog.

"I can't believe we live right next door to each other! How crazy is that? I've been wondering who was going to move in. The apartment has been vacant for over a month, and between me and you, I'm so glad it's someone normal moving in. The guy that lived there before

24 JENN HYPE

you was so creepy and he listened to this terrible eighties rock music really loud at all hours of the night and it made me crazy."

She talks so fast and so constant that I'm having trouble keeping up. How does she do that? She hasn't even paused to take a breath.

I'm not exactly making the best first impression, considering in the five minutes I've known her I've missed half of what she's said and I've already forgotten her name. *Did she tell me her name? Dammit, I've got to work on my listening skills.*

"Oh my gosh! Where are my manners? I'm Keegan, what's your name?" I stop scanning my new apartment and turn my gaze back to my chatty neighbor, who's holding out her hand for me to shake and smiling broadly. It takes a second for me to snap out of it and put my hand in hers, but I manage to stop acting like a weirdo and return her smile while telling her my name. My smile isn't nearly as wide and pales in comparison to hers, but it's genuine.

"Brailey," she says my name slowly, her eyes drifting away from mine for a brief second and she looks deep in thought. Then she smiles widely again and claps her hands excitedly. "I like it! You and me, Brailey," she says as she loops her arm through mine and pulls me further into the apartment, "we're gonna be great friends."

CHAPTER
TWO

"Alright, c'mon," Keegan orders as she drags me out of my new apartment. An apartment I got to look at for all of two seconds before she starts ripping me right back out of it.

"Where are we going?" I may as well have not bothered asking. By the time the last word is out, she's already opening the door to her own apartment.

"I'm starving and there's no better way to bond with a new friend than over food that's incredibly bad for you. How do you feel about pizza?"

"Uh, it's okay, I guess."

"Preference?"

Anything other than disgusting Mayford cafeteria food is my preference, I muse to myself.

"What's Mayford?"

Or maybe I mused out loud.

I'm saved when someone starts talking on the other end of her phone call and I hear her order one pizza with the works and one plain.

"So what's Mayford?" She asks again as soon as she ends her call. *Guess I'm not off the hook after all.*

"Um, where I used to work." Please let that be enough of an answer for us to move on.

"Oh, you mean the asylum a couple hours north of here? What did you do there?"

"Uh, I was a nurse."

"Holy crap! You're kidding!" Keegan knocks over a little table housing some framed photos in her excitement. She doesn't even spare it a second glance. "You're a nurse?! I'm a nurse, too!"

Would it be rude to groan out loud right now?

"Yeah, I was, but I don't, um…the thing is…"

"Is that why you moved? To switch jobs?"

There's my out. It's not a lie, really. I *am* switching jobs, but it's not the reason for my move. To lie or not to lie…

"No, I was in an accident." I didn't consciously make the decision to tell her that. I might have to consider gluing my own mouth shut.

"Oh no! Are you okay?" True to her profession, she already starts examining me as if the accident happened a few minutes ago.

"Yes, I'm fine. Well, mostly. I lost my memory."

Keegan shockingly sits quietly while I explain what happened. Or at least what I was *told* happened. She doesn't even ask a question until I take a decently long pause.

"So you were a patient there? What was it like?" The question is tinged with a bit of hesitancy and curiosity. Can't blame her for being curious. Unless you've been inside, I can see why most people would assume those places are just like the movies.

"In some ways it wasn't as bad as you probably think, but in other ways I'm sure it was. I was only there as a patient for a few weeks and I don't remember my time working there, but I saw enough in my short stay to know it's not someplace you want to be."

Keegan just sits there staring at me when I don't continue. I really want to just put all this behind me, but maybe talking about it will help. Sounds like something Mark would say.

"I had a lot more freedom than most. We all had areas we were restricted to, ate at certain meal times and had a time to report to our rooms at the end of the day, but for the most part, we did what we wanted. They had different rooms with activities, like painting or reading. No computers, so I spent a good amount of time glued to the television, trying to get caught up with the world and hoping to remember something.

"The rest of the time I wandered a lot. They did a good job at preserving the original structure and it's beautiful. The main corridor has an open balcony that faces the courtyard which is well kept by the landscaping crew. A lot of the patients also help with the flowers and weeding as one of their activities, so parts of it are so lush and green that it looks more like a painting than a garden. Parts of the building have been abandoned and aren't taken care of, but those areas are restricted. I tried to sneak in once just to explore and got busted almost immediately. Damn security cameras."

"So sounds like something I would do," Keegan says with a twinkle of mischief in her eye that makes me laugh.

"Yeah, luckily I didn't get in much trouble. I'm not sure what they do for punishment in those situations, but I saw people disappear for a few days after causing a scene or making a mess, so I'm assuming it's some sort of solitary confinement or something. It's already so eerily quiet there, I can't even imagine how horrible it would be to be locked in a room by yourself."

Keegan and I both shudder at the same time, giggling at our commonality. Maybe it's Keegan, or maybe I'm stronger than I thought, but telling her all of this isn't nearly as difficult as I thought it would be.

"Anyway, the patient wings are pretty sterile looking. Single rooms with a bed and bathroom, though some rooms don't have the bathroom, depending on which wing you're in. The common areas are the beautiful parts. Very serene. It's unfortunate that they've created such a hostile environment in a place that has so much beauty."

My mind catches, like it's stuck between the past and present. Hands down, the most annoying feeling of all time. The only way I can describe it is to compare it to déjà vu or even just an intuition that has you teetering in limbo, unable to tell if you're really calling forth a memory or just indulging an active imagination.

A knock at the door breaks the silence, and I ask to use her restroom while she pays for the pizza. I look up into the mirror while I'm washing my hands, wondering if there will ever be a time when I don't see a stranger looking back at me.

"So, when are the movers coming?" Keegan asks me as I walk back out, her mouth already full of pizza. I plop down on the floor next to her and grab a piece straight out of the box, putting the paper towel she hands me underneath as I take a bite. I assumed we came over here because she has furnishings and I don't, but here we are, sitting cross legged on top of a very soft and smushy rug, square in the middle of her living room floor.

After a few minutes of going back and forth about whether or not she's going to let me help pay for the pizza, she finally asks her question about the movers again.

"Um, actually, I don't have anything. I'm kind of starting from scratch, so I have to go buy pretty much everything at some point this weekend."

That's weird, right? Having absolutely nothing to my name, but enough money in the bank to furnish a mansion? I might be concerned about her reaction if I hadn't already told her my whole damn story. She didn't balk once the whole time I told it though, so when she squeals and jumps up and down while clapping her hands, I'm not at all shocked.

"Oh my gosh! *Really?!*" Keegan jumps up so quickly that she knocks her plate onto the floor, sending pizza flying in every which direction. Instinct – *or habit?* – has me on my feet and cleaning up the mess before the last pepperoni hits the floor.

"Oh stop that, I'll get that later. There's no time, we have to get going."

Apparently I'm a 'we' now. Walked out of Mayford leaving behind my only friend just earlier today, not realizing someone was waiting to strong-arm me into being a part of her 'we.' Keegan's already moving around her apartment in a flurry, putting on her shoes and grabbing her purse. I, however, continue to just sit there, staring after her and trying to figure out what in the hell is going on. When Keegan finally notices that I haven't moved from my spot, she rolls her eyes and walks over to me, grabbing my hand and pulling me to my feet.

"What are you doing just sitting there? We have to go!"

"W-where are we going?" I stutter out, still being pulled by Keegan out of her apartment and down the stairs. We only live on the second floor so the elevator isn't necessary.

"Shopping, silly!" Keegan is already flagging down a taxi before I can even register what she's talking about. I've only known her an hour, and in that hour she's basically railroaded my life already. She didn't invite me to her apartment for pizza, or even ask me if I already had plans. She just told me what we were doing and dragged my ass over to her place, and I have been so stunned and thrown off since she first knocked me over that I haven't been able to figure out if I even *want* to be around her.

Pretty sure I do, though.

Sure, I could try and pretend to be all independent and just dandy on my own, but the truth is I'm really grateful that she seems to have adopted me. Like a lost puppy. Since waking up in Mayford, I've been fighting every damn day to figure out my place in this world, and I may not have a clue what I'm doing, but I've been adamant about needing to do it on my own. It's why I wouldn't let Mark help me, and why I insisted on working.

So fumbling through my days until I figure things out isn't *really* a plan, but it was *my* non-plan all the same. Keegan, however, has managed to completely blow my plan to bits in the matter of minutes since meeting her. Part of me wants to be annoyed, but a much bigger part of me is grateful. She's so confident and charismatic that I find myself just doing whatever she says - like a little lap dog. *Again with the dog analogy. I think I need to come up with one that is less insulting.*

From what little I know of myself already, I can tell Keegan and I have very similar personalities. The main difference being she has the confidence to really let her true self show, whereas I'm too busy being unsure about everything thanks to all the pieces missing now that it tends to take my self-esteem down a few notches.

The day passes by as quickly as the first hour with Keegan did, and turns out that Keegan is not only hospitable, but she's also extremely thoughtful. I half expected her to railroad me the entire shopping trip, making all my decisions for me, but I totally underestimated her. She had to prompt me with questions about what I liked or my preferences, but she always made sure I felt like the decisions were mine – even if they really weren't. How was I supposed to be all decisive and confident when I have no freaking clue what I even like?

She never came out and asked what I could afford, but I could tell she was gauging my reactions to things to try and figure it out. The life insurance money was the only part of my story I left out. I might trust her already, but that's one detail I would prefer and keep to myself until I know if that trust is truly justified.

Another surprise from Keegan is her ability to bring calm and peace to the atmosphere, which is a direct contradiction to the overwhelmingly energetic person I spent the first couple hours getting to know. Her innate ability to read my thoughts and quickly de-stress a situation made it a lot easier for me to enjoy our shopping excursion.

Thank God our building has amazing water pressure. The hot water beating down on me is doing wonders on my aching muscles. We didn't even get back until after dark, and my legs, back, arms and pretty much every part of my body are in agony. Who knew a massive shopping spree was such a workout?

At least my energy wasn't wasted, since I bought just about one of everything in that damn mall. In just a few days my apartment will be fully furnished, useless appliances and all. Don't know what I would have done if Keegan hadn't insisted I buy myself that coffee pot that you can control remotely from your phone. You know, for the days when you're too lazy to get out of bed to push the button on the coffee maker yourself. Considering it didn't come with a barista who will actually bring it to me and I'll have to get up to pour it in a cup anyway, seems silly to control it from the next room.

Funny how Keegan was programming her phone to control the coffee machine before I'd even downloaded the app. Maybe if I give her a key she'll bring me my coffee in bed, eliminating that whole barista issue.

Scrubbing my face down with the fancy, and extremely overpriced new soap I bought, I can't help but laugh thinking back on how excited Keegan got about everything. Like a kid in a freaking candy store, she would dart around from one thing to the next. Once she realized money wasn't an issue, it was no-holds-barred for her. If I nixed a suggestion, she would just shrug and move on to the next crazy thing that caught her eye.

The only frustrating part of the whole extravaganza was feeling like I was sitting on the edge of familiarity, but not being able to fully remember anything. Like with my phone, I would see something and sense a vague familiarity. I could tell you how it worked and what it was for, but couldn't actually picture myself using it. Maddening.

All of the big items won't be delivered until Tuesday, so I'm sleeping on a pile in the middle of my bedroom floor until then. Keegan offered her couch, but I'm ready for some time alone, so I politely declined. She looked like she wanted to press the issue but thought better of it.

After stepping out of the shower and drying off with one of my new fluffy towels, I take in all the scattered cosmetics lining my vanity. Picking up a canister of the face cream and giving it a sniff, I reluctantly start lathering my skin with the potent smelling concoction. The trip to Sephora was an adventure. Keegan was like a kid in a candy store, flitting around the store, filling a canvas shopping bag with what was probably at least one of everything in the store while one of the workers gave me a tutorial on how to use said eyelash curler. I nodded and listened politely, and even though I bought the damn thing, I will not be using it. It looks more like a torture device than a beauty tool.

Slipping on my new cotton nightgown from Victoria's Secret, I wince, remembering how humiliating that particular part was. Keegan was quick to ease my discomfort by joking around and distracting me with conversation, but it was still a tad awkward.

The clothing part...ughhhh...that was the worst. It wasn't the same as picking out a couch. Two hours at the mall made it glaringly obvious that clothing choices mattered a lot more than room decor.

One look at the vast sea of clothing had me wanting to puke all over the tile flooring right there in front of the jewelry counter. So many different styles and colors to choose from. *How the hell does anyone make a decision?* Keegan once again jumped to my rescue by grabbing item after item off the racks and shoving them at me. I'm not even sure if she really looked at anything she picked up, but not even ten minutes later my arms were so full I was about to topple over.

It took hours to try on every piece of clothing, but I ended up buying almost all of them. Turns out Keegan has really great fashion sense, and maybe even I do too, because I passed some kind of test when I started drooling over a pair of hot pink Jimmy Choo's. From there, my confidence had risen and Keegan started following my lead instead. Yay me.

The amount of money I shelled out today is sickening, and along with a dozen bags of crap – with plenty more on the way - I also came home with a gut full of guilt. Mark has been telling me I shouldn't feel bad about spending the money I was left from Shaun, that he would want me to be happy, but I don't know how he could possibly know that. Mark knows as much about Shaun as I do, which is nothing. Even with all the personal facts Mark has been able to fill in for me, Shaun was not included among them. They'd never met.

Keegan didn't have any guilt eating away at her,

however, so she had a blast swiping my charge card everywhere we went. It was a cheap shortcut, but with Keegan making most of the decisions it felt like she really was spending the money and not me, which helped alleviate some of my guilt. Another thing that helped ease my guilt was buying the expensive bottle of perfume I'd seen Keegan eyeing dreamily when she thought I wasn't looking. To me, it was the least I could do to repay her for not only helping me, but for going out of her way to make me feel comfortable the entire time. She shrieked and hugged me so tight I couldn't breathe when I gave it to her, reluctantly accepting after trying to insist it was too expensive.

All in all, I'd say my first day on my own – sort of – was a pretty awesome day. So awesome, in fact, that I pass out from exhaustion, forgetting to take my sleeping pills.

Even as an employee, I don't get access to every part of Mayford. Found that out the hard way when I went looking for a patient I hadn't seen for a few days. Mayra was one of my favorites, and I truly felt she didn't belong at Mayford, but she didn't have any family to care for her. She was placed at Mayford by the state, though I didn't know exactly why. That part of

her file was restricted, even from staff. A month before she was about to turn eighteen and could make the decision for herself whether or not to continue staying at Mayford, I talked to Shaun and we decided we wanted to help her get on her feet if that's what she wanted to do. Problem was, I couldn't find her.

For the most part, all the staff at Mayford kept to themselves. The few friends I had there didn't know anything about Mayra or where she'd gone. After the fifth day of not seeing her anywhere, I decided to go looking. Maybe they had transferred her to a different wing or something. Whatever the reason for her absence, I was worried and needed to know.

Mayford is pretty massive. They've added on to the original structure several times throughout the years, and several of the older sections have been abandoned. The staff is always told that those areas are restricted, mostly for health and hazardous reasons. I never understood why they would just let parts of the building go. Why keep adding on instead of renovating?

After trekking across the entire campus and not spotting Mayra, I was more determined than ever to figure out where the heck she'd gone. Maybe she'd wandered into one of the restricted areas and got hurt? The more I thought about it, the more worried I became, and soon I was on my way what I thought was an abandoned extension of the west wing.

Normally there is a guard on post here, but he must have been called away for something because he was nowhere in sight. One glance down the creepy hallway and I almost turned around and went back, but *then I heard someone calling out.*

At first I thought I was imagining it, thinking it seriously strange that any person – even the patients – would wander down the dark, narrow hallway. Only one flickering fluorescent light was working in the drop ceiling, but it was enough to be able to see where I was going. The linoleum flooring was peeling with huge pieces of it missing, as if someone had started to tear up the flooring and then stopped halfway. The ceiling looked like it was literally about to cave in, and had probably suffered some sort of water damage.

The paint on the walls was chipping, a faint line of a different color paint running across the middle of the walls, like a banister or railing had been torn off, leaving behind exposed pieces of drywall. The voice calling out had stopped, and I again considered just getting the hell out of the creepy hallway. Swallowing thickly, I took one more tentative step forward, my head jerking up when I heard another faint cry echo through the long hallway.

I definitely wasn't imagining it, and whoever it was sounded like they were in pain, and before I knew what was happening, I was running in a full-out sprint.

"You can't be in here," a booming voice says at the same time that someone grabs my wrists and yanks me backwards.

"Let me go, someone needs help." I struggle against the guard's hold, which is entirely useless. Mayford hires guys big enough to be in the WWE. No way in hell someone as tiny as me could escape one of them.

"Yeah, sure lady. Let's get you back to your room and I'll have the nurses bring you some of your crazy pills. Apparently you missed yours this morning."

Asshole.

"Quit being a dick, I clearly work here," I bite out as I show him the ID hanging from my lanyard. "You can also get your giant paws off of me. You're going to leave bruises."

The jerk didn't loosen his grip on my wrist and continued to drag me in silence until we reached Director Mayford's office, where he shoved me so hard my butt hit the hard corner of a wooden chair, sending a sharp pain down my thigh.

"Boss'll be in here in a minute. Little advice, free of charge – don't try and sneak off again. Got cameras everywhere. Boss doesn't take too kindly to people sticking their nose where it don't belong."

The devil herself walks in right after he finishes giving me his 'advice.' The monstrous man who was just trying to intimidate me is now cowering because a five-foot-nothing middle-aged woman just walked in the door.

Wuss.

"So, Brailey," she-devil said with a saccharine smile, clasping her hands together on the top of her desk. "I hear you were trying to go on a little adventure."

"You make it sound like I set out with the intent to cause trouble. I was looking for a patient who I haven't seen in several days, I was worried. I didn't intend to enter a restricted area, but I heard someone calling

out like they were in pain. Not really my fault that your guard wasn't at his post."

Her smile slipped just a little.

I had no business talking to her like that. I couldn't afford to lose my job, but I never did take too kindly to people trying to bully me. I'd only met the director a handful of times, and each time I left with a bad taste in my mouth. Something was just off about that woman. Never could put my finger on it, but my intuition about those things was rarely wrong.

"Oh? And which patient is that?"

I could have sworn she already knew the answer to that question. Wouldn't surprise me really. The woman had eyes and ears all over Mayford.

"Mayra Haines. She's been a patient in my assigned wing for over a year now, and suddenly she's gone. Her file gave no information as to where I could find her and no one else has seen her."

Her fake smile fell completely, her lips thinning into a line. With narrowed, angry eyes, she stared me down as she stood from her chair, placing her palms flat on her desk and leaning over to put her face closer to mine. Her big-ass desk was massive, so she was still a good distance away, but her body language got the point across all the same.

"This is your only warning, Brailey. I do not appreciate your show of distrust for our staff and your obvious lack of respect for me. Do you think I would have just lost a patient? That someone could just disappear and I would not know? It would be foolish of you to make such assumptions. Not a thing goes on at Mayford

that I don't know about, and when something is your
concern, I will tell you. Until then, do the job we hired
you to do. In case you forgot, we hired you for your
nursing degree, not your investigative skills.

"Along with a warning, I'm giving you one day of
unpaid suspension, which you will serve tomorrow. Go
home, Brailey, and don't come back unless you plan on
accepting your place here at Mayford."

Dismissed.

Yeah, okay, I could see why people would find her
intimidating, but I was raised in foster care. After some
of the crap I saw and dealt with growing up, Director
Mayford was about as scary as a baby bunny in com-
parison.

I would take my stupid day off, and I would return,
but it wouldn't be to follow orders. The she-devil was
hiding something, and I was going to figure out what it
was.

CHAPTER
THREE

My back is aching from sleeping on the hard floor, though it probably doesn't count as sleeping really since I spent most of the night tossing and turning, restless from dreaming. I seriously need to remember to take my sleeping pills next time I go to bed. Was that dream a memory or simply just a dream? It certainly *felt* real.

I arch my back, hearing a few pops along my spine when I stretch my arms high above my head. The bags from our shopping trip are scattered all across my empty bedroom. There are so many things I forgot to buy – like hangers. I might have to borrow a few from Keegan or initiate another outing for supplies, otherwise I'm going to show up on my first day looking like a wrinkled mess.

My phone buzzes, and of course the only person it could be is Mark. Honestly, I'm not really in the right frame of mind to talk to him right now. Our lives are moving in separate directions now, and I don't know where he fits in. Hell, I don't know where *I* even fit in, so how can I expect him to want to remain a part of it? Despite the amount of reassuring he's done, I still feel like I'm putting him through unnecessary pain. Somehow, him not pressing the issue of our past relationship only amplifies my guilt, and it's that guilt that keeps me from reaching out to him like I really want to.

Would it be cruel to move on without him, or would it be a good thing for both of us in the long run? Wouldn't continuing to have me in his life only cause him more pain, knowing I might never remember? He won't open up to me about it, not wanting to 'pressure me', as he puts it, so I can't really know what he's feeling. The buzzing stops before I can even come to a decision on whether or not I'm going to answer.

Oh well, I'll call him later. Maybe tomorrow. Hell, I don't know.

If I had a comfortable bed to lay in I'd just sleep the day away, but this floor is killing me. Damn. Maybe I will take Keegan up on that offer to sleep on her couch tonight.

Speak of the she-devil. I assume that relentless banging on my door is Keegan. Someone trying to rob or murder me wouldn't be drawing that much attention to themselves.

"Brailey, c'mon! I'm hungry!"

We didn't make breakfast plans, yet she acts like she's waiting on me. I fully intend to snap at her when I swing the door open – because it should be illegal to bang on someone's door before seven am – but she's holding out a cup of coffee for me, and all is instantly forgiven.

"I didn't know how you take your coffee, so I just made it like I take mine."

Pretty sure I get insta-cavities with my first sip. "Holy crap, Keegan. Is there any coffee in this or is it just sugar?"

"I think I put a couple teaspoons of coffee in there,"

Keegan says with a laugh. "You can get yourself a coffee the way you like it at the diner. I need pancakes."

And so went my morning. Mix in a little guilt for not answering Mark's call combined with my zombie-like state thanks to a restless night, and I was pretty miserable company.

"B, what's your deal. You've been distracted all morning," Keegan asks me when I ask her to repeat herself for the third time on our walk back to our apartments. "All through breakfast it was like you were in another world. I'm pretty sure everyone in the restaurant just thought I was talking to myself."

"I'm sorry, I've got a lot on my mind. Let me make a call real quick and then I promise I'll focus on you and whatever guy it was you were just rambling on about."

Keegan jokingly nudges my shoulder and feigns offense. "Hey, his name is Dirk and he happens to be very good with his- "

"Yeah, yeah, okay, you can tell me after this," I interrupt her. Keegan stops along side me on the sidewalk and we move out of the way so other pedestrians can keep going. I pull up Mark's cell number, and when he doesn't answer, I decide to call his office. Maybe he's at work.

"Hey Marky," I say when his voicemail picks up. He hates that nickname, and I get evil pleasure from using it whenever I can. "I'm sorry I missed your call this morning. I meant to check in with you last night like you asked but I had to go out and get all the stuff missing for my apartment, which was, ya know, everything. Anyway, I'll try you again later."

I slip my arm through Keegan's and tug, pulling her attention away from her phone and back to me. So weird that we only just met yesterday. Less than twenty-four hours, but it feels like I've known her for years. Of course, we've done a helluvalot of talking in that twenty-four hours, so I already know tons about her. Keegan is not stingy when it comes to sharing. In fact, she's a little bit of an over-sharer. There are definitely some things I know about her that I would un-know if that were possible.

Keegan spends the remaining three blocks talking about Derek - or whatever his name is - going into way too much detail yet again. Our arms are still linked together, so when Keegan comes to an abrupt halt after rounding the last corner, I'm jerked backwards, our bodies colliding into one another.

"What in the world? You okay?" I ask Keegan as her arm slips out from mine. She's staring blankly with her jaw gaping. I follow her line of vision, but all I see are boxes littering the sidewalk and an unmarked moving truck.

When she just continues to stand there slack jawed, I start searching the area to figure out what's managed to shut Keegan up for what has to be the first time in her life.

A man steps out from the side of the truck, and now there are two of us frozen in place, causing people on the sidewalk to grumble and complain when they have to go around us. My legs quit working the moment I understand what elicited such an unusual reaction from Keegan, and no amount of nudging or intentional shoulder bumping from angry passersby can unglue my feet.

My jaw drops open and mimics Keegan's, and maybe a little drool slips out when I mutter, "holy hotness." Strong, muscular arms flex as a box is lifted. I follow those arms up to broad shoulders that are covered in a tight, plain black tee shirt that does nothing to hide how built this man is. I slowly travel up his neck and land on his face. A face that's so striking that it literally sucks all the breath out of my lungs.

His hair is dark, the shadow of facial hair on his face softens his sharp features, and my face tingles, wondering how his scruff would feel if I were to rub my cheek against his. Bright, almost incandescent blue eyes rest above prominent cheek bones. One drop of sweat is slowly dripping down from his temple to his jaw and my tongue darts out to wet my lips, my taste buds begging to taste the salty sweetness of his skin.

Keegan has recovered herself, but I'm still literally slurping away at his imaginary sweat when his startling eyes lock with mine. I suck in my tongue quickly like some kind of sex crazed lizard. His mouth tightens and his eyes crinkle in the corners, but he's not able to mask his expression enough for it to go unnoticed that he's trying not to laugh.

Damn. Am I that obvious?

"Yep," Keegan chirps, answering the question I didn't mean to ask out loud. She practically skips in his direction, looking at him like he's been dipped in chocolate and she's got a craving for something sweet. His eyes never leave mine, not even when Keegan is standing right in front of him. I keep trying to will myself to look away, afraid I'll drown in those blue

Keegan clears her throat loudly, and I'm tempted to take advantage of their distraction to run inside and hide. I don't have much in the way of instincts, but knowing what is and is not considered proper social etiquette appears to be one of them. Probably a good thing generally, but at this very moment, I'd much prefer to play the part of awkward weirdo if it meant not having to introduce myself to the intensely intimidating man standing next to Keegan.

It's not even his ridiculously sexy face or absurdly toned body that makes me literally afraid to approach him. There's just something that seems almost...dangerous about him. I can't put my finger on what's making me feel that way though, and I've now spent so much time debating whether or not to bolt that I've lost my opportunity.

"Brailey!" Keegan beckons me over. "This is our new neighbor, come say hi!" He reaches out his hand to shake mine, making the large box in his arms wobble, forcing him to yank his hand back to keep the box from falling.

"Wyatt," he responds tersely with a nod. I can't tell if he's annoyed that Keegan is trying to talk to him when he's clearly busy or if he's just getting tired from holding a heavy box, but either way, Keegan is oblivious to the frustration he's not even *trying* to hide.

"Okay, well it was nice meeting you. Welcome to the building. We'll be seeing you around," I say as I tug on Keegan's arm, dragging her away from our new neighbor and into the safety of the building. My lungs start working again once I'm a safe distance away from Wyatt, and I prop myself up against the wall next to the stairwell.

"Holy shit, B. Our new neighbor is delicious." A deep throated chuckle reverberates from behind us, and I don't need to turn around to know who it is. I can easily tell its Wyatt from the way the air thinned and my head got dizzy. Keegan makes a dramatic fanning gesture with her hand, and when I let myself steal a look backwards my cheeks immediately go a deep shade of red. *Good God, he's sexy.*

Keegan starts dramatically swooning and gushing over him, pretending like she's trying to get loose from my grip so she can run to him as I drag her up the stairs. Sometimes I wonder if Keegan has an endless amount of confidence, or if she simply just doesn't care what people think. More than half of the things she willingly does in public would be the cause of nightmares if it were me.

Do you know how weird it is to be standing next to an almost six-foot-tall woman with the energy of a Chihuahua while she gushes over a stranger, showering them with endless compliments? She's drawn to beauty like a moth to a flame, like a compulsion. She doesn't discriminate against gender either, which had me having to outright ask her what her sexual preferences were.

"Oh Brailey," she'd said with a laugh. "You're so uptight. Beauty is beauty, and people deserve to know it. I might be the only one that tells them that day, or month, how attractive they are. Everyone loves to feel attractive."

It's not the only way she gives back, but it's definitely the weirdest one.

She's still going on and on about how good look-ing Wyatt is as we walk into my apartment. There's no use in me trying to deny it, because it's totally true. Keegan may dole out compliments like it's her job, and I don't always agree with her opinion, but she's right on the mark with this one. Wyatt is hands down the sexiest man I've ever seen in real life. Although to be fair, my memory only goes back about forty-five days, so it's not like I have much to go on.

"Yes, he's very attractive," I say with a laugh, which of course earns an eye roll from Keegan. Something about admitting just how attractive I find Wyatt feels a little like exposing myself. I'm insecure in a plethora of ways, most of which I blame solely on the memory loss. I don't know enough about myself to have any self-confidence, and Wyatt's the first man I've felt an intense attraction to since waking up. I'm not really sure how to handle the whole situation, and until I figure it out, I'm not ready to openly swoon like Keegan currently is.

"You should totally hit that,"

"What?! No! You're crazy! I'm not hitting any-thing. Besides, he's way too hot for me." Okay, so I hadn't intended to freak out and get all defensive and self-deprecating, but she made the remark so casually that something in me panicked.

I shouldn't have said he's too hot for me. It's not that I don't find myself attractive, because I can see my appeal to the other sex. However, I am definitely a few levels beneath Wyatt on the hotness scale. His appeal is more intense and fiery, whereas mine is more tame and casual. It would be plain to any outsider to see that Keegan would make a much better fit with him physically.

My hair is its natural color - which is a light blonde - falling just below my shoulders, with a light natural wave. Keegan's is a platinum blonde with deep waves that fall just above her ass. I'm average height at about five and a half feet with a very small frame, with my decent sized chest being my only noteworthy asset. Keegan is just under six feet with dangerously long legs and a body full of curves.

We couldn't be more different if we tried, and I don't find myself comparing us very often, but when she throws out comments about me having sex with Wyatt? Yeah, that calls for a little fact facing.

"B, you've got to quit doing that. You are gorgeous. How you don't realize it is beyond me, but seriously, he would be lucky to hook up with someone like you."

I don't really want a pep talk. As much as I appreciate Keegan's overeager desire to make me feel better, I'm still coming down off the lust-high I felt in the two seconds I was near Wyatt. I'd rather just plop down on my couch and have a F.R.I.E.N.D.S. marathon the rest of the day. (I'm fairly certain I loved this show before the memory loss. And if not, then I don't even want to get reacquainted with my old self.)

"What are you doing?" My butt hasn't even hit the cushion before Keegan yanks on my arm and is dragging me behind her.

"Get changed. We're gonna get to know our new neighbor." Arguing with Keegan is pointless most of the time anyway, but seeing as how she's already picked out something for me to change into, it seems I've lost this argument before it even started. Doesn't mean I'm not going to give her at least a *little* resistance.

"Oh no we're not! I'm exhausted. I'm staying right here and minding my own business." My phone starts buzzing in my pocket, but Keegan throwing my clothes at my face knocks it out of my hand. By the time I pick it up I have a missed call from Mark.

"No, we're going to be neighborly and go help him move all his crap into his new apartment and make him be our friend. Just like I did to you the first day you moved in, and look how much better your life is for it," she winks at me playfully. "So you and I are going to do the same thing for him. Now get your ass in there and change. You can't help him move his stuff in that little dress of yours. I'll be back in five and you better be ready."

Keegan's body is replaced by a puff of smoke. The little brat bolted from my room before I had a chance to put up any more of a fight. Throwing my head back and growling loudly at the ceiling does little to relieve my frustrations.

"I heard that!"

Damn these paper thin walls.

My reflection stares back at me, taunting me with imperfections. My fingers itch to pick up the compact sitting on my bathroom counter, but we're just moving boxes. I'll probably get all dirty and sweaty, so what's the point in fussing with it? No amount of compressed powder is going to turn me into the kind of knockout who earns the attention from guys like Wyatt.

Why am I acting like an insecure thirteen-year-old girl? I'm attractive enough, and I don't need to camouflage who I am to impress a man I don't even know. As an adult woman I can understand the need for the dozens of beauty products scattered all around my bathroom, but that's only when the time calls for it. Certainly a day of manual labor is not the type of occasion that warrants mascara and lip gloss. *Right?*

Keegan returns to my apartment, making her presence known without having to say anything. She's like a little ball of energy, just bouncing around like a pinball, knocking stuff over any time she's in a confined space. Time's up. Keegan knocks around my kitchen long enough for me to brush my teeth and throw my hair into a messy ponytail.

"C'mon, let's go stare at that cute butt while it carries boxes up the stairs. Did you see his ass? Even through his jeans it looks delicious enough to bite." Keegan's blunt comments always catch me off guard. No matter how many times she says something totally unexpected, I never get used to it. Judging by the enjoyment Keegan gets out of my spontaneous laughter every time she does it, I'd say I'm giving her the exact reaction she's looking for.

Keegan changed from the shirt dress she was wearing into a pair of extremely short shorts and a tight fitting tank. The clothes she threw at me were similar, but I put those back and ended up throwing on a pair of jeans and a baby doll tee. No amount of eye-rolling from Keegan is going to get me to go back inside and change, and thankfully she lets it go. I just want to get this awkward day over with so I can put it behind me.

Keegan strolls right on over to Wyatt's stuff and grabs a box, but I don't see him anywhere. I send up a quick prayer, hoping this guy doesn't have an issue with boundaries, because Keegan likes to put herself all up in people's personal space.

"Uhhhh, are you trying to rob me?" I jump when I hear Wyatt's voice right behind me, and a high pitched squeak pops out of my mouth.

"I don't know, got anything worth stealing?" Keegan jokes. Wyatt's lips turn up at the corners into a slight smile, pulling all my focus to his mouth. I bet he could do wonderfully sinful things with that mouth. Things that I don't have to remember actually having done to me to know I want them now – and from him. The way just looking at him pulls such a strong physical response out of me is sort of alarming.

"Which apartment do you live in?"

Wyatt's smile fades and shifts into a look I can't read. If Keegan notices the change in him, she ignores it, just rolling her eyes and starting towards the door we just came out of.

"Hurry up, playboy, this shit's heavy," she barely gets out before he swiftly swipes the box out of her hands. Keegan doesn't even react other than to let out a huff before marching back to the moving truck. She picks up a few boxes to test out their weight before picking one light enough for her to carry.

"Seriously, what are you doing?" He looks and sounds genuinely confused.

"We're helping you move, dumbass, what does it look like?" Wyatt looks stunned when Keegan starts muttering under her breath while shaking her head. "I swear; the pretty ones never have any brains. Probably bad in bed, too."

Those startling blue eyes of his just blink. Once, twice. The longer he goes without reacting, the more nervous I get. He wouldn't be the first person to take offense to one of Keegan's off-color jokes. I was witness to a handful of altercations between her and unsuspecting strangers while we were shopping, and that was all in just one outing.

All I know about Wyatt so far is how stupidly attracted to him I am. Everything about him gives off a bad boy vibe. I can't even put my finger on why I feel that way, but something about him just seems a little... dangerous.

I think I'm the only one sitting on pins right now, but the intense vibe going on is really freaking me out. I'm two seconds away from doing or saying something incredibly stupid just to ease the tension when Wyatt throws his head back and busts out laughing before walking over to the truck to pick up a box of his own. Keegan smirks at him and winks while I stand here like an idiot, not understanding in the slightest what the hell just happened.

My pulse picks up and my fingers start tingling, something that feels a hell of a lot like jealousy coursing through my veins. I don't like it, so I busy myself by running to the truck and grabbing the first box I see. Not even one step away from the truck, and the stupid curb just comes out of nowhere and tripping me. The box I'm holding breaks my fall before anyone has a chance to catch me.

The corner of the cardboard is stabbing me in the side, but luckily whatever is inside must be soft because the box pretty much just caved in beneath my weight. Nope. I am not going to be that girl who trips all over herself, making herself look like an idiot just because a hot guy is around. I'm also not going to be looking up anytime soon, because I'm embarrassed enough without having anyone see my face blushing furiously.

Keegan none so discreetly clears her throat several times before I realize she's trying to get my attention. It's no longer just my face that's blushing when I realize I'm sitting on top of a pile of Wyatt's underwear. No, that blush is quickly spreading down my neck and over my entire body. When I see the condoms scattered amidst some seriously sexy boxers, I'm afraid the blush is going to turn into hives.

I can't even bring myself to look at him. It's not that underwear freaks me out or anything - I'm not twelve - but all I've done since meeting him less than an hour ago is act like an idiot. I manage to shuffle out of his way, watching from my still crouched position as he fixes the box and fills it back up.

When he's finished he closes up the box and his eyes meet mine. There's humor in them and I can't tell if he's just amused by the situation or if he's actually laughing at me. His face is inches from mine as he remains in a crouched position that mimics my own. The wind kicks up, sending the most heavenly scent straight to my nose.

He smells clean sweat with a hint of cologne or after-shave. It's potent, not because it's strong, but because it has me envisioning having my face buried in pillows that smell like him while he grips my hair from behind and...

Keegan clears her throat, stopping my fantastically bad timed fantasy, luckily before I did something stupid like moan out loud. I'm not sure how long we stay like that. Probably only seconds, though it feels like hours. Keegan's eyes flash, her head tilting like she's trying to tell me something. I look over just in time to see Wyatt shake his head like he's trying to snap himself out of a similar trance. The thought that maybe Wyatt is as affected by me as I am him is a heady feeling, and I take a second to remind myself that hyperactive hormones have no place in my life right now.

Wyatt stands and holds his hand out for me to take, offering to help me up, but I push up without taking it. My body feels stiff, and I arch my back, trying to stretch it out. Wyatt's eyes dart down to my chest, and I might have let his eyes linger a little more than appropriate.

He squeezes his eyes shut for at least three Mississippi's – yeah, I counted – and when he looks at me again, his eyes are glazed over. That's definitely lust I see lurking in those blue eyes, but he also looks...angry?

Well, that's confusing. Maybe I'm reading him all wrong. I try not to dwell on how disappointing it feels, knowing this attraction could be totally one-sided.

With a hand on my hip, I hold my free hand out, palm up. "Gimme your credit card," I say flatly, thanking the Lord above for my voice coming out sounding confident and normal. I thought for sure it was going to sound all breathy and husky, giving away the internal struggle I have going on with my libido.

"Uhhhh, what?" Wyatt raises one eyebrow and looks at me like I'm crazy. I feign annoyance and pretend to be irritated, because feeling anything towards him other than lust makes it so much easier to not be affected by how gorgeous he is.

"You guys can carry all the stuff; I'll start unpacking it. But first I'm going to order a pizza and you're buying since we're helping you move. So, I'll need your card."

I see Keegan beaming out of my periphery, smiling at me like a proud mamma. I've impressed her with my sassy attitude, and I actually feel a little proud of myself for finding the confidence to look directly into Wyatt's bright blue eyes without melting into a puddle on the ground.

"My, my, you ladies are a couple of bossy ones aren't you?" Keegan snickers behind him, but his full attention is on me, his eyes never leaving mine as he pulls his wallet out of his back pocket and slides out a plastic card. He places it in my hand, and when his fingers make the briefest contact with my skin, a shiver racks my body in a very obvious - and humiliating - way.

Wyatt chuckles and shakes his head, leaning down to pick up the box he'd put down a minute ago. "Lucky for you both, I happen to like a little bit of attitude in my women." My breath catches when he winks at me. It is seriously unfair to the rest of mankind how good looking he is.

"Buddy," Keegan starts in, "trust me, *you* are the

lucky one. Now if you two are done eye fucking each other, I'd like to get going before I get too tired to help and end up planting my ass firmly on Wyatt's couch while he does all the work."

My head jerks to Keegan and I give her the dirtiest look I can muster, walking over to her and punching her in the arm before walking through the door.

"Ow! Dammit, Brailey, that hurt!" Keegan whines.

"What floor?" I ask Wyatt as the elevator dings and the doors slide open.

"Fourth," Wyatt calls out over his shoulder as he walks in the direction of the stairway, earning himself a laugh from Keegan.

"Yeah right, you take the stairs if you want, playboy, but I'm not carrying boxes up four flights of stairs." Wyatt opens his mouth to respond, but Keegan cuts him off. "And don't you *dare* make a comment about it being good exercise, because I will turn it into you calling me fat and pretend to be offended just to spite you. So unless you wanna hear me bitching at you all night while I complain about my fat ass, then you should probably just shut it and get on the damn elevator."

Wyatt wisely doesn't argue, just nods his head and offers a, "Ladies first," before following us onto the elevator. The ride to his floor is quiet and uncomfortable. Uncomfortable for *me*, at least, which seems to please Keegan who is wiggling her eyebrows up and down at me the whole time, her eyes darting back and forth between me and Wyatt's ass.

My head falls back in frustration just as the doors open and Wyatt steps out first, calling back to us over his shoulder. "I'll go first this time so you guys can get a better look at my ass."

Freaking Keegan.

Keegan calls after him, but I zone out and don't hear what she says. I'm too busy wondering how in the hell I'm going to survive this night.

CHAPTER
FOUR

The night actually went pretty smoothly at first. Keegan did indeed plant her ass on Wyatt's couch and watched him do all the heavy lifting, just like she'd threatened. Wyatt didn't seem to mind, probably because Keegan kept making sexually inappropriate comments about his ass every time he would walk through the room. I'm sure his ego is already big enough and he didn't need the boost, but he seemed to enjoy it anyway.

I busied myself with unpacking the boxes labeled for his kitchen so we would have dinnerware to eat off of when the pizza came. I was also just a little afraid to open any other boxes. My luck, I'd come across one filled with bondage toys.

Keegan and Wyatt spent a half hour fighting over what to get on the pizza until I got annoyed and ordered so many different variations that we could have fed the entire fourth floor.

Having just moved in this afternoon, Wyatt's kitchen was understandably void of food, other than the beer he somehow snuck into his fridge. I have no idea what my tolerance is to alcohol, but I know I haven't had it since waking up at Mayford.

With my track record so far with Wyatt, I figured alcohol probably wasn't a good idea. Seemed logical at the time, but when I kept either stuttering or melting every time he so much as looked at me, I started to reevaluate that whole abstaining from alcohol idea.

It was the jealousy that made me yank the beer bottle out of Wyatt's hand. Not one he was offering, because that would make sense, right? No, he was already drinking this one and it was halfway to his mouth when I stole it and walked off.

First bad decision of the night.

Beers number two, three and four were my next bad decisions.

I'm currently nursing bad decision number five, but the time to worry about bad decisions was like, three decisions ago, so I'm cool with my choices now. "People are so dumb!" *Okay, that came out a little more slurred than I thought it would.*

"What people?" Wyatt laughs from behind me. I'm thinking sitting on the floor right in front of him was bad decision number six, because his legs part slightly when his body shakes with laughter and I slip right between them. Not a particularly intimate position, but I've been fighting off lustful feelings all night, and being closer to the object of my lust isn't doing me any favors.

"The stupid criminals on the show! Duh." We're watching Cops, which started out hysterical in the beginning of the night, but now that the alcohol has kicked in, I'm just getting annoyed. Annoyed is good. Annoyed is better than lust drunk. "These idiots try to run from the cops, even though they *have* to know it's a waste of time, and then they have the stupidest excuses. I mean, if you're going to do something as dumb as drive around with drugs in the console of your car, then at least have a contingency plan in place. Sure, it makes for good television, but these poor cops. I don't know how they do it."

Laughing that damn laugh of his that makes my insides tingle, Wyatt leans forward to grab his drink off the coffee table sitting in front of me. He and Keegan wisely switched to water after one beer. At the time I thought, "Great! More for me!"

Idiot.

His large frame practically engulfs mine, and is it just me, or did the heat just kick on? He's taking forever to grab his stupid drink. I'm going to suffocate in his scent if he doesn't hurry up and pull away. Okay, in reality, it's only maybe been a few seconds, but I swear every time I breathe him in, my blood alcohol levels spike. Don't know how that makes sense, but it's how I feel.

The second he pulls away from me I'm jumping to my feet. Jumping would be bad decision number seven. Gravity apparently hates me when I'm drunk, and sudden movements have become my enemy. So when my hand reaches out for something to grab on to, that fickle bitch known as fate sticks my hand right on his crotch.

Ho-ly crap. That is *definitely* something to grab on to.

Blushing something fierce, I quickly right myself and fumble my way past Keegan and towards the small hallway. His apartment is exactly like mine, only the layout is flipped, so the bathroom should be easy enough to find.

"Whoa, where you going, Peaches?" I scrunch my nose at the endearment, but still halt in my tracks. I haven't heard him call Keegan 'Peaches' all night, so does that mean the nickname is unique to me? Why do I so badly want Wyatt to have given me a cute nickname?

I'm twenty-six, so I'm sure I've lusted for men before, but not in my 'new' life. Mark is attractive, and I'm sure some women would even consider him sexy, but I just can't bring myself to see him that way. No matter how much I try, all I see when I look at Mark is a companion. He wore his expensive suits well, and it's easy to see his appeal, but I'm sad to say I feel nothing even remotely more than friendly towards him.

Wyatt is *all man*. He's rugged and rough around the edges, with his jeans that hug his muscular thighs in a way that has me picturing them flexing while he holds up against the wall, driving into me over and over. The basic cotton tee he's wearing shouldn't do much to add to his appeal, but it stretches taut across his chest, making my finger-tips tingle, imagining how it would feel to trace those lines down his chest, across his hard stomach and down to his…

My lust for him feels so raw and primal, so all-consuming that it feels impossible to think or even breathe when he's near, so basically I've been suffocating all day.

Keegan has a naturally flirty personality, and it probably doesn't mean anything, but do I really know her well enough to make that assumption? Every time she laughs at something he says or touches his arm lightly, I have the bizarre desire to scratch her eyeballs out with my fingernails.

"Peaches?" Wyatt's voice snaps me out of my trance, and I realize I've been staring at him the entire time I was zoned out.

Wait...what did he ask?

Oh yeah, bathroom.

"Knock it off with the cutesy nickname," I spit out when I manage to find my voice. "I just need to use the restroom, if that's okay with you."

"I'll show you," Wyatt says as he moves to stand. I'm unreasonably annoyed by his show of hospitality, but recognizing how unreasonable it is doesn't keep me from getting pissed off at him for acting like I'm a child who needs supervising.

"All these apartments are basically the same. I got it."

The stupid floor is uneven and it's making my legs all wobbly. I can hear Keegan and Wyatt laughing behind me and it takes everything in me not to literally growl.

"Haven't unpacked the toilet paper yet! It's in a box in the bedroom!" Wyatt calls out and I growl after trying a third door and still not finding a room with boxes. Similar or not, navigating an apartment that's a mirror image of your own is extremely difficult while inebriated. Finally, I see a mattress on the floor behind door number four. There are several boxes scattered around the room, but my vision is blurry and I don't feel like trying to figure out which box is labeled bathroom, so I just start tearing into them carelessly.

When I come across the box filled with condoms and boxers I laugh. The next box I open steals all the laughter right out of me, though, when I come face to face with a handgun. I know it's not uncommon for people to own guns and I have no reason to be afraid of

Wyatt, but really, what do I know about him? And if I'm being truly honest with myself, it's not so much the fact that he owns a gun that bothers me, as much as it is the realization of just how irresponsible I'm behaving.

Forgetting all about the bathroom I walk back out to the living room, prepared to make up an excuse to get myself and Keegan out of there, but I come up short when I see them laughing together on the couch. Keegan leans into him and says something low in his ear, and when his mouth turns up into a sexy smirk, I hit my limit.

Two days. I've been on my own two days, and I'm a freaking mess. Screw excuses, I just need out of here.

"Hey, where are you going?" Keegan yells after me when I bolt to the door, but I'm too upset to stop. I'm fully aware of how random it is for me to just go running out of his apartment without saying a word, but I need some time alone. Time to reset and sober up and I don't know, freaking get over myself or something.

I'm already down a flight of stairs when Keegan catches up to me. I didn't want to wait for the elevator and risk having to explain my sudden departure in front of Wyatt, so the stairs seemed the best option. Only now that I'm on them I'm thinking it was a bad idea, considering how I'm struggling to stay upright.

"Hey, stop, what's going on?" Keegan asks pulling on my arm, jerking me back. Not hard, but enough to make me stumble.

"He has a gun!" I shout a little too loudly in the confined space. Hell, Wyatt probably even heard me.

"So?" Keegan looks at me like I've lost my mind. *Well, maybe I have!*

"So it's a gun!"

"Yeah, people own guns, Brailey. It's in the freaking constitution. Owning a gun doesn't make him a bad guy."

"But we don't know him! He could be a psychopath or something!"

"Unless you found a meat locker and a machete, I'd say we're okay. Pretty sure psychopaths tend to get a little more creative than just using a gun."

I can't do this in the middle of the stairwell while I'm drunk and all mixed up in my head. "Whatever. Just let go, Key. I'm just going home to go to bed. I'm tired." I don't sound tired, I sound whiny. Plus, I don't even technically have a bed, but I can't ask to stay on her couch like I'd planned. She'll keep trying to talk to me and talking is the last thing I want to do right now.

"Knock it off, B. I know what you're doing." I'm still making my getaway, but Keegan is hot on my heels. I manage to make it to my apartment without falling and breaking my neck, but when I drop my keys, Keegan bends down and gets them before I can react. She opens my door and pushes me inside. "Sit," she barks at me.

With a mock salute I take a seat on the floor – *because, ya know, no couch yet* - and watch Keegan's face go soft when she sits down next to me. I immediately don't like the look she's giving me; I've seen it many times from the staff at Mayford. That look is called pity.

"Don't look at me like that."

"I'm not looking at you with anything except understanding, so shut it."

"Huh?" I shut my eyes tightly because suddenly

Keegan has three heads. "Why the hell am I so wasted when I've only had like…" I start ticking off beers on my fingers, but stop when it gets to four because math is hard.

"Sweetie, you had six beers. My bad for not cutting you off, didn't realize you were such a cheap drunk."

"Math is stupid." Yep. Totally blaming math for being the reason for my drunkenness. "I'm sorry I'm acting like a crazy bitch," I apologize and give her a pouty, puppy dog face.

"No apologies necessary, B. I shouldn't have flirted with him so much."

I smile at her, because Keegan really does seem like she's going to be a great friend to have, and I…

"Wait - what are you talking about? You're free to flirt with whoever you want. He's obviously into you. You should head back up there, I'm sure he would appreciate some alone time with you, now that the third wheel is gone."

"If anyone is the third wheel, it was me."

"What? Are you drunk, too? I could have sworn you only drank like, one beer."

"I swear, you are so blind sometimes, B. Were you paying attention at all?"

"What are you talking about?" She's not making any sense, and I'm in no frame of mind to be trying to figure shit out on my own.

"He was only talking to me because you weren't talking to him. *At all*. If I hadn't kept the conversation going it would have been quiet and weird. But he spent the entire night staring at you, which you would know if you bothered to ever look in his direction. I flirted, hoping it would motivate you to make a move on him or something. It backfired. Even drunk you're too stubborn to act on your attraction to him."

"You don't know what you're talking about," I say on a yawn.

"Come on, let's get you in bed," she says as she lifts me and wraps my arm around her shoulders so she can support me while she all but drags my limp body to my bedroom and lays me down on my make-shift 'bed' consisting of a pile of blankets.

"I'm sorry I wanted to punch you in your face tonight." Keegan chuckles at my confession and pulls the covers over me. My eyes are closed and I feel myself starting to drift off.

"You wanted to punch me?"

"Yeah. A lot." I hear Keegan laughing as I drift out of consciousness, but I don't miss the last thing she says before I fall asleep completely.

"Jealousy can make people do some crazy things."

WYATT

One minute I'm laughing with Keegan on the couch, waiting for Brailey to get back from her extremely long trip to my bathroom, and the next thing I know both girls are running out of my apartment like it's on fire.

I'm tempted to go after them but decide against it. Today was bizarre and completely unexpected. I'm only supposed to watch Brailey, stay close to her, not completely infiltrate her life. I'm not sure what the repercussions of getting too close to her will end up being, but

I have a feeling I'm not going to have a choice in the matter.

Brailey was quiet and seemed uncomfortable all night, but her loud friend kept the conversation flowing. I lost count of how many times I had to apologize when I would get distracted by something Brailey was doing and wouldn't hear what Keegan was saying. She never got annoyed, she would just smirk like she was in on my little secret.

She doesn't know my secret, though, and if letting her think my attention for Brailey was out of attraction will keep her from getting suspicious, then so be it.

Not that Brailey isn't desirable. I'd seen pictures of her before I moved into her building, but none of them prepared me for what she would look like in person. Keegan is gorgeous in a runway model sort of way, while Brailey has more of a girl-next-door look to her. The two of them couldn't be any different, but watching them together it was clear to see how well they fit as friends, balancing each other out.

When Brailey spilled my boxers all over the sidewalk and her face turned the most adorable shade of pink, I couldn't help be take the opportunity to get close to her. Maybe I could have left a little more distance between us when I bent down to repack the box, but something about her, something I felt since I laid eyes on her that very first time out in front of the building, kept tugging me in her direction. The need to be near her was strong and foreign, unlike anything I've ever felt towards a woman, especially one I'd never met.

As soon as I was actually near her I realized my

mistake. The dress she wore made her look feminine and delicate, and the modest amount of exposed skin shouldn't have been such a turn-on, but almost instantly I felt my dick getting hard in my pants. My mind automatically started picturing what her soft skin would feel like if I ran my fingertips teasingly across her shoulders, down her chest, dipping into the V between her breasts that look like they would fit perfectly in the palms of my hands.

She smelled like peaches and sunsets; an obscure and tantalizing scent that had me wondering what would happen if I were to replace my hand with my tongue, trailing a wet path down her breasts, over her stomach and not stopping until I found the most intimate part of her. Would she taste as sweet as she smells?

Indulging in unrealistic fantasies involving Brailey is a waste of time, and if I don't find a way to keep those fantasies at bay, then I'm going to be spending more time taking cold showers than actually doing my job.

Avoiding her and keeping watch from a distance isn't a possibility anymore. Both her and Keegan pretty much railroaded their way into my life on the first damn day, so I just need to find a way to keep my dick in check and focus on the task at hand.

The task at hand meaning my job, which doesn't require me to go after Brailey. Seeing the look on her face before she ran out my door put an ache in my chest and a restless energy in my legs, the desire to run after her and make sure she's okay entirely too strong for having just met her today.

To keep from giving in to my unprofessional and

inappropriate urges, I busy myself with unpacking my sheets, making my bed so that I don't have to sleep directly on the mattress. I still have to put my bed and a bunch of other shit back together, which I'd planned on doing tonight, but that was before I met the two women who just waltzed into my life and turned all of my carefully laid plans for Brailey to shit.

"Yeah, I guess just put it over there."

The delivery guys are being less than enthusiastic about helping me. I'm pretty sure if I hadn't bribed them with twenty bucks each then they would have unloaded my crap and left it sitting right there on the sidewalk. Apparently I should have tipped them a little better still, because they just keep dropping boxes and furniture in random places instead of where I ask them to sit it.

In fact, the more I try to guide them, the more annoyed they seem to get with me.

"Ow!" One of the jerk movers shoves me out of his way with his shoulder, sending me flying backwards into the doorframe.

"Hey! Apologize to the lady." I don't know where he came from or how he got inside my apartment without me noticing, but Wyatt has the jerk by his collar and looks like he's about to pound the guy's face in. The mover guy has at least thirty pounds and a couple inches on Wyatt, but he's more blubber than muscle and his big belly protruding over his pants is definitely no match for Wyatt's meaty arms. You can practically see Wyatt's muscles through his long sleeved tee.

"S-s-sorry," the guy stutters, and I almost feel a little sorry for him. But then my shoulder aches from where he just threw me into the wall and that pity evaporates.

"Now put the box where the lady asked," Wyatt orders. I'm a little too dumbfounded to speak, so I just stand back and watch as Wyatt orders them around until the truck is finally empty.

"Well crap," I mutter as I take in my box filled apartment.

"Problem?" Wyatt asks coolly as he opens my fridge, helping himself to a bottle of water.

"Uh, I guess I didn't realize none of it would be put together." Probably something normal people would have been aware of – but I'm not normal. Wyatt laughs, but otherwise doesn't push the issue regarding lack of common knowledge.

"Looks like you got most of it from Ikea, so it should be easy enough to put together." He's already tearing open a box, pulling out parts and laying them out. A drop of water sits on his upper lip, and my tongue slips out, swiping my own lips while I indulge in a little fantasy of swiping my tongue across *his* lips instead.

"I'm happy to just be your man candy for the day, but it would probably go a lot faster if you helped." *Busted.* My face flames with embarrassment, but his teasing smile is so damn endearing that a laugh slips out.

"Sorry, of course, I'll help. What do we need to do?"

For the next two hours I basically played assistant to Wyatt while he did all the actual labor. He was right – most of it was pretty simple. Or at least it looked simple, since I was more an observer than a participant. Despite having assembled my bed frame, side tables, dresser, and kitchen table, Wyatt looks fresh as a daisy. The man is in good shape. And those hands…those big, strong, capable hands. Hands he used to build furniture while I fantasized about what those hands could be doing to me instead.

"I'm starved. Why don't we order some food and then I'll get your living room furniture done?"

"I'd be happy to buy you lunch, it's the least I can do, but you really don't have to stay and finish the rest. I'm sure you have other things you need to do."

Guess he didn't have anywhere to be, because we just polished off the last of the Thai food I ordered and we're still sitting on my new couch watching the newest Star Wars movie.

"I still think she's going to be Luke's daughter."

"Don't you think that's a little too obvious, though? My guess is that she's Han Solo's daughter and Kylo Ren's half-sister."

Apparently my memory loss did not extend to my knowledge of Star Wars movies. It all came flooding back to me the minute the opening credits popped onto the screen.

"That's stretching it a bit," Wyatt argues. The end credits are rolling and we've been debating Ren's char-acter for half the movie. "Plus the producers have already admitted they don't know where they are going with the story. They could go anywhere with the plot."

Tossing the last Thai container in the garbage, I turn and scoff at Wyatt. "Puh-lease. They probably just say that to keep people guessing. There's no way they don't already know where they are going with the story."

"Maybe you're right," he offers with a shrug. "So do you want to get the rest of this done, or…"

My eyebrow quirks when his sentence trails off and he averts his gaze. "Or what?"

"I've got the first six episodes on DVD in my apartment." He rubs the back of his neck nervously. Dammit. Why is it so adorable when he's nervous? And why would he be nervous? He practically attacked the moving guy for bumping into me, but asking me to watch a movie with him has him acting all shy and uncertain?

Like I said – adorable.

"It's been a while since I've seen them. I could probably use a refresher. Why don't you go get them while I finish picking up in here?"

There isn't a lot to clean up, so it only takes me about five seconds. I spend the rest of the time checking myself in the mirror. Yeah, I'm *that* girl now. Is it even possible for me to pretend I'm not around Wyatt? He's the epitome of sexiness, and turns out, has a pretty great personality, too. He stood up for me and demanded an apology from that mover, then spent half his day fighting with the vague instructions that came with my furniture, and now we're going to have a Star Wars marathon?

Conversation flows easily around him, despite how incredibly on edge I feel when he's near. My whole damn apartment smells like his cologne now, and every time I breathe in my body silently begs to be closer to the source of that delicious scent. Even now, when I inhale deeply, the smell is so strong that I can practically feel his body close to mine.

"Got the movies," Wyatt says from right behind me, making me jump. No wonder he felt like he was actually next to me. My imagination isn't *that* good. "I also brought some bags of popcorn in case we wanted snacks later. Wasn't sure if you already had any."

I don't. I made a quick run to the supermarket yesterday to get drinks and a few necessities, but microwave popcorn wasn't one of them.

Wyatt gives me a few seconds to admire his backside as he bends over to load episode one into the DVD player, which he also hooked up for me before we watched the last movie. He takes a seat at the end of the couch opposite mine, putting a safe amount of distance between us. At least it felt safe at first. The further we get into the movie, the more his distance starts to feel like torture rather than safety.

"Can you pause it? I need to use the restroom."

Wyatt clears his throat and grabs the remote, looking every bit as uncomfortable as I feel. *Is he feeling the sexual tension between us too? Or does he literally just feel uncomfortable around me?*

Not giving myself time to dwell on it, I make the most of my few minutes away from Wyatt by throwing some cold water on my face and giving myself a pep talk about why it's not a good idea to try and seduce my neighbor.

The microwave beeps as I come back into the room and Wyatt is at the sink, washing one of the new bowls that came with the delivery of my dishes today. Why does he have to be so freaking thoughtful and sweet? Why can't he just be an asshole and make it easier to keep my libido in check?

After grabbing us each a bottle of water from the fridge, I plop myself back down on the couch. We didn't get around to assembling my coffee table, and I feel Wyatt take a seat next to me while I'm bent over, putting the bottles on the floor.

Definitely no distance between us anymore. I didn't even realize that when I sat back down, I sat smack in the middle of the couch. Though Wyatt has plenty of room on the other side of him, so practically sitting on my lap had to have been intentional.

Wyatt holds the bowl out to me, and I almost smack my forehead at my stupidity. He just sat close to share the popcorn, not because he's trying to actually be closer to me.

God, I'm such an idiot.

Or maybe I'm not. Don't think it's necessary that he sling his arm over the back of the couch and casually rub my shoulder with the tips of his fingers in order for us to share a snack.

Also, I was wrong before. Being nestled into Wyatt's side, but not being able to kiss him or touch him or climb on top of him? *That* is torture.

CHAPTER
FIVE

I'm hiding out in the laundry room, washing all my new clothes before I start work in a few days. I've been avoiding both of them the last couple days, not ready to face either of them after my day spent with Wyatt.

Keegan has been a nightmare since she walked in to my apartment without knocking and caught Wyatt and I snuggled up on the couch. It was an innocent snuggle, nothing happened between us, but we were definitely cozy. By episode three of Star Wars, Wyatt was laying against the back of my couch with me playing the part of the little spoon. At some point the sexual tension eased into a tolerable need to be close, which resulted in a game of spooning. I call it a game because we were both very aware of what parts should not be touching, and we both made a conscious effort to keep space between them.

I will never admit it to her, but I was so thankful for Keegan's interruption. My willpower was waning, and the longer we laid like that, the more I wanted to just say 'screw it' and flip over, putting an end to the stupid spooning game.

Wyatt jumped up so fast when Keegan came barreling into the room that he almost knocked me onto the floor. He mumbled some sort of apology before bolting out the door, leaving me behind to feel like a teenager who just got caught by her parents while making out with her boyfriend.

Now Keegan is convinced that more is going on between us than there is. I mean, I've only known Wyatt a handful of days, so it's not *possible* for there to be more going on. Right?

Whatever, it's just lust. He's still pretty much a stranger. Yeah, so he's a polite, considerate, sweet and seriously hot stranger, but *still* a stranger. The fact that my body seems to react to him in ways that I'm still not willing to totally admit to yet doesn't change anything. I've not known him nearly long enough to be obsessing over him every waking second. Too bad that's *exactly* what I've been doing.

I wish I could talk to Mark about it, but even with our murky history aside, I'm not sure it would be appropriate. I don't want to hurt him, and even though I have no idea if he has *those* types of feelings for me still, I don't want to risk it. I've been putting off calling him, only taking the time to send a text once in a while, and I know it's bothering him because he's clearly agitated in his messages, which makes me feel horribly guilty.

I throw in another load of clothes into the washer in the lower level of my apartment building, and decide to just get it over with and call him while I wait.

"Hey! Finally!" I yell excitedly. He laughs softly on the other end, but even through the phone I can hear the sadness in it. "I'm sorry, I know we haven't had a chance to talk much. Are you busy now? Is this a bad time?"

He hesitates a second before answering. "No, no it's fine. I was about to head out, but it can wait. Tell me what's going on with you."

"Oh, well I don't want to keep you. Really, it's fine. I can call you later."

Things feel strained and awkward, which is new for us. I've never felt anything but completely at ease when talking to Mark. It's my fault that we haven't talked much, and the distance is putting a wedge between us, but I'm not sure how to fix it. I'm not even sure why I'm avoiding him to begin with.

"Stop it, I told you it's fine," he says with a sigh, his words having a little snap to them, which surprises me.

"Okay...well, tell me how things are at Mayford."

He spends a few minutes giving me a recap of what's going on, but he sounds disinterested or distracted...I'm not sure which. I wish he was here in person so I could see his face and maybe be able to figure out what's bothering him, because there's no way he's that upset over not talking to me in a few days.

"So, that's about it. Enough about me and my boring life, tell me about your new place. You ready to start your job? Make any friends yet?"

"Yeah! Her name is Keegan and she's great, you would just love her Mark. I can't wait for you to come visit." I didn't mean to sound so overly enthusiastic, and the exaggerated pep in my voice makes me cringe. Good thing he isn't here to witness in person just how forced my response was. I prattle on about Keegan for a few minutes, intentionally leaving out any details that involve Wyatt. I know when Mark comes to visit he'll most likely end up meeting him, but I don't want Mark to read into things too much, especially with this weirdness between us right now.

"Yeah, about that. I was thinking I might try to come up next weekend if you don't have anything going on."

"Oh my gosh! Really?!" *That* enthusiasm is not forced, and I'm practically jumping up and down with giddiness.

"Hey, Brailey, got a minute?" I whip around and see Wyatt peeking his head into the laundry room, looking apprehensive. His nervousness distracts me, and I miss Mark's question.

"Brailey?" Mark asks through the phone, getting my attention again.

"Oh, I'm sorry, what did you say?" I hold up a finger to Wyatt, asking him to wait a minute, and turn my back to him. I don't have a shot in hell of focusing if I'm looking at Wyatt.

"I asked who that was. I heard a man's voice."

Shit. Um. Am I a good liar? Dammit, I don't know! Think Brailey, think.

"Oh, um, that was just the uh...maintenance guy! I was having a problem with my plumbing and he is going to fix it."

I startle when I feel Wyatt's arm brush against mine, and out of the corner of my eye I see him smirking at me.

"Okay well, let me call you back, okay? I've got to um, let the maintenance guy do his thing. Bye!" I hang up without waiting for Mark to say bye, my heart beating a little faster than is really necessary.

"Boyfriend?" Wyatt asks, crossing his arms. I don't answer. Instead I start refolding a stack of clothes I'd just finished folding, just to have something to do with my hands.

"What's up, Wyatt? You need something?" I try to sound casual, but it comes out a little breathy.

"Well, I was going to ask you if-"

My phone rings, cutting him off, and I pick it up to hit ignore, only I miss and hit the answer button instead.

"Hello?"

No one answers, but I can hear crackling noises on the other end, so I know someone is there. I say hello a few more times, and just when I'm about to hang up, someone finally speaks up.

"Brailey! Put the phone down and come play with me!"

It sounds like a little kid, but it's so muffled and staticky that I can barely make out the words. The voice is familiar but I can't place where I know it from.

"Just do your thing and ignore me, Shaun!"

My own voice comes through the other line, and a sharp, stabbing sensation shoots through my abdomen and up to my chest when the little boy's voice rings out again.

"Come on, please! We need a fourth!"

"Okay, okay, buddy. I'm coming."

I absentmindedly rub the spot on my chest that's restricting in pain, desperate to hear Shaun's voice again, but I hear a clicking sound and the static disappears.

The call ends suddenly, and I start hyperventilating, my shallow breaths doing little to help ease the panic coursing through my veins. I'm still holding my phone up to my ear, my hand clenching it so tightly that my fingers start to ache, so I loosen my grip and let it crash to the floor. Tears start gushing from my eyes and my chest aches so hard I could swear I'm actually having a heart attack.

It's not until I feel strong arms pull me up against a warm body that I snap out of my haze and spring into action. I start screaming at the top of my lungs, thrashing and kicking, trying to free myself of the tight hold some-one suddenly has me in.

"Leave me alone! Why are you doing this?! Get away from me!"

"Brailey!" Keegan's cry stops me mid-scream and my body stills instantly. I watch as she runs over to me, looking over my shoulder and speaking to whoever is holding me. "I've got her, let her go. Seriously, I've got this, just go."

My breathing starts to deepen and my heart rate be-gins its descent back to normal speeds while I stand there with Keegan's arms around my shoulders. I'm dizzy and weak from my panic attack and all I want in that moment is to be laying in my own bed. Luckily, Keegan notices my body starting to droop and she pulls me toward the door, but my legs give out again and she's not strong enough to hold me.

Next thing I know, I'm being scooped up into the air and carried over to the elevator. My head is heavy and if the person holding me is intending to kill me, then their job will be an easy one because I no longer have it in me to fight back. I let my head fall to the chest of whoever is carrying me, and curiosity gets the best of me, so I open my eyes and I'm stunned to see Wyatt staring back me.

My eyes widen a fraction before falling closed again, and they stay that way until I feel him laying me in my bed. The last thing I remember is Wyatt kissing my forehead right before I fall asleep.

"There she is! Have a good night, sis?" Shaun asks as I toss my keys on the counter and plop down on a stool across from him. I snatch a grape out of his bowl, almost dropping it when Shaun swats at my hand playfully.

"Shut up. I don't want to talk about it."

"Aw, c'mon. I haven't seen you do the walk of shame since college. Who was the lucky guy?"

My forehead slams down on the counter hard enough to make a loud thump. I don't care. My head is already pounding so hard I barely feel it.

"You know you'll tell me eventually. Save us both the trouble and just tell me now so we can move on."

"Fine," I grumble. "It was Mark."

Shaun looks away, searching his mind to figure out who Mark is, his eyes going big as freaking dinner plates when it finally registers who I'm talking about.

"Mark as in your co-worker Mark?"

I still can't believe it myself. When I got the call from the bank saying the loan I applied for to pay for Shaun's surgery was denied, I was too devastated to deal. For months I've been working my ass off - getting letters from employers, friends, businesses I frequent - anyone and everyone who could say something positive on my behalf, I begged them to help. My credit is already shot because of all the debt I've wracked up in medical bills, and it was a long shot anyway, but it's still upsetting as hell to know I've failed Shaun. Again.

Not once have I ever felt like Shaun was a burden. After our parents died, I willingly took over the role of parent for Shaun. He's the best brother anyone could ever ask for, and if our asshole foster parents had paid enough attention to us, he wouldn't be in the condition he's in now. I told them for weeks that something wasn't right and Shaun needed to see a doctor, but they never listened. It wasn't until he ended up in the hospital with Rheumatic Heart Disease from untreated strep that CPS stepped in and removed us from the home.

Shaun recovered and we moved on with life. Then a few years ago for his eighteenth birthday I took him to play laser tag to celebrate. We'd never gotten to do those fun things growing up and he got to invite a bunch of friends. It was a great day - until Shaun collapsed. I was already in nursing school, thank God, and I gave him CPR until the ambulance got there.

I'll never forget the minute the doctor walked in and the grim look on his face. I knew it was going to be bad, that our lives would never be the same. Shaun needed a new heart. Only eighteen years old and he was given only a few more years to live if he didn't get a transplant. That damn strep throat from when he was a kid had de-stroyed his, all because our foster parents were too lazy to get him some antibiotics.

"Sis," Shaun says, placing his hand over mine and

pulling me out of those dark memories. "Where did you go just now?"

How am I going to tell him I failed again? How am I going to tell him that it's looking more and more like he's not going to be alive much longer, and there's not a damn thing I can do about it?

My room is pitch black when I jolt out of my dream, my clothes damp from sweat. I hear voices coming from just outside my bedroom door, which is slightly cracked, allowing a sliver of light to stream across my bedroom floor. My head is pounding and my muscles ache like I've ran a marathon, but I've been through the after effects of a panic attack a time or two and I push past the pain and make my way over to the door.

I freeze when I hear Wyatt's voice. I don't mean to eavesdrop, but what he says gives me pause long enough to catch part of his conversation. His back is to me as he stands in my kitchen, talking on his phone, and by the sounds of it, whoever is on the other side of the conversation is pissing him off.

"No, she's fine. I don't know if she remembered anything, all I know is that she flipped the fuck out. It needs to stop, this isn't right. No, I understand the-… yes sir."

I don't have a chance to react before he turns and sees me standing in the doorway. He doesn't look surprised, almost like he knew I was there and either wanted me to or didn't mind if I overheard him. He takes a tentative step towards me and I look around, realizing we're alone in my apartment.

"Who was that?" I ask cautiously, my voice barely above a whisper.

"No one." He looks worried but his words come out brusque, making it clear he's not going to tell me anything.

"Alright...well thanks for helping me out. I owe you. I'm fine now, though, so you can go."

"I'm not going anywhere until you tell me what happened." I take a step in his direction this time and don't bother masking my anger. How *dare* he demand I open up to him when he was obviously just talking to someone about me, but won't tell me about it.

"Yeah, not really any of your business. I don't know you and I'm not keen on sharing the personal details of my life with strangers."

"We aren't strangers, we're neighbors. We hung out and you drank all my beer a few nights ago, and then we spent all day bitching about Ikea while putting together that table you're leaning on, remember?" He moves towards me with one more step, a smirk lifting at the corner of his mouth. My attention is immediately pulled down and I have to bite down on my tongue to keep from licking my lips. "You can't tell me you forgot about the part where you laid in my arms, torturing me through one of my favorite movies. Don't think I'll ever be able

to watch that episode without thinking of you now...
Peaches."

"Yes, of course I remember, and I appreciate your
help and everything, but that doesn't make us friends.
We still barely know each other." I can't comment on
the part where he said I was torturing him. I'm too distracted by that mouth of his and thinking about kissing
that cocky smirk off his face.

"So let's hang out," he says casually with a shrug.
I'm all hot and bothered over here, and he's just shrugging like the temperature in the room didn't just jump up
twenty degrees. "You need me to spend time with you
so you can get comfortable opening up, then that's what
we'll do. Because like it or not, you're going to tell me
what happened down there, and I'm a man of little patience. So help me out and tell me what I can do to speed
up this whole 'becoming friends' process."

Wyatt closes the distance between us, his eyes darting to my mouth before he brings his hand up and rubs
the pad of his thumb across my bottom lip, then pulling
down and letting it go with a quiet 'pop.'

"If spending time with me was so torturous, then
why are you trying to do it more?" *Stupid, stupid girl.
You finally find your voice and* that's *what you say?*

"What can I say? I like a challenge. And I don't
mind torture when it's as sweet as you, Peaches."

Somehow we've moved to standing only inches
apart, so close that I can feel his breath fanning on my
face. His head dips down, our foreheads touching and
then our noses, and I let my eyes drift shut. I can feel his
mouth closing in on mine; so close that if I were to in-

hale through my mouth, I would probably be able to taste the cinnamon left behind from his toothpaste or gum or whatever lucky substance it was that got to take up residence in that mouth I want to taste so badly.

After a few seconds – that feel more like hours – I open my eyes, not at all expecting to see the pain looking back at me. Pulling back, already hating the loss of his heat, I notice it's not just pain in his eyes. He looks… conflicted?

My mouth is suddenly painfully dry and for some strange reason, I feel tears pricking at the back of my eyes. Wyatt just stands there, unmoving, and watches while I run to the kitchen and down half a bottle of water in one drink. The whole atmosphere suddenly feels uncomfortable and awkward, and I feel like I'm slowly suffocating under his stare. I need him to leave. Only the thought of him leaving makes me feel a little panicked and I know if he tried to walk out my door right now that I would end up begging him to stay. My thoughts are so jumbled it feels like I'm drunk again, but this time I have no excuse. Nothing to blame my feelings on other than my hormones and inability to control them.

"You get some rest and I'll see you tomorrow." Wyatt's voice startles me, and I wonder how much time has passed with me leaning against the counter and staring at my half empty bottle of water. The urge to leap on his back to keep him from going is pretty fierce, but I manage to not act like a lunatic and respond with only a curt nod as I take a sip of my water.

It's not until he reaches the door that it sinks in what he just said. "Wait. What? Why would I see you tomorrow?"

"You're making me lunch and I'm going to hang up those paintings and put together those tables we didn't get to yesterday," he says, nodding to the large paintings sitting on my living room floor, propped up against the wall next to the unopened boxes.

"Uhhhh, I don't remember asking you to do that." My mind scrambles to remember if I did something dumb, like ask for a favor in the midst of my stupid panic attack and just don't remember.

"You didn't," he responds before pulling the door shut behind him, not giving me a chance to argue.

"What do you mean Mayra's been transferred? Why would that even happen? Where did she go?"

"I'm sorry, sir, but that information can only legally be obtained by a blood relative. I'm not permitted to divulge that to a friend of a patient without her permission."

"I'm not just a 'friend'. Surely this means something to you."

I'm eavesdropping, but I can't help it. As soon as I heard her name, I had to listen.

"While I can appreciate you providing your work identification, without a legal document stating we are

legally obligated to release this information to the bu-
reau, then I still can't tell you. You addressed yourself as
a personal visitor, so I'm assuming this is not an official
visit."

I can't see his face, but his voice is so loud and angry
that I think it could crumble walls of stone if he wanted
it to.

"Oh, I can get something official for you if that's how
you want to handle this. I can also make things incred-
ibly difficult for you, and that's not an empty threat. This
is unacceptable. You act like I'm some sort of creep off
the streets. I can provide you any personal information
about Mayra you want to prove how well I know her. It's
just a waste of time to make me go through the hoops of
acquiring a warrant." Silence.

I gotta hand it to Becky, the receptionist. She's been
holding up well under his booming, scary-ass voice. The
only sound now is his heavy, harsh breaths, and I picture
a fire breathing dragon on the other side of the door, or
in the least, someone very big and threatening.

"I-I'm s-sorry, sir. I-I'd help you if I could." I cover
my mouth when a snicker escapes my lips at the sound
of her stuttering. Mean, I know, but seriously. Becky is
actually kind of a bitch. It's funny to hear her getting shit
dished back out at her.

"This isn't over," he threatens, his voice no longer
loud and yelling, but rather calm and menacing.

I hear the door close behind him, and I step into the
entryway where the receptionist sits.

"Becky," I greet her. "Do you know who this wallet
belongs to?" I ask, bending over and pretending to pick

something up.

She's too shaken up to notice I'm not actually hold-ing a wallet. I could be stark naked right now and she wouldn't notice, so I take advantage of her being dis-tracted and tell her I'm going to see if the gentleman who just left dropped it.

I see him stepping up to a big pick-up truck just as I step outside, and I call out to him.

"Wait, sir! You forgot this!" I take off running down the path to where he's standing. When I finally reach him, he slowly turns to face me, and I suddenly lose the ability to breathe.

"Excuse me?"

I'm a little winded from running down the steps, which tells me I definitely need to quit skipping the gym. Although, to be fair, I'm pretty sure I quit breathing the second the man in front of me turned around.

Holy snacks, he is delicious. I don't think I've ever seen someone this hot - at least not in real life - sans Photoshop.

His hair is dark and a little long on the top, but it looks intentional, not like he skipped a haircut. His eyes are so dark they're almost black, and his chiseled face makes my mouth water. He's a few inches taller than me, and we'd probably be the same height if I wore high enough heels, but his shoulders are so broad that he seems much bigger.

He lets me blatantly check him out, not seeming at all affected by my drooling over him. He's probably a cocky sumbitch, but he deserves to be, because holy hotness, Batman.

"Okay, sorry," I say, shaking my head and forcing myself to look him in the face again.

Nope. One more quick gaze down his body and back up, thanks.

"Anyway." This time when I look at him he's smirking, the cold and emotionless expression softened just a smidge. "You're hot. It would be a crime not to appreciate it. Thanks for letting me," I say seriously, and he laughs.

"You said I forgot something?" He asks, and my panties melt just a little at the silky smoothness of his voice. Yeah, I heard him talking to Becky, but he was practically growling. Which was also hot, but this is totally different.

"Yeah, I lied. I just wanted to talk to you." His smile grows, and I realize how that sounded. "Shit, not to hit on you. Not that you're not worth hitting on, but...oh my gosh...you make my brain go all kinds of stupid," I say, flailing my arms around, expressing how exasperating he is. I close my eyes and start talking again. "I didn't mean to eavesdrop, but I heard you back there talking to Becky."

When he doesn't respond, I open one eye to make sure he's still there, then close it back when I see him still standing in the same place. "Um, hello? Did you hear me? Should I just go on?" I need to get back to work, and he's really not easy to talk to.

"Why are your eyes closed?" He asks, and I can hear the smile in his voice.

"Because I can't talk when I'm looking at you. All I can think about is licking you like an ice cream cone and

it's very distracting."

He laughs again. "You always this honest?"

I slowly open my eyes again, because, well, it's getting weird. "Why not? There are worse qualities to have than being brutally honest."

"Unless you're brutally honest about stuff that hurts people."

"I'm not a bitch, if that's what you're implying," I snap. I'm not really irritated with him. I just want to see how he reacts. He throws his hands up, and all I can think about is how big his hands are and how they would feel on my body. "My, my, grandma, what big hands you have."

He raises a confused eyebrow, but I don't bother finishing my thought. 'The better to spank you with, my dear.'

"Listen, it's been real, but I gotta get back to work. Here's my number. Call me tonight." I shove a piece of paper in his hand that has my number scrawled on it. He looks at it and then back at me.

"Awfully bossy, aren't you? What if I have a girlfriend?"

"Awfully full of yourself, aren't you?" I ask, rolling my eyes. "I want to talk to you about Mayra, dumbass, not go on a date. I get off at seven, so call me after that!" I yell over my shoulder as I run back inside.

This day had started out so terrible. After making that huge mistake this weekend...just the thought of having to face Mark was enough to have me debating whether or not to call off. Damn bills. Luckily I've been able to avoid him all day. Unluckily, right as I come back inside, my mood considerably perkier after the little exchange with hot stranger guy, I come face to face with Mark, essentially zapping all that perkiness right out of me.

"Hey, I'm sorry Mark, I don't have time to talk right now. I'll come find you before my shift is over, okay?" I blurt out without slowing, just barely making eye contact, though I at least looked long enough to catch that angry glare he sends me. Not wanting to hear his response, I literally take off jogging. It's shitty of me to avoid him like this, I know, but my life's way too damn complicated already without adding work drama to the mix.

CHAPTER
SIX

Thanks to another restless night, I'm having to blare music from my iPhone just to stay awake while I redo the laundry I left behind yesterday. Plus, the music is keeping me from dwelling on remembering the reason why this laundry was left behind in the first place.

"Holy shit, Wyatt! You scared the crap out of me!" I yell, yanking out my earbuds and smacking him on the arm. He's laughing at me, and I'm so entranced by the carefree sound of it that for a second I forget I'm pissed at him for sneaking up on me.

"I'm sorry," he says between laughs. "I called your name three times and you didn't hear me, obviously. I didn't mean to scare you." He casually puts his arm around my shoulders and pulls me in for a side hug. It's a meaningless gesture, something a friend would do, just an apology hug. But knowing that doesn't stop the tingling sensation from spreading throughout my body, and it doesn't prevent my knees from weakening when his fingertips brush lightly on the bare skin of my shoulder.

"Ugh, whatever. You suck," I pout, shoving him off of me. I hope he thinks I'm pushing him off of me in a playful way and doesn't realize I'm doing it because if his arm stays around me much longer I might melt into a puddle of goo in the middle of the laundry room floor.

"Okay, okay, sorry. No sneaking up on Brailey, noted. Anyway, I was just wanting to see if we could push lunch back to dinner? Something came up and I have to step out."

"We don't have to do either, considering you invited yourself over in the first place." I'm just teasing, but when his face falls I feel horrible, so I quickly try to reassure him. "Not that I'd ever pass up someone offering to help with manual labor. If you do a good enough job then you might end up getting roped into other various household things, like fixing my faulty plumbing and changing light bulbs."

Wyatt laughs nervously as he moves to stand next to me again. Nervous Wyatt is sexy as hell, but now that he's so close to me I'm the one getting nervous. He picks up a shirt out of my basket and starts folding it distractedly and I just stare like an idiot, watching him fold *my* laundry.

"Hey, just because you dubbed me the maintenance guy to whoever you were talking to yesterday doesn't mean I actually have to do all of that."

"Okay, smartass, then what is it that you do?"

"Maybe I'm an international spy, like James Bond." I roll my eyes at him and he laughs. "Tonight, Peaches. I'll tell you all about myself, you tell me about yourself. Since we're friends and all now, remember?" He says with a playful wink.

Oh. Right. Friends...

"Friends...not a date..." I muse to myself, then immediately blush when I realize I've just said that out loud. "Just wanted to make sure you understood that." I spit out, hoping he doesn't realize I hadn't actually meant to say that out loud. His knowing smile tells me he's not buying it, and words come spewing from my mouth before I can stop them. "Not that I wouldn't want to date you! I mean, I don't, but you know...you're attractive and all that. I can see why some girls would want to date you. Just...not me, because you know...friends."

I bury my face in my hands and hide from him like a two-year-old. I keep expecting to hear him laughing at me, but after a long moment of pure silence, I think he might have just bailed when I got all weird. I crack my fingers enough for me to peek out and see a very amused Wyatt standing there, dangling a bright pink lacy thong off the tip of his finger.

I snatch the dangling panties away from him and toss it back in my basket, groaning and wishing like hell I could punch myself in the face right now.

"We don't have to call it that if you don't want, Peaches," he says with a wink as he backs away from me towards the door. "I'll text you when I get back. Oh, and you wouldn't hear me complaining if you wore that sexy little number tonight." *What the hell?*

I'm so tempted to yell at him for assuming that one, it would matter what underwear I have on because there is no chance he's going to see them. Well, okay, there's a good chance, but he shouldn't just assume that. And two, for giving me that hot smoldering look he does that has me needing to change out my panties anyway.

Really, what I *should* do is tell him to go to hell and put a stop to whatever game he's playing. My spastic brain chooses door number three and I hear myself blurting out, "You don't have my phone number!" The biggest shit-eating grin spreads across his face, and in that moment it becomes glaringly clear that I may never have the upper hand when it comes to Wyatt.

Wyatt pulls his phone out of his back pocket and types something, then my phone buzzes where I've laid it on the counter. I look at it and sure enough, there's one unread message notification looking back at me. Sender's name is Sexy Neighbor. A slow smile creeps up my face while I waver between wanting to kick Keegan's ass and kiss her for giving Wyatt my number and putting his into my phone.

Wyatt pops his head around the doorway, catching me grinning like an idiot down at my phone.

"Hey, you buy tools yet or should I bring my own?" I startle at the sound of his voice and he laughs when I blush.

"Um, huh?"

"Tools. You know, like a hammer and nails. For the paintings." He mimics the movements of hammering something like I'm an idiot.

"I know what a hammer and nails are, you didn't have to do the motions. And no, I don't have any."

"Okay, I'll bring mine. See you later, Peaches," he says with a wink before disappearing again.

An hour later I'm back in my apartment and trying to talk myself into texting him to cancel when my phone dings and the song "Sexy Back" starts playing. I snatch my phone up and don't bother looking at it before storming over to Keegan's apartment and banging on her door.

"Jesus, where's the fire?!" She yells as she yanks open the door, but she winces when she sees it's me.

"Sorry, I wasn't thinking." Honestly, it didn't even occur to me to be bothered by her choice of words. Maybe if I actually remembered being hurt in a fire then hearing that expression might elicit some sort of emotional reaction, but that's definitely one memory I'm thankful not to have.

I push past her and hold my phone into her face when she turns around to face me, closing the door behind her.

"Uhhhh, cool. A phone," she says in a bored tone.

"Yeah, it's *my* phone. Why did you mess with it?" Keegan's nose and eyes scrunch up and it's clear she isn't faking her confusion. She has no idea what I'm talking about. Since I haven't opened Wyatt's last message, my phone starts playing "Sexy Back" again and the phone lights up with his name. Errr, what was saved as his name in my phone.

Keegan snatches the phone out of my hands and ignores me when I yell at her to give it back. She's laughing hysterically, but I'm failing to see the humor.

"I didn't do this, babe. He probably did it yesterday when you had your freak out. He had it in his pocket when he brought you back to your apartment."

"Ugh, of course he did," I groan, tossing my head back and looking at the ceiling. "You guys are gonna be best friends, seeing as how much you both love to invade other people's privacy." Keegan cracks up like my dig at her is a joke, but I totally mean it.

"Have you read this message?" She asks, drawing my focus back to her.

"No," I say with a shrug, trying to pretend like it's

not killing me not knowing what it says. I've been obsessing over it like a teenage girl since he sent it, but there's no way I'm going to admit that.

"When were you gonna tell me you guys were going on a date tonight?"

"What!?"

I could smack that grin right off her face, but instead I yank the phone out of her hands, glaring at her and growling loudly when I read his text.

Don't even think about trying to back out of our "non-date" tonight...I know where you live. Plus, you can't hide from me and my super-secret spy resources. I would find you.

Keegan disappears into her bedroom saying something about figuring out what I should wear, but I'm too busy trying to sort out the reasons why butterflies are assaulting my stomach after reading his message. *Is he flirting with me?* I mean, stranger things have happened, but he is seriously out of my league. He's probably just one of those naturally flirty guys who doesn't even know he's doing it, and making it into something it's not is just going to end in humiliation.

"It's not a date!" I shout, interrupting Keegan's ramblings about finding the perfect outfit.

"Yeah, I know. It's a "non-date", whatever that means. You don't have to explain now, but you can bet your sweet ass that I will be getting every damn detail tomorrow. I don't like you holding out on me," Keegan calls out from inside her closet.

"I'm not holding out on anything! When he left my place last night after bringing me back to my apartment he invited himself over for lunch saying he was going to hang those paintings I bought at Pottery Barn and put together the rest of my furniture. Honestly, I wasn't sure he really meant it until he showed up downstairs while I was folding laundry and asked to push it back to dinner. He was being all charming and sexy and you know how I get around him. I clammed up before I could argue with him."

"Oh, he's really not holding back is he?"

"I hope that's a rhetorical question, because I have no idea what you mean."

"Honey, you are so clueless. It's both endearing and annoying as hell. Trust me," she says as she grabs my shoulders firmly with both hands and looks straight into my eyes so I know she's being serious. "This is a date."

"Ughhhhhhh," I grumble and fall back on her bed. She's wrong, I know she is, but obviously it's not going to do any good to keep arguing with her. All I can do is give in and let her play dress up with me, which doesn't end with just clothes. An hour later, barely an inch of me isn't covered in Keegan - clothes, makeup, hair products and even perfume. Sitting still while she plucks at my eyebrows and shoves pins in my hair is only making me more anxious. What if she's right? What if there is a little more to this than just him trying to be friendly?

"Voila!" Keegan pulls me out of her bathroom and into her bedroom and plants me right in front of her floor length mirror. As hesitant as I was to let her help me, I have to admit I'm a little impressed.

She used just enough eyeliner and mascara to make my eyes pop, and a hint of blush paired with a light pink lip stain makes me look fresh and flush. She's dressed me in my favorite dress of hers, which has a light grey top and high waist with a coral skirt that flares out, stopping just above my knee. It's silky and makes me feel feminine, but is still casual enough to not make me look too dressed up. My blonde hair is straight and shiny, the sides pulled together and pinned with sparkly clips just above the nape of my neck.

Two hours later I'm wringing my hands nervously while pacing around my living room floor in nude, sparkly ballet flats when a knock sounds at the door. Taking a deep breath, I remind myself that Wyatt is just a friend. A really, really hot friend, but still just a friend, so I don't need to be nervous.

Only when I open the door and drink in his appearance, my brain turns to mush and I wouldn't be able to tell you what the definition of 'friend' is, because the only word I can process right now is 'sexy.' He's wearing black jeans and a plain white t-shirt underneath a black leather jacket and he looks positively sinful. His dark hair is mussed like he's been running his hands through it, and his bright blue eyes aren't blue at all. They're almost black, and I watch them glaze over as he takes in my appearance slowly, an inch at a time at an agonizingly slow pace.

I'm no expert at reading people, but I'd have to be blind to not notice the desire written all over his face. My nerves have me frozen in place, too torn between wanting to run and hide and wanting to throw myself at him to move. When the tension between us becomes so intense that breathing is actually painful, my survival instincts kick in, willing my legs to move and put some distance between us.

Wyatt apparently doesn't feel the same need for distance, because despite the ample amount of room I made for him to be able to walk past me and into my apartment, he makes it a point to brush up against me. If I still questioned his desire for me before, I don't anymore, because I just felt his desire rubbing against my stomach.

"Okay, well, I'll get started on dinner," I choke out, my voice sounding way too breathy and husky for my liking. Clearing my throat, I quickly head towards the kitchen, anxious to put some distance between us. "Do you want anything to drink?" I call out without looking back.

"Actually, I brought this." His deep voice sends chills down my spine, his body close enough for me to feel his breath on my neck and his heat against my back. After a few stabilizing breaths, I force myself to turn and face him, simultaneously taking a step back.

"Um, thanks. I actually don't have wine glasses," I say with an apologetic smile, taking the wine from his hands and looking it over, even though I have no clue if it's a nice bottle or what kind it even is. Unlike Star Wars trivia, wine did not survive the blow to the head, so my knowledge of it is absolutely nil. It must be clear on my face, because he smiles at me in a way that makes me feel embarrassed and small.

"I guess maybe I should have asked how old you are before I brought alcohol over. I just assumed since you drank the beer at my apartment…"

"I'm twenty-six, for your information. Although, I

don't think me not owning wine glasses should make you question my age. There are a few things I still haven't bought. I'm not a big wine drinker," I half lie. My voice is defensive, but not because I'm offended. I'm just a bundle of nerves, afraid that any second I'll either say or do something really stupid or just attack him and start tearing at his clothes.

Wyatt chuckles and closes the gap between us, and I instinctively take a step backwards, bumping into the counter. My kitchen isn't large by any stretch of the imagination, but it shrinks in size by at least half when Wyatt presses his body against mine and lifts his hand towards my face.

The only sound in the room is the loud gulp as I try to choke back some of those pesky nerves when Wyatt leans in and puts his mouth to my ear. "Excuse me," he whispers, his warm breath tickling my neck, and to my horror, I giggle. I might only be able to remember as far back as a month, but I've never, not once in that time, giggled. I'm not a giggler. Or at least, I wasn't. *Dammit.*

Wyatt pulls back and I see he has two coffee mugs in his hand and I feel foolish. He wasn't leaning in to be close to me, he was trying to reach the open-faced cabinet behind me that houses all my dishes. Of course, he could have just asked me to move instead of getting all up in my personal space, but it's clear I'm just reading into everything and making more out of this than it is. *Damn wishful thinking.*

"Is it at least safe to assume that since you didn't have wine glasses, you don't have a corkscrew, either?"

"Yeah, that would be a pretty accurate assumption.

I'll run next door and borrow Keegan's." I push off the counter and grab the bottle of wine to take with me before moving past him towards the door. His hand reaches out and his fingers wrap around my wrist, catching me off guard when he tugs on my arm hard enough to pull my body against his. "Ummmmm," I mutter dumbly, looking from his hand to his face.

He opens his mouth to speak but immediately closes it, like he isn't sure what he wants to say. Uncertainty flashes in his eyes, but it's gone as soon as he blinks. He drops my wrist and clears his throat, tugging at the collar of his shirt. *Crap.* He's being adorable again. Big, masculine, muscly men should not be allowed to be adorable. It's just not fair.

"So um, where do you want me to hang these?" He asks as he walks over and picks up one of the paintings.

"Um, I was thinking that wall over there," I say, pointing to the wall behind my sofa. Wyatt makes a funny face and I blush. "I mean, or wherever you think it would look good. It doesn't matter to me," I throw in quickly, trying to sound nonchalant about it, but my voice is high and shaky.

Too anxious to wait for Wyatt's response, I just reach for the door handle and yell "be right back," over my shoulder.

"Go away," Keegan says from the other side of the door when I knock.

"It's me, Key," I respond impatiently.

"I know who it is, I have a peephole, dumbass. You're supposed to be next door on your date with Wyatt, so go away."

"Keegan! Seriously!" The door swings open and Keegan glares at me.

"Better be good, B." I push past her and roll my eyes, heading straight for her kitchen and pulling open the drawer where I know she keeps her corkscrews. I grab the first one I see then close the drawer a little too roughly. I put the corkscrew and wine bottle down and grip the edge of the counter to brace myself before leaning over and taking a deep breath.

"He brought wine!" Keegan shouts and I can see her bouncing up and down out of the corner of my eye.

"Keep your voice down, he's right next door. These walls are thin. And so what?" Why does my voice sound all breathy, like I had to jog a few miles to get to Keegan's instead of walking all of ten steps to get from my door to hers?

"It's totally a date."

"It's not a date," I argue, picking the corkscrew and bottle back up and making my way to her door.

"He brought wine, Brailey."

"Yes, I'm aware. I have to get back." My patience wanes when she blocks the doorway, crossing her arms defiantly and narrowing her eyes at me.

"Why would he bring wine when he's just coming over to hang up some paintings and crap? And don't try to pretend like you don't want it to be a date."

"I don't know, my ability to remember if I have experience with this sort of thing is kind of lacking, you know that. I think you're just reading into it." Maybe if I keep shrugging like none of this is a big deal I might actually start to believe it. Whatever it takes to keep from hyperventilating, which I've been fighting not to do for hours now.

"I call bullshit," Keegan say with the flick of her wrist. "Oh my God! Is this the wine he brought!?" She yanks the bottle out of my hand and I lift my hands to my ears to check and see if they are bleeding. "Shit, Brailey. This is nice wine. You are in so deep," she taunts as she hands the bottle back to me.

I roll my eyes and gently push Keegan out of the way and step into the hall. "Reading into it, Key!" I call over my shoulder.

"You keep telling yourself that, sweetie!" Keegan yells back, and I glare at her before walking back into my apartment. I managed to calm my nerves a fraction while I was at Keegan's, but when I walk back into my apartment, any semblance of composure I gained in my time away just flies right out the dang window.

The leather jacket Wyatt wore is tossed casually over the arm of my sofa. He's too busy holding the large painting up to the wall like he's trying to determine if it's the right place to hang it to notice that I've returned, so I take the opportunity to try and memorize the glorious-ness of his finely sculpted body.

With his arms outstretched, his tight fitting t-shirt is lifted just enough to give me a sensational peek of his well-defined torso. The canvas he's holding, a replica of Monet's *Water Lilies*, looks about as impressive as a finger-painting by a kindergartner in comparison to the exquisite work of art that is Wyatt's arms and shoulders.

Every muscle from his wrists to his shoulders are flexing and twitching beneath the weight of the oversized painting, not from strain, but just from being put to use. My tongue slides across my lips slowly, imagining what it would be like to trace each line of those muscles, taking my time tasting the salty sweetness of his skin.

My thighs instinctively press together tightly, trying to ease the pulsing between my legs. I swear, I'm so on edge, that just clenching almost pushes me right over that cliff. Giving the door a more forceful shove than I intended, the door slams shut loudly. Wyatt – always so composed – turns and gives me a warm smile, not at all startled by my booming entrance.

"So, I've never used one of these. You mind opening the bottle while I get started on dinner?" I ask with a shaky voice as he props the painting back up against the wall. When his back is turned I make my way into the kitchen, feeling all hot and bothered once again. *How the hell does he affect me like this?*

"No problem," his husky voice says from right behind me, making me jump for the fiftieth time since meeting him.

"Dammit, Wyatt! You're like a freaking ninja. Quit sneaking up on me." Wyatt doesn't laugh at my lame joke. He just looks all intense and angry. "Uh, you got something against ninjas?" He quirks an eyebrow at me, so I do the same. "I was just teasing. Why do you seem angry all of a sudden?"

"Why are you so jumpy? Are you afraid of me?" Maybe it's his question, or maybe it's just the sudden vulnerability and uncertainty in his voice, but I'm completely shocked.

"What? No! Of course not! I don't know, I'm just...

ugh."

What do I say here? *Dammit, where's Keegan when I need her.* I could make up an excuse, but I'm not so good with the lying. If I take much longer to decide what to say, it's just going to make it even weirder, and something about the tender way he's looking at me has me wanting to just fess up to the truth. Every second in this man's presence so far has been painfully humiliating. What's one more embarrassing moment to toss on the pile?

"You make me nervous, okay!?"

Okay, that didn't come out how it was supposed to. Shouting and throwing my arms up in the air while looking and sounding extremely frustrated wasn't really what I was going for. *Oh well, gotta go with it now.* An apology for my outburst is on the tip of my tongue, but his expression - or lack thereof - has my mouth clamped shut. If my confession affected him in any way, he's hiding it well, because he's just staring right through me with a blank expression.

I'm not sure where he just went, but he can stay there. Him being distracted just gives me time to steer the conversation to a safer subject. Before he snaps out of his trance, I pull open a drawer and pull out a knife and point it at him. Making a face at him that I hope comes across as menacing when I say seriously, "Now I've got a sharp object in my hand, so unless you want one of us to lose a finger, do *not* sneak up on me. Capisce?"

Wyatt gives me a mock salute and chuckles as he turns to open the bottle of wine. I pull out the cutting board and pull the carrots I cleaned before he arrived from the colander in the sink and start chopping away.

This time I sense Wyatt approach me slowly from behind and my body reactively stills. He doesn't say anything, but he's close enough that I can smell a hint of cologne and feel heat emanating from his body to mine.

"What are we having?" Wyatt reaches an arm around my body and snags a carrot, grazing my arm with his as he pulls back to pop it into his mouth. I take a deep breath and turn to face him, but he's so close that my hip rubs against his torso and when I'm fully facing him, I'm practically caged in between him and the counter. Again.

So far tonight I've realized Wyatt has several habits that make me uncomfortable: sneaking up on me, caging me in against the counter, and whispering in my ear in a voice that makes me want to turn my head and bite his neck.

The fact that he knows the effect he's having on me irritates me enough to snap me out of my lust filled haze. My efforts to push past him are useless, because he easily stops me by pulling his arms closer together on either side of me - those same arms that I was envisioning licking like a lollipop just minutes ago. The large knife I was using is still in my hand so I point it at him again, and to my relief - and disappointment - he puts his hands up in surrender and moves out of my way. I can feel his eyes on me while I sit the knife down to open the fridge and pull out more of the ingredients I need for the dish I'm making.

The cool air hits my face when I lean down, and I close my eyes for a second, pretending to be looking for something while he can't see me. After giving myself a few seconds to enjoy the cold air on my overheated skin, I reach for the butter and pull back quickly, causing me to bump against Wyatt's hard body. He snuck up behind me when I came over to the fridge and I didn't even notice.

"Wyatt! I told you to quit sneaking up on me!" Wyatt just chuckles behind me and I try to turn so I can punch him or slap him or...something, but his hands had automatically moved to my hips when I bumped into him a second ago. Instead of holding me in place or letting go altogether, he loosens his grip, so his palms graze my stomach like a caress, and when I'm finally face to face with him it puts our bodies flush together. A very impressive erection is pressing into me just under my bellybutton, but instead of being embarrassed, I have to fight the urge to grip his shirt and pull him even closer.

"Sorry," he whispers, making a shiver trickle down my spine, and something in me just snaps. I might not have any knowledge of my experience with guys, but I know his constantly whispering in my ear isn't something people do when they are just being friendly. He's intentionally trying to get a response from me, and it's starting to feel like he's toying with me to feed his own ego. I mean yeah, he's obviously aroused right now, but to keep flirting but never making an actual move just makes the whole thing frustrating.

I spin out of his hold and put several feet between us, narrowing my eyes and pointing at him.

"You. Enough with the funny business. For the rest of the night you stay on your side of the kitchen. Touch me again and you'll lose a finger for sure, only it won't be an accident." Wyatt's eyes widen in surprise, and knowing I can throw him off his game a little boosts my confidence.

That is, until he tilts his head back and barks out a laugh. *Asshole*. Grabbing a handful of the carrots I just carefully chopped, I toss them at his head, nailing him with a few before he has time to duck.

Of all the things I never could have predicted happening tonight, a food fight would be at the top of the list. But that is most certainly what happened after I threw a bunch of carrots at Wyatt.

An hour later, we're both laying on our backs in the middle of my floor, panting and winded from laughing, with dinner spread out all over my apartment. Wyatt has lettuce in his hair and I giggle when he can't find it, so I lean on to my side, reaching over and pull it out for him. The movement puts my face inches from his and my smile falters when I see him staring intently at my mouth.

Being propped up on an elbow, hovering slightly above him and rolled halfway on my side, my body instantly relaxes into his when he reaches up and rubs his thumb across my cheek.

My eyes stay locked on his while he pulls his hand away from my face and puts his thumb in his mouth, licking off the chocolate syrup that was meant for dessert. I have to bite my lip to keep from moaning, wanting so badly to yank his thumb away and replace it with my tongue. When he reaches his hand to my face again, I jerk back before he can touch me and jump to my feet. If I don't put some space between us then I know I'm going to end up doing something dumb, like ripping my dress off and straddling him.

"Well um, I guess I won't be making dinner," I state, pointing out the obvious, while smoothing my dress down nervously. My eyes dart nervously around the room searching for nothing in particular, just trying to avoid looking at Wyatt. It dawns on me that he didn't bring his toolbox with him like he was supposed to, and I realize Keegan was right. This really is a date, but instead of being happy about that, I'm actually a little nauseous.

My eyes track Wyatt's movements in my periphery as he walks in my direction. I can't be near him right now and not do something stupid, so I back up - because he's seriously done sneaking up on me - and use my kitchen island as a barrier. My phone dings and I lunge for it, more than thankful for a distraction.

I don't lunge fast enough, though. The phone is on Wyatt's side of the island, and he snatches it up right as I reach for it, and without asking permission, he reads whatever is on the screen. Whatever it is, he doesn't like it, based on how his eyes narrow and his brow furrows.

"Quit screwing with my phone, buddy. Off limits." I'm teasing, but apparently I didn't do a very good job of conveying that, because if anything, Wyatt looks even more agitated.

"Who is Mark," he asks angrily as he shoves my phone into my hand. There is nothing about him that is okay right now, not to me. The way he says Mark's name like it's a dirty word, the venom in his voice and the way all his muscles are taut, like he's ready to pounce on someone. The whole thing reeks of jealous boyfriend behavior, and if this is how he reacts to a guys' name when we aren't even technically dating - because let's face it, if he didn't call it a date, then it's not really a date - then he and I have no possible future together. Non-date over.

"I think it's time for you to go," I say firmly. Wyatt doesn't respond. He just walks to the couch and grabs his coat, pausing when he reaches my door. "See you around," he mutters without even looking back, and I just stare at the door trying to figure out what in the hell just happened.

CHAPTER
SEVEN

WYATT

I have to fight the urge to break shit when I make it back to my apartment. I let things get out of hand back there and I have no one to blame but myself. I knew what I was doing when I invited myself over. Hell, I even bought an expensive bottle of wine to bring! It wasn't until I was standing in her apartment that I realized I hadn't even brought the damn tools to hang up the paintings. Luckily she didn't notice, because I didn't have a good excuse to give her. Not a truthful one, anyway.

I'm not sure what it is about her, but I've never been so out of sorts around a woman. It's like she makes me lose my damn mind, and after only a few minutes in her presence I forget why I'm here to begin with.

I can't keep letting this happen. I have to focus, stay on task. I have a job to do, and it doesn't include a naked Brailey lying underneath me and screaming out my name, no matter how badly I might want it.

That text message sobered me up quickly, thank fuck. I didn't mean to turn into an asshole all of a sudden, but I was so damn angry. Angry at myself for acting like a hormone crazed teenager instead of the grown ass man that I am. I should have better control over myself than that.

Having her hate me is going to make this more difficult, but it will still be easier than having to deal with her looking at me like she wants me to tear her clothes off and ravage her - which she does. I'm not arrogant, she just doesn't hide it well. At all. And every time I see her eyes glaze over and her lips slightly part while she stares at my mouth...*shit!*

I've just got to get it together. I pull out my phone and call Garrett, who is currently sitting in an unmarked van on the curb outside the building. I tell him I failed tonight, and tell him to meet me outside in a few to come up with a new plan.

"Oh my gosh, who is that with Wyatt?" My hand is in the air, hailing a cab, when I look back over my shoulder and see Wyatt walking out of the building and up to a tall blonde man who could easily be mistaken for a real life Ken doll.

"How in the hell would I know?" Yep. I'm being a bitch. If only a damn cab would respond to my frantic waving and pull over to whisk me away from Wyatt and the uncomfortableness now wedged between us.

I waited for a few minutes after Wyatt walked out of my apartment, a little too stunned and confused to move at first, but as soon as I snapped out of it, my butt was planted in front of Keegan's door. Much to my dismay and extreme frustration, Keegan used this opportunity to be the one time she ever in her life didn't offer up an opinion. She just grabbed my hand and pulled me into her bedroom, ripped an outfit out of her closet and threw it at me, and told me we were going dancing.

Dancing and daiquiris sounded like the perfect plan for getting Wyatt out of my head for a while. I've never had a daiquiri but it's the only drink off the top of my head that starts with D and I'm in the mood to be cute - even if it's only in my head. Or at least I *was* feeling like stepping out of my comfort zone and letting loose. Why does it feel like Wyatt is freaking *everywhere* all the time? Is it *that* impossible for me to catch a break?

I see my fast getaway looking more and more less likely with each step Wyatt and the eager-faced Ken doll make towards us. Oh, the urge to look heavenward and let loose a few expletives or tear my hair out is strong, but somehow I manage to keep my hands at my side and dial my screaming back several notches so that it only comes out as a low growl.

"Hey guys, this is my friend Garrett. Garrett, this is Keegan and Brailey," Wyatt introduces us, sounding a hell of a lot more bored and annoyed than is necessary. The jerk doesn't even bother looking at me, even as he says my name. To be fair, he didn't really acknowledge Keegan either, but not the point. *He's* the one that turned into a crazy person out of nowhere like some kind of Jekyll and Hyde impersonation. One minute we're laughing and having a really awesome time, and the next minute he's so pissed off that I'm seriously worried he's going to turn green and bust out of his clothes like the incredible Hulk.

Why do I keep comparing him to fictional characters that suffer from some kind of bipolar disorder?

If only I were the kind of girl who was comfortable flirting with a guy just to make someone else jealous. Though now that I think about it, playing games just to get a reaction out of someone sounds incredibly immature and not at all like something I want to do. No, what I really wish is that I would meet someone else that actually drew my attention away from Wyatt, someone I was truly interested in, even though dating isn't necessarily high on my priority list.

Garrett is definitely attractive in a pretty boy, surfer kind of way, but not really my type physically. He's apparently Keegan's type though, if her blushing and giggling are any indication. Seeing Keegan all shy and nervous is a side of her I've not yet seen. It's makes me feel better to know I'm not the only one who gets a little unnerved around attractive men.

When Garrett takes my hand in his and brings it to his lips, placing a chaste kiss on my knuckles, a blush creeps up my cheeks. My eyes automatically flicker over to Wyatt in time to see him avert his gaze, like he's trying really hard *not* to look at me.

"Where are you stunning beauties headed to tonight?" Garrett's question elicits another giggle from Keegan, but I'm too distracted to hear her response. I'm already back to trying to flag down a cab and then cursing every single one of them that keep going as if I'm invisible. Is it so much to ask for just a little distance, a small reprieve from the anxiety and confusion and rage and lust I feel every time Wyatt is near?

Apparently it is, because my underworked arm muscles are burning from me franticly waving at cabs like a crazed person. Maybe that's the problem - all the drivers think I'm just saying hello instead of trying to get a ride somewhere. At this point I'd rather call it a night and go back upstairs for a hot soak in the tub, but the second I tune back into the conversation and hear yet another giggle, I know there's no way she is going to let that happen for me.

"We were just gonna head to a bar down the street, but how could we possibly decline an invitation to go dancing with two gorgeous women, right Wy?" This guy is laying it on a little thick, in my opinion, but Keegan looks a little too smitten to notice - or care. Garrett's too busy making sexy eyes at Keegan to turn around to look at Wyatt, so he doesn't see the murderous glare Wyatt is giving the back of his head, but I do. *Jerk*.

One flick of Garrett's wrist and not ten seconds later two cabs come to a stop right in front of us. No one notices my exaggerated eye roll. *Freaking cab drivers*. Keegan and I take the first cab and agree to meet them at the club, and I don't even wait until the cab pulls away from the curb before I start laying into her.

"What the hell! Why did you invite them? You know how badly things went with Wyatt. You *know!* I wanted to spend the night trying to forget how much things suck with Wyatt, not spend it being pissed at how he's working so hard to ignore me even though *he's* the one who was a jerk!" The cab driver gives me a funny look in the rearview mirror when I let loose an animalistic growl when Keegan's response is to roll her eyes and flick her wrist at me dismissively.

"Whatever, your night went great. Trust me, you don't want to pass up the opportunity to shake your cute ass in front of Wyatt."

"Were you even listening when I told you what happened? What exactly was so great about him suddenly turning into a massive dickhead and then taking off? I may not have any past experiences to compare it to, but I'm pretty sure if things had been great, then I wouldn't be so freaking angry at the thought of spending more time with him. And if you hadn't been so distracted making googly eyes at Garrett then you would have noticed just how much Wyatt doesn't want to be around me either."

My rant actually helped me feel a little better, and so did spending the whole ride to the club pouting with my arms crossed while quietly plotting my revenge on Keegan for putting me in this horrible situation. I can understand why kids are so prone to tantrums.

When Keegan yanks me out of the cab and drags me inside, it's decided - screw daiquiris, I need some hard liquor. Time to work on building up my tolerance to alcohol. "I'll have two of whatever will get me drunk the quickest!" I yell to the bartender.

"No she won't. She'll take an appletini," Keegan tells the bartender who makes a hasty retreat before I can argue with her. Whatever. I'm too distracted by Wyatt and the fact that he hasn't quit staring at me since he walked in, and how much I wish he was avoiding making eye contact like he was before. It's really unnerving to catch someone looking at you, and them *not* look away.

Avoiding him has been a nightmare. He was even waiting right outside the bathroom door when I came out a few minutes ago, though that time he at least had the decency to pretend like he was doing something else when I walked out.

Things are tense and awkward between us and we still haven't said one word to each other. It's starting to really grate on my nerves not knowing what the hell his problem is, but I'm nowhere near confident enough to just come out and ask him. Eventually it gets too much to handle, so instead of addressing the elephant in the club, I just grab Keegan's hand and drag her out to the dance floor with me.

I can feel Wyatt's eyes on me the whole time we dance. Every time I glance in his direction, his eyes are narrowed and hard, like he's scrutinizing every move I make. Garrett keeps trying to talk to him, but I'm not sure if Wyatt even hears him because he's too busy acting like an asshole to notice.

Letting the song take over my senses, I close my eyes and try to block out thoughts of Wyatt, but it's not even half a song before the feeling of him staring at me becomes too much to bear. He's not at the table with Garrett anymore, though, and I spin around looking for him only to come up empty. He must have gone to get a drink or to the bathroom or something. So why do I still feel like someone's watching me?

Keegan's found herself a dance partner and is otherwise occupied, and I spot Garrett talking to a tall brunette next to the bar, but still no sign of Wyatt. Something grabs my attention out of my periphery, and my head jerks to the right. It's too dark to see his face, but I can tell his build that it's not Wyatt, and I don't know how I know since I can't see his eyes, but I'm absolutely certain he's staring at me. Standing stock still in the middle of the dance floor, I engage the dark stranger in some sort of uncomfortable stare down. Goosebumps spread over every inch of my skin, and not the good kind.

It's possible I'm being paranoid, though I don't know where the paranoia would be coming from, but something about the dark stranger has my whole body locked up tight in fear. Pulling from a bravery deep inside me that I didn't know existed, I take a step towards him, but when he notices he quickly disappears into the crowd.

Probably not the best decision I ever made, but I have to know who he is and why he was staring at me, so I go after him. After searching for a few minutes it's clear I'm never going to find him. Even if I did come across him, I didn't get a look at his face, so I would have no idea what he looks like.

"Miss," one of the waiters that tend to the tables says to me, holding out an appletini, waiting for me to take it.

"Oh, thank you," I say absent mindedly, assuming Keegan just ordered me another one and pointed him in my direction. Weird, though, because she's still out on the dance floor. Maybe it was Wyatt or Garrett? I turn back to ask the waiter who ordered it, but he's already gone. Luckily the crowd parts for a second and I spot Garrett back at our table.

My drink sloshes a little a few drops spilling over the top, dripping down my wrist. I lick up the green liquid, trying to avoid getting it on my borrowed clothes from Keegan, and continue to inch my way closer to the guys. The second I hear one of them shout my name, I down a big gulp of my drink, needing the liquid courage to be able to handle whatever I'm about to overhear.

"What do you think you're doing Wyatt!? You're going to screw everything up and you know he will kill you if he finds out. You need to find a way to make this just a job, man. Disassociate. I'm not spending all my time cooped up in a fucking van…"

"Hey guys," I interrupt, not wanting to eavesdrop any more than I already have. "Thanks to whichever of you bought me the drink." Raising my glass in a toasting gesture, I take another big gulp, spilling a good amount of it on my dress when it's ripped out of my hands.

"What the hell, Wyatt?"

"We didn't buy you a drink. I thought you were out there dancing with Keegan!" Wyatt's practically screaming at me, then he starts muttering to himself and looking around like he's trying to find someone or something to punch.

"What's the big deal? Maybe a guy bought it for me," I offer meekly with a shrug. I was just trying to make him calm down, but my suggestion only makes him angrier.

Screw him. I'm not going to stand here and keep being subjected to his pissy attitude. Spinning around, I grab the first guy I see, yanking on the neck of his shirt to bring his face down to mine. "Wanna dance?" His eyes widen, probably taken aback by my forwardness, but he nods his head and lets me drag him out to the dance floor.

We walk up next to Keegan, who joins in when she sees us dancing. I'm not really interested in dancing up close and personal with anyone, let alone a stranger, I just wanted to piss off Wyatt and get away from him for a minute. As luck would have it, the random guy I forced onto the dance floor also happens to be really freaking hot, so when the effects of the alcohol start to kick in and my thoughts go fuzzy, I give in to his advance. His hands find my hips and I don't hesitate to lean in closer to him and close my eyes, thankful to have a body helping me stand since I'm starting to feel a little woozy.

My first drink of the night barely did anything to me, but this second drink is kicking my ass. I'm about to excuse myself for a minute, but then I feel his hands start to roam out of the neutral zone and down to my ass. It feels like the world is moving in slow motion, and for some reason my arm isn't getting the signal to slap this guy's hand away from areas where it's uninvited.

Turns out I don't need to slap him away, because I'm suddenly being yanked away from him and being pulled off the dance floor.

"Hey man!" My dance partner shouts at Wyatt, pulling on my other arm hard enough to yank me backwards and tear me from Wyatt's grasp. Since I've lost control of my own limbs, being tossed around like a ragdoll puts the world at a tilt, and I fall sideways into another patron, causing his beer to spill all down his shirt.

"It's his fault!" I yell defensively and point with a weak arm towards Wyatt, who's got ahold of my arm again. The big guy covered in beer gets in Wyatt's face long enough to distract him, and I yank out of his grip. Okay, maybe I didn't yank so much as gave in to gravity, because when Wyatt lets go of me to ward off the angry beer guy, my legs give out and down I go.

I don't make it all the way to the ground, though. Oh, no. Wyatt in all his knight-in-shining-armor glory comes to my rescue once again, scooping me up and throwing my arm around his shoulders.

"It's time to go, Brailey," is all Wyatt says before he starts pulling me to the exit again.

"Keegan!" I yell-slash-slur, not wanting to leave without telling her where I'm going.

"Garrett's got her," Wyatt says over his shoulder as he walks out of the club and into the cool night air. The bright blue dress Keegan made me wear is short and sleeveless, made of a thin fabric that's covered in matching lace, and it does little to ward off the cold air, causing my skin to break out into goosebumps.

Wyatt hails a cab quickly and holds the door open for me to climb in, then he surprises me by pulling me into his arms after he gets in after me. His hands are rubbing up and down my arms vigorously while my cheek is pressed tightly to his hard chest. He smells amazing and feels even better, and the last of my defenses vanish when I feel his cheek come down to rest on top of my head.

I relax and lean into him, my eyes getting heavy and harder to keep open as the seconds tick by. I must have drifted to sleep because I'm suddenly being lifted out of the cab and carried up the stairs, cradled in his ridiculously strong arms. Wyatt digs my keys out of my purse, which he must have thought to grab before we left the club because I certainly didn't have it in my hands when he tore me out of the building.

After kicking the door closed behind us he walks over to the couch and gently lays me down. I miss the warmth of his body as soon as he pulls away and I reach out to him, snagging his arm and trying to pull him back to me. My arms feel as heavy as lead, and as soon as I tug on him, my hand slips off and hits the side of the couch with a loud thud.

"Where are you going?" My words are slurred and my voice is whiny, and I might actually care if I wasn't too busy trying to find the energy to even breathe.

"Home," he responds curtly, but he makes no effort to keep moving.

"Stay with me," I mumble weakly.

I lose the battle to keep my eyes open, but I remain awake, and I feel Wyatt scoop me up into his arms and pull me to his chest once again. It feels like being wrapped up in a warm, sexy, *irritating* cocoon. When he tries to place me on the bed he has to go down with me, because I cling to him with all the energy I have left, refusing to let him put any space between us.

"You can let go, I'm not going anywhere. Promise," he whispers.

His voice is sweet and reassuring, a total contrast to how he's acted the whole night. I feel the bed dip as he makes himself comfortable next to me, never loosening his hold. I'm so unbelievably tired and still can't open my eyes, but I somehow manage to move my body closer to his - or maybe he pulls me closer, I can't tell at this point. I bury my face in his neck and breathe him in deeply. My lips are touching his skin and I want so badly to place a kiss to his neck, but by the grace of God, even in my drunken stupor, I manage to resist.

His heart is beating hard and loud in my ear and his body stiffens a little when I drape my arm over his waist and force my leg in between his thighs, effectively removing whatever small space still remained between us. The small movements steal every last bit of energy left in me and I sigh deeply and relax even further into him, treating him like my own personal body pillow.

"Are you an angel?" My words come out a little slurred, either from being tired or the alcohol, I'm not sure which. I feel Wyatt's laugh rumble in his chest and it makes me smile.

"What?"

"Are you an angel?" I ask again, my voice almost a whisper as I fight to hold sleep off for a few more minutes.

"Why would you ask that?" His voice is soothing and I feel his hand start to stroke my hair, making me even more sleepy.

"I don't know. Bad things are just always happening to me. Only you…you're always there, always saving me, taking care of me. I just thought maybe you were an angel."

He whispers something in my ear, but I'm already being sucked under, unable to fight off sleep any longer.

Chapter
EIGHT

What the ever-loving-hell is wrong with me?

Last I checked, my eyes fit perfectly within their sockets, so why do they feel like they've grown about ten sizes too big for my face all of a sudden? Pretty sure I'm either seriously dehydrated, or someone was scrubbing my tongue with sandpaper while I was sleeping. I really don't remember joining the MMA, so why does it feel like my body took the beating of a lifetime? Also, whoever is making that stupid ringing sound needs to stop before my ears start bleeding.

I'd like to open my eyes and make sure I haven't fallen down the rabbit hole and landed in some crazy-ass world where everything spins and gravity is about a hundred times more powerful than normal, but unless that creepy caterpillar is going to be waiting for me with an explanation, I think I'll just stay right here in bed.

My bladder, however, has different plans for me. Halfway to my bedroom door I hear voices. No, not the crazy kind that live in your head. Actual voices.

"Yeah I sent it in for testing, and you were right."

"Five minutes. Five fucking minutes I asked you to keep an eye on her for me, Garrett, while I took a leak and this happens. I should have your head."

Wyatt's doing his best to keep his voice down, but it doesn't do anything to lessen the bite of his words. If anything, it makes him sound more menacing. I would hate to be in Garrett's shoes right now.

I push the door open a little wider, not for the sole purpose of eavesdropping, but because...okay whatever, I'm eavesdropping. They don't want me to hear what they're saying? Then they should have thought about having their conversation somewhere other than my living room.

"Where is she? Is she okay? How the hell did you let this happen, Wyatt!?" Keegan comes bursting through the door and goes straight up to Wyatt, pushing his chest as hard as she can. He doesn't even budge. Keegan would have better luck trying to move a brick wall.

Wyatt puts up with the shoving for a minute, but when her movements get frantic, he grabs her wrists and holds them firmly up in front of her. Keegan struggles just a little before choking back a sob.

"Just tell me she's okay," she says quietly, her voice cracking. Wyatt releases her and she takes a step back, squaring her shoulders.

"She's fine. She'll be dehydrated and weak for a day or so, but no permanent damage or anything."

"Why would someone do this to her?" I hear Keegan ask.

"Don't worry about that. I'm taking care of it."

"Yeah, you're gonna have to give me more than that. This shit's too crazy for me to take your word on it. I get that you like being mysterious and broody and all that, but I don't know you. More importantly, I don't know if I can trust you, so unless you can give me a reason to trust you, then you can bet your sweet, delicious ass that I'm not going to let Brailey go anywhere near you."

"I don't answer to you, Keegan. Now, I don't want to come across as an asshole, but you need to understand right now that you can't keep me out of Brailey's life. It's not your decision." Wyatt's in Keegan's face and the look he's giving her could light a fire, but she's not backing down. Instead she takes a step towards him, eliminating the little distance between them, and pokes him in the chest hard with her finger.

"You listen to me, dickhead, you will not bully me. I don't know why you've got such a hard-on for Brailey since you just met, but you don't know her well enough to get all alpha male, protector caveman on her. Unless there's something you aren't telling me, which I assume is probably the case. So the way I see it, you can fess up and tell me everything, or you can get the hell out and stay away from my friend."

My phone dings, and Wyatt backs away from Keegan and walks over to the counter. When he picks it up and reads whatever is on it I clench my fists and vow to punch him in the neck for continuing to touch my phone after I warned him. Once I'm functioning at full capacity, that is.

"How much do you know about Mark?" Wyatt asks Keegan, running his hand through his hair and tossing my phone back down roughly. She shrugs and crosses her arm, looking a little too happy to have the upper hand. "Fine. I'll find out for myself," he mutters under his breath, taking his phone out of his pocket and typing some kind of message.

I can't believe that asshole is trying to snoop on my freaking phone right now. If I wasn't already so weak and dehydrated and much closer to death than I should be, then I would be kicking his ass right now. Screw it. If I'm going to die today, I'm going to do it knowing I got in a solid junk punch to Wyatt.

"Brailey!" Keegan yells before running over to me. I missed the mark a little. Wyatt was much further away than I anticipated, and after about three steps my body just collapses like a marionette. Keegan tries to lift me, but I'm dead weight, so Wyatt steps up to help her. I can't kick him in the nuts, but I can give him a death glare. Wyatt takes the hint, even though the jerk is trying really hard not to smirk at me. Garrett leans down instead and takes my other arm, and together with Keegan they hoist me up and walk me over to the couch.

"Sorry I'm late to the party," I deadpan. "Anyone wanna tell me what's going on?"

Keegan starts to speak up, but Wyatt cuts her off.

"You got really wasted at the club and I brought you home. Keegan and Garrett stopped by to check on you, that's all." Something about his response feels forced, like he's rehearsed it, and Keegan confirms my suspicion.

"Tell her the truth, Wyatt," Keegan warns.

"Enough!" He barks at her and she actually flinches a little. "Just rest, Brailey," Wyatt says softly, taking my hand in his and kneeling before me. My brain sends fierce signals to my hand, telling it to pull away, but it's like I'm paralyzed, and instead of trying to get away from Wyatt, my eyes close and I'm dead to the world again.

When I wake up again it's dark outside and my apartment is quiet. My eyes open easily this time and I see a glass of water and a bottle of pain medicine sitting on my bedside table, right next to my phone which apparently has been getting blown up while I had my mini-coma.

One text from Keegan telling me to take the medicine and rest and that she'll be by after her shift. Five texts from Mark, each more frantic than the last. Freaking hell. The absolute last thing I want to be doing right now is trying to explain to Mark why I haven't been returning his messages, because I have no intention of telling him about whatever the hell happened last night. The other night? What the hell day even is this?

My memory is blurry at best with missing spans of time scattered throughout it. I'm so damn sick of trying to remember stuff. It's bad enough when I can't remember things prior to the accident, but to lose bouts of time presently? That just annoys the crap out of me.

Keegan is a nurse in the hospital's rehab facility, and depending on the needs of the patient, sometimes she works late. Today must be one of those days. I take three pills and down the entire glass of water. My muscles still ache and there's a lingering thumping in the back of my head, but I don't feel at all like I did the last time I woke up.

What I really want is a long bath and a few gallons of water, but when another text from Mark comes through, I figure I may as well just get this over with.

"Finally! What the hell, Brailey? I've been asking you to call me for days. Are you okay? What's going on?" It didn't even ring one full ring before he answered, so his yelling through the phone catches me off-guard, bring back that stabbing feeling in my temples.

"I'm fine, calm down. Things are just really crazy. I'm still trying to get settled and get things ready for when I start work. I didn't mean to ignore you or stress you out." He lets out a relieved sigh and I feel a stab of guilt for worrying him. "You don't have to worry about me, Mark. I'm fine, and if I weren't, I would tell you."

"Okay, but you really would tell me if you need anything at all, right?"

"I promise. So what's up? Is everything okay? You sounded pretty upset in your texts." He pauses for so long before responding that I pull my phone away to check that we're still connected.

"Yeah, everything's fine, just wanted to hear your voice." That's an unusually personal admission for Mark, and it kind of throws me for a loop. For weeks he made sure to not say anything that resembled anything other than friendship, but you don't just want to hear someone's voice that you don't have feelings for. I don't know how to respond to that, and a tiny spark of anger chips away at the guilt I usually feel when it comes to Mark. Instead of saying something I'll end up regretting, I decide to just change the subject.

"So I've got a new pain in the ass neighbor," I say with a scoff. Mark doesn't say anything again and his long pauses are making me feel insecure. "Anyway, if you're busy I can call you later. I didn't mean to interrupt anything."

"No! No. I'm sorry, I'm not busy. I was just distracted, but I'm paying attention, I promise. So tell me about this new neighbor." It's so very unlike Mark to be distracted. He is the best listener EVER, which I suppose is a really good thing considering he gets paid to listen to people. *Why is he acting so weird?*

My palm flies up to smack myself in the forehead when I realize that in my haste to find something to talk about, I've just brought up Wyatt - a topic I've been specifically avoiding talking to Mark about. Now I don't know what the hell to say without it sounding like I'm trying to make him jealous or hurt him, and he's already being so sensitive and strange, so try to play it off like I hate Wyatt. Which isn't too hard since I'm actually pretty pissed at him still.

"Well all I know about him so far is that he's kind of an asshole. I mean, I guess he's nice at times. I don't know, I don't really know him. I just haven't met many people here yet. Keegan is great, though. We went out the other night and-"

"What do you mean he's an asshole? Has he said or done anything to you?"

"No, no, nothing like that. Actually, he's been looking out for me, which I'm sure you would be grateful for, but it's starting to annoy the piss out of me. I don't know...there's just something about him. Like he's moody or something and I can't tell if he likes me or hates me."

"I'm sure he doesn't hate you, no one can hate you, it's not possible."

"Not everyone can see the best in people like you do, Mark. I guess it will just take time with Wyatt. I'm just not good with people yet. It's hard to be able to read other people's emotions when you're trying to figure out your own."

"You'll get the hang of it, Brailey, give it time. Have you made any other friends?"

"Actually…" A knock at the door cuts me off, and if I don't answer soon, Keegan will just start banging relentlessly. She's so impatient. "Hey, sorry Mark but someone's at the door. Can I call you tomorrow?"

"Yeah sure, just be careful Brailey." The seriousness in his voice warms my heart, reminding me again how lucky I am to have him in my life, looking after me.

"I'm being careful. Promise." Keegan knocks on the door again so I hang up without waiting to hear Mark's goodbye.

"I'm expecting company, so whatever reason you're here for, make it quick," I say, more annoyed than surprised when I open the door to find Wyatt standing there instead of Keegan.

"Yeah, I know you're expecting company. That's why I'm here." Wyatt laughs at my confused face before pushing his way past me. "Keegan can't make it, so I'm here in her place."

"How would you know that? Is she okay?"

"Yeah, I just came from her apartment. She had a really difficult shift and was exhausted so I offered to come over and check on you so she could rest." That jealous bitch inside of me raises her claws, slicing my gut violently. He was at Keegan's. Why would he be at Keegan's? They aren't close, and last I heard, they were at each other's throats in my living room.

Plus, Keegan obviously knows I'm attracted to him, considering how many hours she's spent talking to me about him in the weeks since he's moved in. Of course, I couldn't fault her for going after him since I've also spent every day since meeting him trying to deny that I feel anything towards him other than annoyance.

"Well, as you can see, I'm fine. So you can go back over there and tell Keegan you did your job and you guys can continue whatever it was you were doing." *Whoa*, that came out sounding a hell of a lot more bitter and resentful than I meant it to.

"Now Peaches, if I didn't know any better, I'd say you were jealous." I contemplate denying it, but he reaches up and lightly caresses my cheek, my words getting stuck in my throat. "I ran into Keegan on my way up here to check on you, she was just getting home. She looked exhausted so I told her not to worry and get some rest. I didn't mean to make it sound like I was just spending time with her."

All the muscles in my body uncoil, an absurd amount of relief washing over me. It shouldn't matter this much. How he chooses to spend his time, and whoever he spends it *with*, is none of my business. We are nothing to each other. Why do I care so damn much?

"You want to tell me why you call me peaches?" I ask, trying to change the subject to something safer, less complicated.

"Nope, not really," he says with that cocky grin of his. He's so damn charming when he wants to be that it makes it hard to keep denying how much he really affects me.

"Alright, well, thanks for coming by, I appreciate it. I'll see you around," I say quickly, hoping he'll take the hint and realize he's being dismissed. He doesn't. Instead he leans against my kitchen counter and crosses his legs at the ankle.

"Have you eaten?"

"Uhhh...yes," I lie, just wanting him to leave so I can be alone.

"You suck at lying," he says with a smirk while his eyes take a long, slow look over me. Dressed in only light blue silk pajama bottoms and a matching tank, it's not until his eyes stop at my chest that I remember I'm not wearing a bra.

"Ugh, I know. I'm just not in the mood for company right now," I lie again.

"You were in the mood for company when it was Keegan coming over. So what you're saying is, you're just not in the mood for *my* company." He's still wearing his damn smirk as he calls me out on my lie...*again*...but there's a little bit of uncertainty in his eyes now.

I *hate* how well he can read me. And I *hate* how much I want to kiss his cocky mouth right now.

But damn, I *love* how he looks in the tight jeans he's wearing.

I feel my body start to hum and react in ways I'm not able to hide in what I'm wearing, so I look away from him and try to distract myself. He's not having it though, because he walks over to me and grips my chin with his fingers and turns my face so that our noses are so close they're almost touching. The way he's looking at me, for a second I really think he's going to kiss me.

Ha! Good one, Brailey.

I'm such an idiot. Of course he doesn't kiss me. Instead he pulls his hand away and nudges my chin in a casual way that makes me cringe. He may as well have called me "sport" when he did it, and I'm getting so freaking sick of him treating me like a child when all I want is for him to see me as a desirable woman.

I close my eyes and hold back a growl when he steps back and moves around me towards the sitting room. When I hear my TV come on, I turn to see Wyatt with one arm draped over the back of the couch and the remote in the other hand. He's flipping through channels casually, as if hanging out in my apartment is something he's done a hundred times. The whole scene is baffling and I'm not quite sure what to make of it. It would seem he's not leaving any time soon, though, so I plop down on the opposite end of the couch and watch quietly as he flips through channels so quickly that I can't even tell what shows he's skipping over.

"Slow down your trigger finger, bud. How can you tell if you're not skipping something good?" Wyatt shrugs and then holds the remote out to me and I hesitate, looking at the remote like it might bite me if I reach out to take it from him.

"Here, you find something. I don't care what we watch, I just wanted something to do while I waited for you to realize I wasn't leaving." How can he be so bluntly honest one minute, and then guard so many secrets the next? He can take his honesty and shove it, because I don't need a babysitter.

"You know what? No. You can watch what you want. Help yourself to anything in the kitchen, the bathroom is through that door, and most importantly, please don't hesitate to let yourself out. I'm going to bed and unless you're truly an asshole, you'll leave me alone and let me rest." With that I storm into my bedroom and slam the door behind me, quickly locking the door.

I know it's cowardly to just hide from him, but I can't very well force him to leave. That doesn't mean I have to be forced into spending time with him, so if he just wants to mooch off my cable and food, then he can have at it, but I'm not sticking around to suffer through it any more.

"Hello?"

"Ehhem, is this Brailey?"

" 'Sup," I say, a little breathless as I move around our little house with my phone clutched between my shoulder and my ear. I lose my grip and it falls to the floor, and I drop all my grocery bags when I bend to pick it up. "Dammit!" I yell right when I put it back to my ear. "Oops, sorry. Dropped my phone. Didn't mean to shout

in your ear. Who is this again?"

"Um, this is Bryce. You gave me your number today at Mayford. I, uh, we talked and-"

I could be nice here and put him out of his misery, but what's the fun in that?

"At Mayford? Are you sure you have the right number?"

He doesn't respond for a second, and I hear shuffling on his end of the line. My ice cream is melting on my floor, and I'm trying too hard not to giggle to care enough to bend down and pick it up.

"Uhh, the paper here has the name Brailey and this number on it, so yeah...pretty sure I have the right number." He still doesn't sound pretty sure, so I keep probing.

"Hmmm, maybe someone gave you my number? The person you talked to - what did she look like?"

He clears his throat nervously, and I picture him pacing the room he's in. "Um, she had on yellow scrubs. Light blonde hair, pulled up into a messy bun. She had a killer ass and a nice rack," he pauses and though he can't see me, my face flushes. "Her face was okay, I guess. If you're into that kind of thing."

"What the hell! That's a really asshole thing to say! You're lucky you aren't saying that to my 'okay' looking face, because I'd kick you in the nuts!"

When I stop yelling, I can hear him laughing on the other end. "Oh man, you're too easy."

"Trust me, I'm not easy, but I'm definitely worth the effort," I tease, and I hear him choke on his laughter. I wait patiently until his coughing fit subsides, just staring

at my ice cream that's still melting on the floor. I really should clean it up, but I'm kind of frozen in place, mesmerized by the sound of his laugh. It's freaking magical, as stupid as that sounds.

A knock on the door pulls me from my trance, and I ask him to hold on while I get the door, only to find out that he's hung up.

That's weird.

I look out the peephole, but it's dark out and my porch light is out. Dammit, I told Shaun to fix that last week.

I figure if the person standing outside is some kind of crazy killer, then he'll find his way in whether or not I open the door for him, so I may as well just get this over with.

I yank the door back and throw my arms straight up into the air, yelling, "Chop away!"

Bryce stares at me like I'm out of my damn mind. "Oh, hey, didn't know it was you," I say, stepping back from the door to let him in. He walks in behind me, taking his time as he appraises my living quarters.

I busy myself with putting away the rest of the groceries, then make my way over to the melted ice cream once all the bags are empty. Bryce still hasn't spoken, and it's starting to get a little weird.

"Did you just come over to watch me do chores, or did you need something?" I ask him without looking up from where I'm on my knees, scrubbing Rocky Road out of my carpet.

"You said you wanted to talk to me about Mayra," he says nervously, scrubbing the back of his neck with his hand. I look up and quirk an eyebrow at him, which *makes him fidget more.*

"You couldn't have talked to me over the phone?" I ask as I make my way back to the sink, rinsing out the rag I used to clean up my mess. He shrugs, looking everywhere except at my face. "Want something to drink?" He shakes his head, and this tongue-tied, nervous person is a complete contrast to who I met earlier.

I pop the lid on two bottles of beer, handing him one and making my way over to my crappy couch. "So how do you know Mayra?" He hesitates, so I use my finger to tip his bottle up closer to his mouth. "Drink your beer, maybe it will loosen your lips a little."

He finally relaxes a little, and puts the bottle to his beautiful lips. Oh, I wish I was that bottle right now. He notices me staring, so I flick my eyes back up to his.

"Yeah, I'm a...uh...friend. Any idea where they transferred her?" He sits in the arm chair across from me, leaning forward with his forearms on his knees, staring at me intently.

"Not a clue, but something weird is going on there. One day Mayra was there, the next she's gone, and when I asked about it they flipped out. I spent a lot of time with Mayra, so it's not odd for me to be asking about her, but their reaction definitely was. Her chart is already archived so I couldn't even look at it, and I don't have access to the computer files."

His shoulders tense and his hand tightens around the bottle so hard that his knuckles turn white, and I worry he's going to shatter the bottle just by squeezing it. He doesn't say anything, so I continue.

"What makes you think her being transferred is

weird?"

I shake my head, because really it's just a feeling I have and I'm not even sure how to explain it. "I don't know, but patients don't get transferred often. And when they do, it's usually at the request of a family member due to location change or finances. Mayra had no one, so I don't know why she would need to go anywhere. If she was unhappy at Mayford and just wanted a change, she would have told me."

My stomach growls, breaking the silence and pulling us both out of our thoughts.

"C'mon," Bryce says pulling on my hand and leading me to my door.

"Where are we going?" Fumbling with my keys, I eventually get the door locked behind me and follow this sexy, mysterious stranger blindly to his car.

"To eat."

Thirty minutes later we're in a little diner just outside of town. We're seated in a little booth in the far corner of a restaurant, where we're talking about a secret mission to uncover the mystery of where Mayra went. It feels so clandestine, and I wish I had taken the time to change into something more fitting before we left. Maybe some black leggings and a black sweater, with black combat boots and leather gloves.

"What are you thinking about over there?" Bryce asks me as the waitress brings us glasses of water. He tells her we need more time and turns his attention back to me.

"I was wishing I had changed into something you would see a cat burglar wearing."

"A cat burglar?" He asks with a laugh.

"Yeah, you know...like something a modern day Cat-woman would wear. Hey! Do you think that's why it's called cat burglar?"

Bryce barks out a laugh so loud that people turn and stare. "No, I don't think that term specifically comes from a cartoon character, but I do believe it stems from the parallel between cats and the type of thief."

"Uh, you should go on Jeopardy. That's some random factoid you just gave me." I pick up my straw and hold it like a buzzer. "Yes, I'll take 'What is Random Cat Shit' for six hundred, Alex."

Bryce is still laughing when the waitress comes back. She's eyeing him up and down, not even trying to be subtle with her admiration. I don't blame her, he's a freaking sight to behold. Especially when he's smiling like this with his bright, pearly whites showing between his perfectly proportioned lips.

The gawking I get, but when she reaches out and flirtatiously touches his arm and giggles, my understanding takes a big leap out the window.

I've known Bryce for a little over two hours now, and while I'd love nothing more than to take him for a ride, I have absolutely no idea if the attraction is mutual. But I don't need to have actual claim to him - she doesn't know we aren't together, and watching him flirt back with our slutty, albeit very pretty, waitress just pisses me off.

Hello? Am I freaking invisible here?

"Hey, can you guys save the shameless flirting for after I've eaten? I'm kind of losing my appetite with the visual I get watching it, no offense Bryce. I know you can't

help your condition, but it's kind of gross." I shrug, and force an apologetic smile. I'm shooting for pity on my face, and based on the disgusted look the waitress gives him when she sees it, I'd say I nailed it.

She tenses, and all her flirting disappears as she quickly takes our order and runs off.

"Nice cock-block, B-ray. Didn't know you had it in you," Bryce teases. He looks more smug than angry, and even though he's right to feel smug, I still feel the need to try and convince him that me doing that had nothing to do with jealousy.

"Uh, first of all, it's a little early for us to be giving out nicknames, but it's a pretty cool one, so I'll take it. Second of all, I was getting hungry and she wasn't going to give up, so it just seemed the quickest way to get her to take my order. I'll tell her I was joking before we leave so you can stick your man meat in her later tonight if you want."

I pretend to mess with my phone, not wanting him to see just how much I want him to say he doesn't really want her. I don't really have a reason to look at my phone though, so after a few seconds it just looks weird, so I put it back in my purse and force my eyes to meet his.

His smug smile is gone, and I definitely did not expect to see heat reflected back at me in his eyes. He shifts in his seat, obviously rearranging himself inside of pants so he's more comfortable in his seat.

Dammit, he did want her.

"I'm sorry, it was rude of me. I'll go apologize now," I say as I move to get up. I place my napkin on the table and push out of the booth, but Bryce grabs my wrist and

pulls me back down. His hand slides from my wrist to my hand, and his fingers twine with mine.

"She's not the one I want." His voice is low and sultry, and I feel it all the way to my core. When his thumb starts to rub soft circles on my wrist, I have to clench my thighs together, trying and failing to give myself some relief. He notices, and lust flashes in his eyes, and it takes everything in me not to jump up and drag him to the bathroom.

The waitress returns with our food, and I pull my hand from his, though he tightens his grip just enough that I have to tug hard to get my hand out of his.

Our plates drop heavily onto the table, and the waitress huffs before walking away without asking us if we need anything else. I don't know if she's still grossed out by what I said, or if she's realized I was lying and is jealous of our hand holding, but I'm too elated to care.

That uncertainty about the mutual attraction is gone, that's for sure. It's a little intimidating with how affectionate he got all of a sudden, but I've been laying it on pretty thick since we met, so I guess I can't get all bent out of shape when he reacts to it. It's not like I've been over here playing hard to get. And based on the way he's looking at me now - like he'd rather skip dinner and take me home and eat me instead has me squirming in my seat.

Yes, please!

The next hour is spent with Bryce explaining how he knows Mayra. She was part of a raid he did for the FBI, only a small child at the time being forced to live in miserable conditions, helping her criminal, drug addict par-

ents cook meth, of all things. They kept in touch and she reached out to him a few days ago sounding upset, so he took a few days off to come check on her, only to find out she was gone.

"Let me handle this, Brailey. You aren't trained for these things," he bosses when I offer to do some digging.

"Well too bad you can't stop me, huh?"

When he doesn't answer, I roll my eyes and wipe my mouth delicately with my napkin, and excuse myself to the restroom. The door hasn't even closed behind me when someone pushes it open and walks in. I don't think anything of it until I hear the lock turn and feel a body pressed against mine.

Suddenly, I'm being spun around and pushed up against the wall roughly, and when I look into Bryce's hungry eyes, I barely get out a gasp before his mouth comes crashing down on mine.

"Bryce, we're in a public bathroom." I laugh as I playfully push him away. He looks around for a second, like a fog is clearing and he's noticing his surroundings for the first time. When his eyes settle back on mine, my whole body reacts instantly. One look is all it takes to have my legs turn to Jell-O and my heart tripping over itself.

Without speaking he takes my hand in his and leads me straight out of the restaurant. I don't need to ask; I know where we're going. He just better get us there fast.

CHAPTER
NINE

There's no way to know for certain, but these dreams definitely feel like memories. Bad part is, I don't know how accurate they are, and it only raises for questions for me instead of giving me any answers.

Dammit, I wish I had someone in my life to answer these questions.

Well, I suppose it's a good thing my dream woke me up a whole hour before my alarm was scheduled to go off. I had to forego my usual nightly routine last night since I was holed up in my bedroom avoiding Wyatt, but luckily when I came out this morning he was gone and I had plenty of time to get ready for work. My hair is so long and thick that I usually wash it the night before and let it dry while I'm sleeping, otherwise it takes almost an hour to blow dry.

I still don't know what the hell happened the other night, but I've decided I don't care. Ever since Wyatt waltzed into my life, I've been walking around in a fog, unable to think about anything other than all the very inappropriate things I want to do to him - some sexual, some murderous.

Luckily I got everything ready on Friday for my first day at my new job, which I can't believe is today. Not because it feels like time has flown by. Quite the opposite actually. In the short time since moving here, it feels like a months' worth of time has passed.

The building I'll be working in is only a couple blocks from my apartment, and it's a nice day out, so I figure walking will give me a good chance to clear my head and mentally prepare.

Wrong.

I'm only a few steps outside of my apartment building when I hear Wyatt call out for me. My head falls back in frustration, but I don't quit walking. In fact, I speed up. Doesn't matter to me that he's yelling for me to slow down, because he's going to catch up to me soon enough since I'm in heels and he's jogging.

"Brailey! Seriously!" He yells, and when several people on the sidewalk turn and look our way, I finally come to a halt and glare at him.

"Quit making a scene, Wyatt. What do you want?" I ask through gritted teeth.

"I was just gonna see if I could walk you to work. Your first day, right?" He shoves his hands in the pockets of his jeans and gives me a shy smile, and I just want to stomp my foot and growl at how frustratingly adorable he looks. I know no matter what I say he's just going to walk with me anyway, so instead of arguing I just start moving again, this time at a slower pace.

"I don't need a chaperone just to get to work, Wyatt. I know you think I'm helpless, though I can't figure out what gave you that impression, but I can manage walking a few blocks without anything bad happening."

"What? I don't think that." He sounds sincere, but I've seen so many different sides to Wyatt already that I'm starting to wonder if he's a really good liar or just has multiple personalities. There's a good chance one of these days I'm going to end up getting whiplash trying to keep up with how quickly he changes from day to day.

"Really? Sure looks that way to me. You keep swooping in like some white knight, which honestly is getting kind of weird because you always seem to be there when something does happen. Come to think of it, you're just *always* around. Do you even have a job?"

"Yeah, I uh, build websites, but I do it from home so I get to work a pretty flexible schedule. But listen, about the other stuff..." He trails off when I abruptly start walking away from him again, not wanting to hear what's coming next. He grabs my hand and gently tugs me to a stop, and the tingling that spreads up my arm to my chest from his touch is almost enough to make me forget how pissed off he's making me. Almost.

"I guess I have been acting protective when it comes to you, but it's not because I think you're weak or incapable of taking care of yourself, I just...shit, I don't know." He lets go of my hand and runs it through his hair, worrying his lip for a minute before turning back and pleading with me, "Can you just trust me?"

It's an odd question from someone I really don't know and my first instinct is to tell him to shove off, but the vulnerability in his eyes makes it hard for me to say anything at all. When I don't respond right away he grabs my hand again and all my mental strength is spent ignoring the way my body lights on fire with his touch, effectively making me agree to something I may very well regret in a matter of minutes.

"Fine." I watch the relief wash over his body from

head to toe like a tidal wave, and he lets out a big breath that he must have been holding while waiting for my answer.

"Look," I start, not really sure how to navigate myself through this situation, but I feel the need to put some guidelines to this whole 'trusting a stranger' thing. "I'm not good at reading people or situations so I don't exactly trust my judge of character, but I also don't want to be a jerk and not trust you right off the bat before getting to know you. So I have one condition that I'm going to put on our friendship and it's a deal breaker."

He winces at the word friendship, but I brush past that and continue on before I lose my nerve. "Honesty. I don't lie, I couldn't even if I wanted to, I suck at it. And because I'm still a little naive when it comes to other people, I probably won't be able to tell if you're lying, so I'm going to ask you to always be completely honest with me. I'll trust whatever you say, until you give me a reason not to. One lie, however small, and I'm out."

Just like that, Wyatt's whole demeanor shifts. His grip on my hand loosens and he lets my hand fall to my side then looks at the ground, and when he looks back up the pain reflected back at me steals my breath away. Wyatt's face is so expressive, and I'm grateful for that, because I meant it when I said I'm not good at reading people.

"I promise you if I ever lie to you it will only be to protect you. You don't know me, but you can believe me when I say I am loyal and honorable, and I will never hurt you intentionally."

He's skirting around my question and carefully

wording his response in a way that if I weren't paying attention would sound like an agreement, but I'm not a fool. I hear the hidden message loud and clear. Wyatt will lie if it's convenient for him or when he deems it necessary in order to 'protect' me.

"Not good enough," I say shaking my head and walking away from him.

"Brailey, please!" He pleads, grabbing my hand again. I don't pull away from him, but I don't turn around to face him either.

"One shot, Wyatt. That's all you get." I start walking again and he lets go of my hand, not bothering to follow me the rest of the way to work.

To sum up my first day of work? Disaster. I've never felt so incompetent in my life. How I made it through college and managed to get a nursing degree is beyond me. I've been telling myself that today was just one of those days where everything that could go wrong went wrong, and that it wasn't my inability to do the simplest tasks that made the day so bad.

The walk home feels like it takes forever, my feet aching and my body worn down, and by the time I start up the stairs to my apartment all I can think about is taking a long, hot bath. I should have taken a cab home.

Screw the fact that it's only two blocks. Walking is stupid.

"Unless you're waiting to give me a piggyback ride up the stairs, then now's not a great time, Wyatt," I mutter when I see him standing in the lobby, very obviously waiting on me. He turns around and crouches like he expects me to actually jump on, and dammit, it makes me laugh. I don't want to laugh. I want to be tired and grumpy and miserable.

Neither of us saying anything as we climb the stairs silently. "So are you some creepy guy who just sits around waiting for people to go in and out of the building, or am I just lucky?" I ask sarcastically.

"Nope, you're just lucky," he answers with a wink.

"Alright then, thanks for walking me home. I can-" Wyatt cuts me off when he breezes right past me as soon as the key is turned in my door handle. "Please, come on in. Make yourself at home. If you need me, too bad, because I'll be soaking in the tub." Wyatt lets out a low growl and I look at him quizzically, wondering why in the world he thinks it's okay to be frustrated that I'm too busy to talk to him when he didn't bother to let me know he would be stopping by ahead of time.

I hear the TV click on just as I turn on the faucet for the bathtub. While the tub fills up I brush my teeth and strip out of my clothes. The water is so hot it's almost painful, but it quickly helps my muscles relax and I feel myself sinking into a comfortable oblivion.

Just a few minutes of peace is all I'm looking for, but not five minutes after climbing into the tub, a piercing sound startles me, making me sit up so quickly that water splashes over the side and soaks my floor. The door handles to the bathroom jiggles and Wyatt starts banging on the door. He's yelling my name and telling me to come on, but I'm stuck in the tub, unable to move once I realize the sound is the fire alarm for the building.

The building is on fire.

Wyatt's still yelling and banging, but it sounds like white noise to my ears. The room is spinning and my head is screaming at my body to move, but my arms and legs won't comply. The banging and yelling on the door stops and I think Wyatt has given up on me and left to save himself, but seconds later the door to the bathroom bursts open and wood splinters scatter through the air.

I don't even care that I'm naked, I don't have time to worry about it. Wyatt's already pulling me out of the water by my arms and wrapping my white, terrycloth bathrobe around me. When my limp body becomes too difficult for him to move, Wyatt slips his arms behind my knees and lifts me into the air. My skin is slippery and when he starts moving he loses his grip on me, slipping on the wet bathroom floor.

The sensation of falling snaps me back into reality and I scream, throwing my arms around Wyatt's neck. He finds his balance and takes off for the door, and within seconds we are outside in front of the building. My eyes are blurry with tears, but I can still make out Keegan's face running towards us.

"Put her down, Wyatt," Keegan tells him almost hatefully.

"No!" I yell and squeeze Wyatt tighter to me, shoving my face into his neck. I feel myself being lowered, but Wyatt's grip on me never loosens. He's sat himself down on the curb with me in his lap and he's stroking my hair and whispering soothing words in my ear over and over again. I take deep breaths and the clean, masculine scent of his skin starts to calm my heart and my breathing slows.

"How bad is it?" I ask with a shaky voice.

"How bad is what, Peaches?"

I pull back from Wyatt just enough to look in his eyes, but not far enough to be able to see anything besides his face. I can't bring myself to see how bad the fire is.

"The fire, how bad is it?" His eyes look pained and I want to start crying again, but when he cups my face in his hands and presses his forehead to mine, the panic that had started to rise again subsides.

"It was just a small fire in the laundry room. One of the lint traps caught fire in the old dryer, but they got to it in time. I'm so sorry if I scared you. I didn't know until we got outside that the fire was already contained and no one got hurt. You're okay."

I'm not even entirely sure why I freaked out so bad, but I'm so relieved to hear the building is fine and no one was hurt that I don't think about it before I press my lips to Wyatt's. As soon as I feel his body tense up I realize what I've just done, but when I go to pull away, Wyatt's hands on my face hold me in place. His body relaxes and when he starts kissing me back I completely lose myself in the feel of him.

Much too soon Wyatt breaks the kiss and a small whimper escapes me. My eyes are still closed and I feel

Wyatt chuckle, but I don't even care if I seem desperate or pathetic, I need to feel his mouth on me again.

This time when I press my lips to his again he doesn't hesitate, and instead of a slow, tender kiss like the one before, this one is full of hunger and need. When Wyatt drops one hand from my face to my waist and pulls my body even closer to his, I let out another moan and he uses the opening to slip his tongue into my mouth.

I know without a doubt that if we were alone in my apartment right now, I'd be tearing at his clothes, ripping them off his body as quickly as possible. If it weren't for Keegan clearing her throat behind me, reminding me that we are in fact not alone in my apartment, then I might have started stripping him down anyway.

When Wyatt pulls back and presses his forehead to mine again we both laugh. His bright blue eyes hold so many emotions as I stare into them that it's almost painful to look into them, so I look down to our bodies pressed up against each other. It's that moment that I realize I'm outside, in Wyatt's lap with people all around us, completely naked except for my tiny bathrobe that's not even tied.

Wyatt shifts underneath of me and it's clear that he is very much aware of just how naked I am, and when a blush creeps up my face I bury my face in his neck to hide my embarrassment.

"Take me home, please." My mouth is pressed up against his skin and my words come out muffled, and I can feel the effect my hot breath on his neck is having on him. I can't stop myself from pressing a soft, wet kiss to his neck, smiling when he groans.

Wyatt stands effortlessly with me still cradled in his arms and I hear Keegan tell him she will be by later to check on me. When we reach my apartment door it's still flung open since Wyatt didn't bother closing it when we thought the building was on fire. He kicks it shut behind him and walks over to the couch and sits. I start to pull away from him, but he tugs me back and holds me tightly.

"Wyatt, at least let me put some clothes on."

"I think you're fine the way you are," he says seriously, but he has a teasing glint in his eyes.

"And I think you've seen enough of my naked body for one day." Wyatt growls and pulls away from me, then slowly peruses my body, lingering on my breasts, making it painfully obvious that he's soaking up the view before it's gone.

"I think I should be the judge of whether or not I've seen enough." I grip his chin and pull his face up so he has to look at me and not my half naked body and laugh when he pouts. "Fine, if you insist, but so we're clear... if it were up to me, you'd be wearing less clothes, not putting more on." All the teasing is gone from his eyes and his pupils dilate, and I swear my heart is pounding so loudly that he has to be able to hear it.

"Alright now, get on with it before I change my mind," he says as he lifts me off his lap and slaps me on my ass.

Once I'm in my bedroom the weight of the last hour hits me so hard it knocks the wind out of me. Everything seemed okay when Wyatt was holding me, but now that I'm alone in my dark, cold bedroom it feels like someone is sitting on my chest. I grab a set of pajamas; a silky, strappy top with matching shorts so short they may as well be underwear. I'm playing with fire – no pun intended – but part of me wants Wyatt to see me in something skimpy. Something that might make him throw me down on the bed and…

My phone that I left sitting by my bed buzzes, and before I can think better of it, I answer.

Emotions I didn't realize were bubbling just below the surface start to spill over as soon as I hear Mark's voice. Things between us might be strained and a little awkward even, but he was the one who sat with me for hours and hours after I woke up in Mayford. Until Wyatt, Mark was my source of comfort, just in a different way. In the scheme of things, this is a pretty small breakdown compared to others I've had recently. By the time I'm done telling Mark what happened, my tears have dried up.

"Do you need me to come to you, Brailey?"

"What? No! I mean, I appreciate it and yeah, of course I'd love to see you, but you don't have to drive two hours to see me just because of some silly overreaction to a fire alarm. I'll be okay."

"I hate not being there to help you through this, Brailey, you know that, right?" Again with the overly personal response that I don't know how to respond to. Maybe it's me. Maybe meeting Wyatt and all the feelings he stirs in me are making me feel guilty and I'm the one putting a wedge between me and Mark.

"I know, but it's not your job to take care of me anymore." How horrible am I for thinking life would actually be a lot easier if Mark truly were just my doctor? Why does someone I held so much affection for just a week ago suddenly feel like a tether that keeps me from being able to move forward?

"I don't want to come there because it's my job, Brailey. I want to be there for you."

I want to groan out loud. I can't do this anymore. Wyatt is waiting on me, and he's who I want to be talking to. As much as it will hurt, at some point – and soon – I'm going to have to let Mark go.

"I um, I have to go. I have company waiting on me." He doesn't respond right away, and when he does speak, his voice sounds angry.

"What company, Brailey." The demanding tone in his voice raises my hackles. I already have a ridiculously overbearing and bossy man in the other room. I'm not really in the market for another.

"It's Wyatt. He was here when the alarm went off." I hate myself a little bit for the bitchy way that comes out, because I've been trying so hard for so long to be sensitive to Mark, but it's getting old - and fast.

"Sounds like you've been spending a lot of time with Wyatt." The agitation in his voice is the last straw.

"Yeah, I guess. Gotta go, call you later," I say quickly, hanging up before he has a chance to say anything else. Throwing my phone down on the bed, I put thoughts of Mark behind me and focus on the man I'm pretty sure I'm about to try and seduce.

Only it turns out, that man is gone.

WYATT

Fucking Mark.

I save her life and what does she do? She calls Mark. Yeah, I know he's her doctor, but that doesn't lessen the stab to my ego when she's in there being comforted by him when I'm sitting right in her damn living room.

No, she wasn't actually in danger, but does it matter? I was the one who was here, the one who protected her. Okay, so I was also the one who set the whole fire in motion, but it wasn't by choice. I hate this. All of it. It doesn't matter that it's my fucking job, because whenever I'm with Brailey, it doesn't feel at all like work.

For a minute I thought she actually wanted me, but she couldn't get away from me fast enough. As soon as she's out of my arms, she runs to her room and calls someone else. A good guy would be grateful that she has someone she can turn to, right? Maybe if I weren't waiting for her while being rudely ignored than I could find it in me to be the 'good guy.'

Was she thinking of him when she was kissing me? Was she picturing his arms around her and pretending it was his voice soothing her?

It doesn't matter, asshat. She isn't yours.

Reminding myself of this fact doesn't help ease the ache in my chest when I think of her. I shouldn't feel this way about her. It's ten kinds of wrong and it's going to end up ruining everything. I have a job to do, and it does not include falling for her. If Bryce were here he'd be kicking my ass the same way I want to kick Mark's.

Our research didn't reveal much about Mark, and as much as I hate to keep prying into her life, I'm going to have to dig deeper. Something just feels off about the guy. Okay, so maybe I haven't talked to him or met him, and maybe most of these feelings stem from jealousy, but dammit, it's my job to make sure she's safe. So at least I have *that* excuse to fall back on.

"Fuck!" I yell when I walk into my apartment. I yank on my hair and I just...snap.

Anything that's not nailed in or too heavy to lift gets thrown across the room. By the time I'm done destroying my apartment, the only things I own that aren't destroyed are the couch and the TV.

I look around me at all the destruction I've just managed to cause in a matter of minutes.

I am so screwed.

CHAPTER
TEN

I'm standing in the middle of my apartment trying to decide whether or not to go after Wyatt and ask him why he just disappeared when there's a knock on my door. Assuming it's Wyatt I run over and swing the door open without checking the peephole.

"Hey, where'd you go?" The question is out before I have the chance to stop myself.

"I didn't go anywhere; I've been next door." Keegan pushes past me with a bottle of wine in one hand and two wine glasses in the other. She's already filling up the glasses before I even get the door shut behind her.

"Sorry, I thought you were Wyatt."

She quirks an eyebrow at me, most likely because of how I answered the door. I may have sort of ran to the door and anxiously yelled out my question, so she might sort of think I was excited to see him.

She would be sort of right.

"Don't look at me like that, it's just been a weird day and he disappeared when I was in the other room without saying goodbye."

"Mmmhmm," she hums skeptically as she gives my skimpy PJs a once over before making her way over to my couch. "That was some kiss you guys shared outside." My cheeks heat up immediately, but this is Keegan and I know I may as well suck it up because she's going to make me tell her every little detail, no matter how much I try to resist.

"Yeah, I don't know what happened. I was just so freaked out at first when he carried me down and then when he told me it was a small fire I was so relieved, and the way he was looking at me, I just...I'm such an idiot," I groan, plopping down next to her and covering my face with my hands.

"You're not an idiot, it was hot."

"Ugh, what if I'm a horrible kisser? Maybe that's why he left, because he was afraid I'd try and kiss him again." I throw my head back and stare at the ceiling, then I feel a wine glass being shoved into my hand, so I turn my head to the side to look at Keegan.

"Sweetie, that kiss was amazing, and I wasn't even a part of it. Trust me, he enjoyed it. Maybe an emergency came up or something," she offers with a shrug, but I'm not sure she's right. Seems like he would have at least called out that he was leaving or something. Just taking off without bothering to yell out a goodbye or something just seems...odd.

"I don't know, he's so hard to read. Not that it would matter if he weren't, because I suck at reading people. I just feel like, I don't know, he's coming on pretty strong right? Like sometimes it seems like he's into me, and then the next minute he's totally closed off or being an asshole. He's so freaking moody, he even chased me down before work this morning and offered to walk with me. Weird, right?"

I turn to look at Keegan when she doesn't immediately jump in with an opinion and I'm shocked when I see her avoiding my eyes and looking nervous.

"What?" I ask nervously. She fidgets and lets out a sigh before facing me with a pained expression on her face.

"I honestly don't know about him, B. On one hand, he seems like a great guy. He's been there every time something has happened to you since he moved in and hasn't hesitated to help, but isn't it odd that he's *always* there? I just get the feeling that he's keeping something hidden. I mean *other* things besides what happened at the club, and-"

Keegan smacks a hand over her mouth, her eyes wide. "What do you mean what happened at the club? You're keeping something from me?" Betrayal - definitely recognize that emotion when it stabs me in the heart. Why would Keegan keep a secret from me - especially if it's *about* me?

"I'm so sorry Brailey. I wanted to tell you, but he and Garrett ganged up on me and I don't know, I guess I thought since you were okay that it wasn't worth it to worry you. But that night at the club when you got really drunk and Wyatt brought you home? You weren't actually drunk, you were drugged."

The world around me starts spinning so fast I can't see straight.

"Wh-what do you mean? How could you even know that?" Keegan squeezes my hand and starts to talk but I interrupt her when I realize she said *Wyatt* convinced her not to tell me.

"Wait," I interrupt her, my vision turning red. "What does Wyatt have to do with this?"

"That's what I'm trying to tell you, sweetie. He's the one that figured out you were drugged, but he made me promise not to tell you."

I'm out the door and taking the stairs two at a time, ignoring Keegan's pleas for me to come back. She's smart enough not to come after me, probably not wanting to be witness to the confrontation that's about to take place.

I bang on Wyatt's door until he yanks it open, and his annoyed expression turns to apprehension when he sees how angry I am. I've never felt pure rage like this before - that I can remember - and it's a little frightening, but the adrenaline coursing through my veins keeps my mind focused on what I came here to do.

"You! I told you. I *told* you!" I yell, poking him hard in the chest, making him stumble backwards. I follow him, poking him over and over so hard that I think my finger might actually break. "I told you that you got one shot with me. I told you that once I found out you lied to me, that there would be no friendship for us. And you stood there keeping a huge secret from me and lied right to my face anyway."

Wyatt throws his hands up in a defensive gesture, but when I go to shove him, he grabs my wrists and holds me in place. I'm using all my strength to escape his hold, but his grip on me is so tight that it hurts every time I yank on my hands.

"Let go of me!"

"Are you going to stop assaulting me if I do?" His calm, unrepentant voice just pisses me off even more.

"You're a lying asshole! Let go of me right now!"

I'm yelling so loud that my throat hurts, and Wyatt quickly releases me, probably afraid the neighbors are going to call the police if they hear me.

"Look, Brailey, I'm sorry. I wanted to tell you. I couldn't, though, it wasn't my decision."

"What the hell are you talking about?" Why the hell wouldn't it be *his* decision? I'm so confused and it's obvious he's hiding *another* secret from me.

"Dammit!" He yells, yanking on his hair.

"You know what, Wyatt, I don't even want to know what you're talking about. It's obvious you're keeping so many secrets from me that you can't even keep them straight. I told you if you lied to me then that was it, so I'm leaving and you better not follow me."

I stomp-slash-run to his door, but Wyatt grabs my wrist and spins me around, pushing me up against the wall in one graceful move, before crashing his mouth on mine. Wyatt is holding both of my wrists above my head and his body is pressed up tightly against mine, and for one brief second I lose my mind and actually kiss him back. When I feel him try to deepen the kiss I come back to reality and push off the wall as hard as I can, the sudden movement catching him off guard, giving me the opportunity to free my wrists from his hold.

Without giving him a chance to even blink, my hand comes up and smacks him across his face so hard that his head jerks to the side. I want to tell him to go to hell and storm out, but instead I immediately start muttering apologies. When he lifts his head to look at me I immediately wish I had run out the door when I had the chance.

"Wyatt, I..." I trail off, because I'm honestly not

sure what I'm trying to say. I just can't stand the silence between us and the frightening look he's giving me. His chest is heaving up and down and his head is tilted down so that he's looking up at me, even though he's almost a foot taller than me. My heart is pounding in my chest and I'm torn between wishing Keegan had followed me up here so she could help, and being grateful that she's not caught in the crossfire.

I take a tentative step backwards, hoping to edge my way closer to the door, but Wyatt notices and his jaw ticks. In this moment I'm actually scared of him and I'm not sure what to do. *Do I make a run for it? Do I keep apologizing and hope he calms down?* I feel tears burning in the back of my throat and I lose the fight to hold them back.

Quiet tears stream down my face and a choked sob escapes me, and I use all my strength to keep from just collapsing onto the floor. I lift my hand to wipe the tears from my cheeks, but Wyatt's too quick and in the blink of an eye he's in front of me, gently pushing my hand away from my face and replacing it with his own.

All the fire and rage from his eyes is gone and all that's left is sadness and remorse, and the way he gently brushes my cheek with his hand almost breaks my heart. How he can go from seething mad to gentle and compassionate so quickly is enough to make me dizzy, but when he tucks a strand of hair behind my ear and whispers that he's sorry, all my fears from just moments ago melt away.

"I'm sorry I hit you, I don't even know where that came from." I'm full on sobbing now and Wyatt continues to brush his knuckles gently down my cheek.

"Don't apologize Brailey, I'm an asshole. I'm the one who's sorry."

"You scared me," I whisper as my tears start to slow.

"I know, I know," he utters, pushing one hand behind my head and grabbing a fistful of my hair and pulling me into a hug. I don't hug him back at first, but I know the gentle squeeze he gives me is a plea for me to return his hug, and after a moment's hesitation, I finally wrap my arms around his waist and hold on tight.

"I'm not angry at you, I wasn't angry that you hit me. I'm frustrated. I'm in an impossible situation and I want nothing more than to be honest with you, but I can't. Not yet." He pulls back and holds my face in his hands, searching my eyes for something, I'm not sure what. "I don't deserve your trust, I know that. I've been all over the place since meeting you and I promise it will make sense to you soon, but I'm begging you to please... just give me a little time and I swear I'll tell you everything."

Instinct tells me not to believe anything he says, especially considering how cryptic he's being. Not to mention the fact that someone I just met shouldn't have huge secrets that involve me already, but since he doesn't appear to be going anywhere and seems pretty relentless, all I can do is agree for now and hope for the best.

"Okay, I'll trust you." His shoulders sag and he lets out a sigh of relief. "On one condition." He quirks an eyebrow at me and his lips turn up into a sly grin. I roll my eyes but can't prevent myself from grinning back at him, he's just too damn adorable when he grins like that.

"Okay, lay it on me," he says cockily.

"You give me some space." His face falls and he opens his mouth to argue, but I hold up my hand to stop him. "Not forever, just give me some time, Wyatt. We just met and you're a little...intense. I need some time to digest everything that's happened. So please, just...give me some distance."

He crosses his arms and narrows his eyes. "How long?"

"I don't know," I sigh, knowing he's going to argue with whatever I say. "It could be a day; it could be a month. Let me reach out to you when I'm ready, okay?" All hope that he would agree goes out the window when he starts vigorously shaking his head back and forth.

"Nope, no way. I'm not going to stay away for a month, that's crazy."

"Ugh, it might not be that long, I don't know! You act like we're dating and I'm asking to take a break or something. We're just neighbors, Wyatt, we barely know each other." His head jerks back like I slapped him again, and he's clearly offended by what I just said, though I have no idea why.

"We're not just neighbors, Brailey," he growls.

"Okay, fine, we're friends. Ish." When he glares at me I hurry to get out what I need to say before I lose my nerve. "Look, let's make a deal. You give me the space I need, and when I contact you I'll tell you everything about me. There's a reason I need this space, Wyatt, and it's not personal. This life...*my* life...it's complicated. I'm still figuring things out and learning to be on my own, and honestly, I can't think straight when you're around. I just need a little time to sort myself out."

"You can't think straight when you're around me, huh?" He asks with a huge smile that lights his entire face. I notice a dimple on his right cheek that must only make appearances when he smiles this big, because I've never noticed it before, and it's entirely too sexy for me to have just missed in the past.

"That's all you took from that?" I feign offense, holding my hand to my chest in mock horror. He rolls his eyes and takes a few steps towards me, closing the gap between us.

"No, I heard you. I'll give you space, even though you make it sound like I'm some creepy stalker," he jokes and I can't help but laugh at his playful tone.

"You are so damn moody, Wyatt, it kills me. And you do kind of act like a creepy stalker." My smile fades and my expression grows serious. "I mean it, Wyatt, I need this."

"Can we at least kiss on it?" Wyatt asks, waggling his eyebrows up and down.

"I think the saying is shake on it," I argue.

"I know, but nothing seals a deal better than a kiss." Wyatt leans in to kiss me, but I playfully push him away.

"Nice try, bud, not happening." I walk out his door, but turn and give him a small smile when I reach the top of the stairs. He returns my smile, but it's one of the smiles I've come to notice are forced.

When I get back to my apartment, I see Keegan has left me an angry message on the magnetic white board I keep on my fridge, so I send her a text and tell her I'm okay and will talk to her tomorrow. My bed is calling, and I intend to answer.

CHAPTER
ELEVEN

Almost a week has passed since I saw or spoke to Wyatt last. The whole space thing sounded great at the time. It's unnatural for me to miss him as much as I do.

I've stopped taking my sleeping pills altogether now. Sometimes I remember my dreams, sometimes I don't, but it's been helping me remember fragments when I'm awake. When I made a comment to Mark about thinking about stopping them he freaked out, so I haven't told him. It feels like lying, even though I know it's just an omission, but guilt still has me avoiding him. I'm ashamed to say that when he texted me this morning saying he was going to be in town for a meeting and wanted to meet up, I pretended to already have plans.

I also haven't told anyone that I'm starting to remember. I don't know enough yet to feel comfortable even describing the memories. Most of the time they are out of order and contorted, half the time not even making sense.

Going out is the very last thing I want to do tonight, too exhausted from not sleeping and not too keen on the idea of possibly running into Mark, but Keegan's been patient with my constant state of apathy, so I kind of owe her. Plus, when I yawned in the middle of a Ryan Gosling movie she lost it and said a night out would do me good. I should just tell her about the dreams, I've told her just about everything else about me, but every time I go to bring it up, the words get caught in my throat.

I'm on my way up from the laundry room on the bottom level, a laundry basket in hand, and when I put it down to open my mailbox in the lobby Wyatt comes strolling in. He's looking down at his phone, but when he lifts his head and sees me, the flash of pain and apprehension in his eyes makes me feel terrible. I don't want him thinking he has to avoid me altogether just because I asked him for space. I really just meant I didn't want him forcing his way into my apartment all the time, not that he had to avoid making eye contact like he's doing currently.

He immediately looks away from me and moves to walk past me, giving me a head nod and making sure to avoid meeting my eyes again. I grab his arm to stop him. I'm not sure why, I don't really feel like talking, but I hate how defeated he looks with his shoulders slumped over like a sad puppy. His head jerks back, and when his wide eyes meet mine an accidental laugh slips from my mouth.

"I'm sorry, your face just now was kinda funny," I say, teasing lightly. His face relaxes and he turns to face me, and though the way I'm holding his arm is somewhat awkward, I can't bring myself to let go. The tingling in my fingertips that started the instant I touched him is spreading through my limbs and into my belly, and the longer I hold on to him, the less I feel the emptiness I've been drowning in for the past few days.

"I was just surprised you stopped me is all. I wasn't

sure if I was allowed to talk to you or anything." He shrugs and says it like it's no big deal, but the uncertainty in his expression tells me he really is insecure about how I would react if he talked to me.

"Oh stop it, I didn't mean you had to avoid me entirely. Come on," I say, finally letting go of him and tossing my mail in the laundry basket on top of the unfolded clean clothes. Wyatt yanks it from my grip, insisting on carrying it for me, so I wrap my arm through his and pull him with me to the stairs.

"Uh, where are we going?" He asks with a laugh.

"You're walking me to my apartment. It's quite a long trek and I could use some company," I tease, melting a little when he smiles sweetly at me. "I'm going out with Keegan tonight, so cancel whatever plans you had, you're coming with." I turn the key in my door handle and Wyatt moves quickly, putting his hand on the door and holding it open for me while propping the basket on his hip with his other arm.

"Demanding little thing, aren't you? Don't talk to me for five days and then force me to go out. What if I had a hot date tonight or something?" I couldn't have kept from scowling if my life depended on it, though I do try to put my back to him so he doesn't see. His cocky grin, that I have seriously missed seeing every day, combined with him just letting me know that he's actually been counting the days since we talked last, has be a little less pissed off at the idea of him going on a date. A little. Okay not really – he better not have a date.

"Are you jealous, Peaches?" His smug face and teasing voice should piss me off, but how can I get mad if he's right? I most definitely *am* jealous at the thought of him going on a date.

I'm about to tell him just that, but as soon as he sits the basket of clothes and mail on my counter, his arm is snaking itself around my waist and yanking me to him. Suddenly his face is inches from mine, and before I can blink his hand cups my cheek, then makes its way to the back of my head and tugs my face to his.

I don't even bother fighting and my body immediately melts into him, my arms going up and around his neck. The kiss starts out slow and cautious, but when I bite down on Wyatt's lower lip, we both lose control. Wyatt's hand comes out of my hair, and before I can mourn the loss of his hands on me, he's dropping both hands to the backs of my thighs and pulling. My legs instinctively wrap around his waist; his hands move to cup my ass.

Sitting me on the counter, he pulls away just far enough to start trailing kisses down my cheek and to my neck. My head automatically tilts to give him better access, and when he bites down on my earlobe, warmth floods my core. All of a sudden it's like I'm possessed by some sort of sex-crazed demon, because I'm yanking at his clothes and stripping him like my life depends on it.

I peel off his button down shirt and lift up the t-shirt he was wearing underneath over his head at the same time that he tugs at my shirt, pulling it off of me with ease. When my shirt drops to the floor and I look back at Wyatt, I gasp. Wyatt stays completely still, except for his twitching muscles, as I lightly trace every line and sinew of his perfect chest with my fingertips.

He's absolutely stunning, and it's like staring at a beautifully sculpted statue. My lips take on a life of their own and start peppering soft, wet kisses over every inch of his shoulders, chest and torso. When my lips graze his nipple I hear his breath hitch and he yanks my head back up, his mouth devouring mine once again.

My brain is mush, I can't form a single coherent thought right now, but luckily I don't need my brain to be fully functioning for me to be able to start pulling at his belt buckle. As soon as my fingertips graze his waist, though, he rips his mouth from mine and grabs my hands.

"I-I'm sorry, I just...I don't know..." I stutter, suddenly feeling insecure and very aware of the fact that I'm wearing only a skirt and my bra and my legs are still wrapped around Wyatt's waist. I drop my legs and move to get down from the counter, but Wyatt stays unmoving between my legs, his hands still holding on to mine.

"Hey," he says, cupping my chin and forcing me to look him in the eyes. "I just don't want to move too fast, that's all. I heard what you said the other day, Brailey, and you're right. We don't really know each other. Trust me, I want you. I want *this*. But I don't want to jump into things too quickly and ruin our chances at...whatever this is that's between us."

He places a chaste kiss to my lips before bending down to pick up his shirt and handing me mine.

"Text me what time you guys are going tonight and I'll meet you down here," he says with a wink, and then he's gone.

An hour later there's a knock at my door, and when I open it I'm standing face to face with a very, very sexy man. He gives me a cheeky grin; enjoying every bit of the blatant appreciation I show for all the hotness standing in my doorway. Instead of being embarrassed I grab a handful of his shirt and tug him inside. Before the door is closed his mouth is on mine, and he's kissing me with deliberate, sensual movements.

Much too soon he pulls away, and I hear him chuckle when I lean forward, my lips instinctively chasing after his. I reluctantly open my eyes, expecting to see Wyatt looking at me with a knowing grin. What I don't expect is for him to be looking at me with adoring eyes, and an emotion I'm unable to place.

I clear my throat and tug out of his grip, walking over to the counter to pick up my phone and purse.

"So where are we going tonight?" Wyatt asks from behind me.

"Just some bar I've never been to that's a few blocks away. Keegan says it's pretty nice and I didn't really want to go to one of our usual hangouts tonight."

"How come?"

My phone dings before I can answer him, thank God, because it was hard enough admitting to Keegan that I wanted to go somewhere I hadn't talked about with Mark because I didn't want to chance seeing him. I'm hoping the fact that Mark doesn't like to go out will mean he probably won't be up for a night out on his own, and my having to explain all that to Wyatt is only going to make the guilt already eating away at me amplify to unmanageable proportions.

"It's Keegan. I guess she's held up at the hospital. She says she will meet us there but it's probably going to be a couple hours."

"That's fine, gives me a chance to take you out to dinner beforehand like a proper date." Wyatt's leading me by the elbow towards the door, and he takes my keys and locks it for me without letting go of my arm.

"Who said this is a date?"

The smile he gives me sparks butterflies in my stomach and I realize just how badly I actually want Wyatt to be taking me on a date. His hand slides down my arms until our hands are touching and he intertwines his fingers through mine.

"If you're gonna throw yourself at me every time you see me now, then I'm at least going to buy you dinner first," he says with a cocky grin. I playfully smack his arm, feigning offense and he chuckles.

It's surprising to me how easy it is to be around Wyatt. The mind-numbing anxiety and knee-crumbling nerves are still there, but in a much more tolerable way. Whereas at first they made me almost afraid to be around him, I find that now I enjoy the fluttering in my belly and the tightening in my chest that I feel when he's near.

Something has shifted between us. My insecurities of whether or not Wyatt is as attracted to me as I am him is no longer there. The kiss we shared earlier, and him actually coming out and admitting that he wants me... it gave my confidence a boost I didn't know it needed.

Where doubt lingered a few hours ago, now is replaced with a newfound boldness. I take advantage of my new emotions by not hesitating to lean my body into Wyatt's as we walk. He responds by letting go of my hand and wrapping his arm around my waist, pulling me tighter against him.

We make casual conversation as we walk a couple blocks to a nearby diner that Keegan and I have frequented a lot – sometimes more than once a day – since I moved in. It's not surprising when we walk in that our Flo, the waitress who almost always ends up with mine and Keegan's table, is the first to greet us.

"Hey, Flo," I say back with a smile. I don't miss the appreciative gleam in her eye as she looks over to Wyatt. If Flo weren't at least twice our age and as sweet as a cupcake, I might feel a jealous – or even possessive – from the way she's practically eating him up with her eyes. And honestly, no matter your age, any woman would find it hard *not* to appreciate Wyatt. His face is gorgeous enough to be on the front of magazines and no matter what he wears, it's clear that underneath is a body that's entirely drool-worthy.

Tonight he's wearing that black leather jacket of his that gives him that mysterious, bad boy edge, but it's paired with a crisp white button-down dress shirt and black pants. It's the perfect mix of casual and dressy, and don't even get me started on how good the man smells.

Without thinking I reach up and tug Wyatt's face down to mine and kiss him hungrily, completely forgetting we're in public. When my hand sneaks inside his jacket, Flo clears her throat and I bury my face in Wyatt's chest, soaking in the soft rumbles in his chest when he laughs at my sudden shyness.

"Don't worry, Peaches," Wyatt whispers low in my ear when we finally break our kiss. "We'll be repeating what happened earlier this evening soon, but next time it's my turn to appreciate *your* chest." I bite down on my lip and my cheeks flush as warmth spreads through my body and my core tightens. My heart rate picks up at the thought of baring myself to Wyatt and I work hard to regulate my breathing. *Why does it suddenly feel like everyone else in the restaurant can read my mind and is judging me for wanting to jump his bones right here at the hostess stand?*

I stay glued to him until we get to our table, and Wyatt seems even more reluctant than me to let go when we're finally forced to break apart.

The middle-aged woman who is normally so chatty and friendly is shifting uncomfortably as she takes our drink orders. She looks like she's trying to hide it, but she's doing a piss-poor job of pretending not to notice how seriously, seriously sexy Wyatt looks tonight. When she finally walks away, faltering a little as she goes, I have to put a hand over my mouth to cover my laugh. Wyatt gives me a funny look and I shake my head.

"Do women always act like this around you?" He raises an eyebrow and looks genuinely confused, and the fact that he's oblivious to the attention he gets from women means he's either too cocky to care or too modest to notice. "It's like every woman who comes within ten feet of you forgets how to function. Flo was clearly drooling all over you."

"Who?"

"The waitress," I explain with a nod in the direction she just left. "Keegan and I have eaten here a lot since I moved in, and she's usually our waitress. I've never seen her so quiet." Right then Flo returns with our drinks, still not bothering to glance in my direction, and she asks Wyatt if we're ready to order. His eyes are locked on mine though and he doesn't acknowledge her. After several awkward seconds pass, I tell Flo to give us a minute. When she walks away without looking at me still, I make a mental note to tease her next time I'm in here without Wyatt.

As soon as she's out of earshot Wyatt reaches across the table and catches me off guard by taking my hand in his.

"Hard to notice anyone else when I can't take my eyes off of you, isn't it?" If words could light a person on fire, then I would have gone up in flames from those. "But if you're going to kiss me like that every time another woman looks at me, then I'm happy to oblige them." I gulp loudly, unsure of how to respond to that, so I pull my hand away and grab my drink. My throat is suddenly so dry I could choke and I down half my water in one drink.

Wyatt chuckles and picks up his menu, asking for my recommendations since I picked the restaurant. He decides on a turkey club and I go with a cheeseburger and fries. Time passes quickly while Wyatt and I get to know each other over our meals, and even Flo starts to warm up to me again. When the check comes a pang of disappointment hits me and I'm sad that we have to

leave. I'm enjoying the new casualness of our relationship where I can actually breathe around him and say
things that don't make me sound like an idiot.

I try to help pay for dinner, but Wyatt again insists
it's a date so he should pay. I blush again at the word
date and look down, but when I look back up at Wyatt
his face has grown somber.

"Can I ask you something without you taking it the
wrong way?" The way he feels the need to preface his
question with that makes me think I'll regret agreeing to
it, but I do anyway by giving him a nod.

"Is everything okay?" I'm not sure what I thought
he was going to ask, but it definitely wasn't that.

"I'm not sure I understand," I reply quietly, unsure
of where he's going with this. He shifts uncomfortably
in his seat and then reaches for my hand again, and my
touch seems to relax him enough to keep going.

"I've seen you a few times this week. You didn't
see me, and I didn't approach you because you wanted
your distance. But every time you just looked so...lost. I
don't know how else to word it. The energy and spark I
saw in you when we first met just isn't there, and then
today when I saw you up close for the first time in days...
you seemed almost sad. And you have dark circles under
your eyes like you aren't sleeping."

I gasp and rear back in shock, caught off guard that
he's able to read me so well. My hand instinctively goes
to my eyes when he mentions the dark circles and he
must see the insecurity on my face, because his hand
squeezes mine lightly and his face softens.

"Don't worry, Peaches, it's not obvious. I've spent

every night dreaming of your perfect face since we met, so I'm probably the only one that notices. Even with those dark circles, you're easily the most beautiful woman I've ever seen."

If we weren't in public, I would jump across this table and ravage him. That was hands down the most flattering and romantic thing I could ever imagine someone saying to me. I'm not sure if opening up to him is the right thing to do, but I find myself wanting to tell him everything, even if it hurts getting it all out.

"I um, I just haven't been sleeping well."

"Is there a reason?"

As much as I hate to dive into this right now, the more time I spend with Wyatt, the more of a connection I start to feel for him that goes beyond physical attraction. If I want to truly put any effort into something with Wyatt, then this conversation would have to happen eventually anyway.

"Honestly? I'm not entirely sure. I was in an accident and I lost my memory. I woke up inside of Mayford Mental Institution - not because I'm crazy!" I add quickly. "I used to be a nurse there, and when they heard of my accident they let me recover there. But lately I've been starting to remember. Mostly when I'm sleeping, but bits and pieces come to me during the day, too. It's just hard to talk about because a lot of it is foggy and like pieces of a puzzle that I don't know how to fit together.

"But you're starting to remember?" Wyatt asks eagerly in a way that catches me off guard.

"I mean; I guess I am. I don't have anyone from my past to confirm whether or not these memories are real or just dreams."

The hairs on the back of my neck suddenly stand straight, my skin tingling with awareness. It's the same feeling I had that night in the club, like someone is watching me. Wyatt immediately tenses when he notices my shift in demeanor.

"What is it Brailey?"

"I don't know, it's weird. I'm probably being paranoid. But that night at the club I saw someone watching me. I couldn't see his face, but I swear he was staring right at me, but he was gone before I could get close enough to look. For some reason that same feeling, like I'm being watched - I feel it now."

Wyatt's out of his seat and scanning the room instantly. "Wyatt, what is it?" He must hear the tremor in my voice, because he whips around and does one of his infamous personality shifts, automatically pulling me into his arms and into a comforting embrace.

"I'm sorry, I just don't like the idea of you being scared," he says with his lips pressed to the top of my head. "Just let me make a call real quick and we'll head out." He turns his back to me and his voice is low, but I catch part of the conversation - enough to tell me he's having someone look into something. I can't help but assume that something must be the possibility of me actually being watched.

"Crap, Keegan's probably already there and waiting on us," I say, grabbing Wyatt's hand as soon as he's off the phone.

We walk the two blocks from the restaurant to the bar, and maybe it's Wyatt's obvious tense stature, but I still feel like I'm being watched. He must sense it, because he pulls me further into his side, giving me the comfort I was too afraid to ask for.

"Bray!" I hear Keegan yell from behind me, but before I can even turn to face her she's attacking me from behind in a bear hug. "You look happy!" I laugh at her excitement, but feel guilty for being out of sorts for so long and worrying her.

"I know, I am. Sorry I've been a crappy friend this week." She waves her hand dismissively while simultaneously signaling for the waiter. Wyatt excuses himself to take a call and I take the opportunity to fill Keegan in on my evening so far. I have to admit it's nice chatting and catching up like normal girlfriends, reminding me once again how lucky I am to be alive.

"Brailey?" A male voice asks, and my head snaps up. I'd know that voice anywhere.

"Mark!" I force enthusiasm and give what I hope is a believable smile. "It's so good to see you!" My brain is running a mile a minute, trying to think up a plausible excuse to give when he calls me out on my lie, but he never does. Instead he just looks genuinely happy to see me, making me feel like an even shittier person.

"I almost drove back tonight, but decided to just let myself have a little fun for once. Something you used to give me a hard time about all the time."

Out of nowhere, major Deja vu hits hard enough to knock me back into Keegan.

"Mark, I'm so glad you came out with us tonight. It only took a year of me pestering you to get you to spend time with your co-workers," I tease Mark, nudging him with my shoulder. He responds with an awkward smile, taking a sip of his beer. The same beer he's been nursing all night while the rest of us have been hammering shots.

"Thanks for talking me into it. I'm having fun."

He doesn't look like he's having fun at all. Maybe I shouldn't have coerced him into agreeing. I just can't help it; I have a soft spot for the introverts. Shaun was always that way, so I can't help but reach out to someone who keeps to themselves, wanting to pull them out of their shell.

Most people at Mayford stay away from Mark because of his aloofness. They think he's creepy, which is funny considering we work with patients who are literally screwed up in the head, but they find the psychiatrist weird? That logic is just backwards to me and only makes me feel even more sorry for him.

"Hey, wanna play a game of darts?" I've been trying to include him all night, but he's preferred to sit out and play 'voyeur' all night instead of participating. I'm not surprised when he shakes his head. I'm also not surprised when I catch his eyes darting down to my chest. That's another reason people tend to avoid him. He's definitely not subtle when he's checking out women - or

ogling, rather, because that's more accurate - but my guess would be he just lacks social skills. No one taught him how to be discreet.

My phone starts vibrating in my pocket, and when I pull it out and see it's the bank calling I excuse myself and step outside. I'm already halfway drunk, but after hearing my loan application was denied for the third time, I'm entirely too sober.

Shaun is at a friend's house tonight, so thankfully I have some time to figure out how to deal with telling him. Right now, all I want to do is forget.

An hour later, I'm drunker than I've ever been, and I'm finally feeling thankful I dragged Mark along for the ride because he's currently the one keeping me upright since everyone else is too drunk to keep themselves up, let alone help me.

I picked Mark up, figuring it was the only way to ensure he came with us, so I have to give him a ride home. Problem? There's no way my drunk ass can drive back to my house, which doesn't even register until we're in his driveway and he's putting my car in park, having driven since he's still sober. I'm pretty sure he never even finished that beer.

"You want to come in for some coffee and try to sober up or something? I can't let you drive like this." I think I answer him, I don't know, it's all getting pretty fuzzy now. "Are you okay? You seemed off ever since you took that call." I don't know if it's his concerned voice or just the fact that someone noticed for once that I'm not really keeping my shit together like I try to pretend, but a dam breaks in me and next thing I know, I'm making the big-

gest mistake of my life.

"Are you sure you want to do this?" Mark asks me between kisses, but I'm too busy pushing him backwards into his bedroom and tearing at his clothes to answer. Once he's down to his underwear, I start with my clothes, and when I'm fully naked I can't help but snicker at the stunned look on his face. He seriously looks lost, like it's the first time he's seen a naked woman, but that can't be possible. He's like, thirty years old, or something. Hell, I don't know, who cares.

Pushing him on his back, I straddle his legs and pull a condom out of my purse. I don't think I could coherently ask him if he has one right now, but at least my brain is functioning enough to remember to use one in the first place.

When I yank down his boxers, at first I think he doesn't even have an erection, but then I realize...he just has a really small penis. Shit, I almost start giggling. Partly from his unfortunate endowment, and partially for me thinking the word 'penis' while I'm this wasted. I swear he almost blows his load when I roll the condom down his shaft, and honestly, it wouldn't have been the worst thing in the world if he did. I have a feeling this isn't going to be good for me anyway, but if I stop now it'll probably destroy his ego.

Thankful that the large condom actually fits over his less-than-large erection, I mount him, and as I suspected, after only a few thrusts, that's all she wrote. The end. Fin. I haven't even worked up a sweat, and my job is done.

I think Mark offers to try and get me off, but as soon

as I roll off him and my head hits the pillow, it's lights out.

"Brailey! What happened? Are you okay?" Keegan is calling out to me when I come to. She's hovering over me, and I realize I'm flat on my back on the dirty bar floor.

"I-I'm not sure. I think I passed out." Keegan rolls her eyes as she helps me try to sit up.

"No shit, B. I want to know *why*. Did you eat today? Has this happened before?"

"Yes, we just came from dinner. No, I've never passed out. I just want to go home. Where's Wyatt?"

Keegan smirks, and I'm well aware it's because I asked for Wyatt, but screw it. He's who I need right now.

"He's still on his phone call," Mark says as he hands me a glass of water, his voice tense and his eyes dark.

"I'm fine, Mark, you don't need to worry," I say on a sigh, taking his proffered hand and wobbling a little when I stand, leaning into his side when he wraps an arm around me. "I haven't been sleeping well is all, I'm sure."

"Do you need a stronger dose for your sleeping pills?" I wince when I realize what I've just done. I've put myself directly in a position to either fess up and deal with a lecture or lie. Reasoning that I deserve a little rest after having fainted, I go with lying.

"Maybe, I don't know. I think I'm just drinking caffeine too late and it's just taking longer to fall asleep is all. I'll cut back."

Mark seems mollified by that explanation, but my relief doesn't last long, because as soon as Wyatt comes back in and spots Mark's arm around me, his eyes turn murderous.

I can't do this right now. I don't have it in me to witness some sort of pissing match, and I need to figure out what the hell that memory was. When did it happen? Was that the beginning of my relationship with Mark? I never could get him to go into the details of our relationship, which I always found kind of odd. Maybe he was embarrassed?

No matter the reason, I need space. He's keeping things from me, and despite how good he's been to me so far, that makes me angry.

Keegan catches the look I give her and moves to intercept Wyatt while I turn to Mark. "Hey, I'm sorry, but I think I'm gonna head back and rest. I wish we could have hung out longer."

"Brailey, you should have told me you haven't been sleeping well," Mark says with his hands on my shoulders. "It feels like you've been avoiding me." His eyes look pained, but his grip on my shoulders tightens, making me wince in pain. Mark doesn't seem to notice, even though he's staring directly at me, inches from my face.

"What the hell!?" I yell when I'm forcefully ripped out of Mark's grip.

"Time to go Bray," Wyatt says in an eerily calm voice that completely belies the way he's practically snarling at Mark.

"Is this the neighbor you were telling me about Brailey? The one you said was an asshole?"

Mark is *never* like this. He's being strangely confrontational and antagonistic, and I'm momentarily too stunned to respond.

"Yep, that's me. I'm the asshole who doesn't like when other guys put their hands on my girl." No time to process Wyatt calling me his girl, because as soon as the word is out of his mouth, Mark is throwing his head back and laughing. *What the hell has gotten into him?*

"Whatever you say, *buddy,*" Mark says when his laughter dies down, emphasizing the word 'buddy' to sound condescending. Wyatt growls, and the next thing I know, Mark is pinned up against the wall with Wyatt clutching his shirt in one hand. Mark's not built like Wyatt, but he's a big guy. Not really the time to be impressed by his strength, but it *is* pretty impressive that Wyatt can hold up a grown man with one arm.

I glance around and see several people staring at the spectacle we're making, but I'm too pissed off and confused to be embarrassed.

"I'd let me down if I were you," Mark says with a cocky smirk, despite the fact that his feet are lifted almost a foot above the ground. I swear, it's like I don't even know Mark at all.

"I'll let you down once I'm sure you understand that you are to stay away from Brailey from now on," Wyatt says through gritted teeth.

"Wyatt." I say his name as a warning, not liking where this altercation is headed. Wyatt's absurd need to watch over me is annoying enough without him physically threatening anyone who comes near me, especially someone who is technically still my doctor.

Wyatt's back stiffens at the sound of my voice, but he doesn't bother responding. Instead he lets go of Mark, while simultaneously pushing him. Mark stumbles a little when his feet hit the ground, but he quickly recovers. By the time he gains his footing, Wyatt already has his hand wrapped firmly around my bicep, which he uses to practically drag me out of the bar.

Mark doesn't relent, and as soon as Wyatt is past him he does a karate chop-type move at the bend of Wyatt's arm which causes him to immediately release his hold on me. Mark takes the opportunity to step in front of me protectively, and the fact that if he fell over he would fall right on top of me is probably the only reason Wyatt doesn't jump him right then.

"Enough!" I yell, stepping out from behind Mark. I put myself between them and I hear Mark say my name gently, coming out as a plea-slash-warning to not put myself in danger. I reach out and touch Wyatt's arm, wincing when he flinches and jerks away from me. It's enough to pull his attention from Mark and back onto me, and when he looks at me his face immediately softens. I touch his arm again and this time he doesn't move away.

"Wyatt, listen to me," I say with a shaky voice. "Please calm down for a minute. Let me say bye to Mark and we'll go. Can you give me a second?"

"Fine," Wyatt grits out through clenched teeth. "But I'm waiting right here by the door, and don't go too far so I can still see you." It takes everything in me not to roll my eyes at his dramatic demands, but right now all I want is to diffuse the situation.

"Thank you," I say on a sigh, thankful to have put a stop to the potential bloodshed.

I pull Mark far enough away from Wyatt that he can't hear us, then start in with the apologies.

"Brailey...honestly, you've hurt me more than that brute." He says he's hurt, but he just sounds angry. "I was being patient, trying to give you time and space to find your footing, not wanting to overwhelm you. I understand you lost your memories, but you have to at least be able to understand how hard it is for me to see you moving on when not that long ago you were telling me you loved me."

My head rears back. Shock, anger, confusion... which emotion to pick? It's probably the wrong one, but I settle on anger.

"You're right Mark, I did lose my memories. And I understand this must be hard on you, too, but maybe if you'd told me anything about our relationship it might be different. Hell, some random nurse was the one who told me, and you only admitted it once I dragged it out of you. I don't want to hurt you, but you're right that I need to find my footing. I'm not the same person I was before, it's like I'm starting new, and I'm sorry if it hurts to hear, but you aren't an active part of this new life. Not because I don't want you to be, but our paths are just heading in different directions right now. So, I appreciate the concern, but maybe you and I need to put some more space between us for a while."

"Fine. Guess I don't have a say in the matter. Just... just be careful with him, Brailey. I don't trust him," Mark says, gesturing with his head in Wyatt's direction.

Yeah, I think to myself. I'm not sure if I do yet, either.

WYATT

There are no words to describe how it felt to walk back into the bar and see Brailey sidled up next to Mark with his arm around her. I would have been jealous, but she looked so uncomfortable. I started to walk over to her and drag her away, but Keegan stopped me and told me the asshole who kept staring at her chest when she wasn't looking was Mark - which I knew - but I had to pretend I was clueless.

It didn't help my already suspicious thoughts when the fucker had the nerve to smirk at me when Brailey wasn't looking. At first I assumed he thought I was her boyfriend and he was enjoying making me jealous, but something in his eyes just seemed...predatory. The way he looked at me like he knew me, knew my secret...I snapped. All I could think about was getting Brailey as far away from him as possible.

I hadn't meant to overreact, shoving him up against that wall like that, but when I saw his fingers digging into her shoulders and then not let up when her body pulled inward from pain, I just lost it. The fact that he had the balls to taunt me, challenge me, even while pinned up in the air by someone twice his size, tells me that he's definitely no good for Brailey.

This would be so much easier if I could just tell her the truth. If she knew everything then maybe she would cooperate.

The longer this drags on the angrier I get. I can't keep this up much longer. I can't keep lying to her and hiding things, it's eating away at me. Denying that I'm starting to develop real feelings for her is useless at this point, and knowing that she's going to hate me when the shit finally hits the fan is killing me.

All I can do is hope that she doesn't hate me so much that she can't forgive me, because I don't know if I can go back to my life as it was before Brailey came into it.

CHAPTER
TWELVE

"Oh, hell no!" If he thinks I'll be joining him in that cab he's hailing, then he's lost his damn mind.

"Hey! Where do you think you're going?" He has the nerve to get pissy with me? *Seriously?*

Who the hell does he think he is acting mad at me when he's the one who just made a scene and acted like a jackass?

"I don't know who you think you're talking to with that shitty attitude, but it better not be me," I say angrily, refusing to stop and talk to him even though he's been chasing after me for half a block.

"Will you please slow down and talk to me?" He pleads and tries to stop me, but I jerk away before he can touch me.

"Don't touch me, Wyatt. I can't even look at you right now, and if you put your hands on me there is a good chance I will break every bone in your fingers." When I hear Wyatt chuckle at my threat, my already fast walking speeds up to almost a jog.

"Oh, c'mon, Peaches. Don't be like this."

"Why the hell do you call me that?" I ask as I spin around abruptly and stab him in the chest with my finger.

"Uhhhh, well…" When he trails off I don't bother waiting for an answer. I just turn and start walking again. "Seriously, Brailey. Just talk to me?"

"About what, exactly?" Wyatt jumps in front of me to stop me from walking, so I push as hard as I can and the jerk doesn't even budge. "Do you want to talk about how you just humiliated me in front of someone really important to me? How about we talk about you acting like a jealous boyfriend, dragging me away like it's your right to dictate who I talk to. Or we could talk about your anger issues and constant mood swings."

Wyatt's eyes narrow and once again, he's acting like a raging lunatic. "What do you mean he's important to you? Who is he?"

I throw my hands up into the air, exasperated by the fact that the only thing he took from that was me saying Mark is important to me.

"None of your fucking business!" I'm making a scene on the sidewalk, but I don't care. I'm way past caring.

Wyatt runs a hand nervously through his hair and after a few seconds of him not responding I just huff and walk away from him again. I can tell he's still close behind me the whole way back to our building, but he at least has the good sense to shut up for a few minutes.

As much as I hate to admit it, by the time we actually get to the building I'm feeling pretty torn between wanting Wyatt to give me some space and wishing he would just push me up against a wall and ravage me. My conflicting desires are making my stomach churn and I'm pissed at Keegan for not helping me put a stop to what happened back there. Come to think of it, where the hell *is* Keegan? She didn't follow us out of the bar. I'm a shitty friend. I should have been less concerned over being pissed off and more concerned about making sure my friend wasn't abandoned at a bar we've never been to before.

When we get inside the building Wyatt continues to trail behind me silently. Since he followed me to my door, I have no choice now but to turn and talk to him, because there is no way he's coming inside with me.

"I'm going inside alone, Wyatt. Let me cool down and we can talk tomorrow."

"Sorry, no can do. We're gonna talk this shit out. I'm not leaving with you pissed at me."

I sigh and lean back on my door, but when it falls open behind me I stumble backwards. Wyatt grabs my hand and keeps me upright, but his eyes widen as he looks over my shoulder and the shock on his face confuses me. I don't even have time to register that I hadn't unlocked my door yet before Wyatt is pulling me to the side and pushing me up against the wall.

"Don't go in there, Brailey," he says in a no non-nonsense tone.

"What? Why?" He pins me in with his arm when I try to move away from him.

"I'm serious. Go knock on Keegan's door, see if she's home. She took off a few minutes before I interrupted you and that jerk."

"You're scaring me, Wyatt," I whisper with a shaky voice. He trails his hand softly up my arm until he reaches my face. He pushes his palm to my cheek and gently rubs the pad of his thumb back and forth, and the soothing motion combined with the tingling I feel where his skin is touching mine, distracts me enough that I forget where we even are.

The sound of Keegan coming up the stairs pulls us out of our little bubble, and we both turn to look at Keegan, who is giving us both a shit eating grin.

"Hey B, you gonna explain to me why you never mentioned Mark is a hot piece of ass?" She asks as she smacks on a piece of gum like a ditzy teenager. Wyatt pushes off the wall and I have to push my back flat against the wall to keep from moving forward, my body craving his warmth like it's necessary for survival.

"Hey Keegan, can you take Brailey inside with you for a minute?" When Wyatt doesn't offer up an explanation for his odd request on my behalf, Keegan takes it upon herself to do some spinny-twirl-ninja-type move to get around him. When she sees whatever it is inside my apartment that Wyatt is hiding from me she gasps and smacks her hand over her mouth.

"Holy shit!" She mumbles through her hand. I make a run for it, but as soon as I reach Keegan's side I instantly wish I had just listened to Wyatt and stayed away.

My entire apartment is trashed. Not just a few broken items and tossed couch cushions...I mean *completely* destroyed. It looks like someone took a knife to my couch and chopped it into tiny pieces, the padding strewn all over the room. All my paintings and pictures are torn off the walls and have been gutted just like the couch. Hell, even the fridge door is open and all the contents are spilled out all over the kitchen floor.

My dishes, my lamps, even the carpet that's nailed to the ground...all destroyed. Why would someone do this? What on earth were they looking for?

"I mean it Brailey, don't keep looking into Mayra. You know you can't afford to lose your job, and after getting suspended for two days just for asking about her, I'm pretty sure if you get caught again you're looking to be standing in the unemployment line."

He's right, I know that. Doesn't mean I'm going to listen to him. So my first day back at work, what do I do? Exactly what I was warned not to. I mean, how could I pass up an opportunity like the perfect one laid out before me?

The director of Mayford, AKA Madame Bitch as the staff likes to call her, just bolted out of her office after being called onto campus for a patient emergency. In her haste, she didn't lock up her office. Her office is always locked. I've been inside a time or two when a little chastising was deemed necessary, so I know what she keeps in there.

Archived files.

Grabbing the tiny little camera Bryce gave me when we first started looking for Mayra, I dart inside without even looking around to see if anyone is watching. I'm taking this opportunity no matter what, and if I get caught then I'll deal with the consequences later.

Every expletive known to man is currently screaming on an unending loop when I find Mayra's file. Reluctantly, I take pictures of as much as I can before I hear voices approaching. Shoving the file back in place, I briefly consider hiding, but screw that...I'll just walk out like I was in her office on purpose and hope no one notices. Fake it till ya make it.

My shift isn't over for another two hours, but screw that noise. Once I safely exit the director's office without being noticed, I make a beeline for my car. Taking out my phone to call Bryce and tell him the good-slash-horrible news, I see he's already left me a voicemail.

"Hey, B-ray. The hospital called while you were at work. They had some sort of anonymous donation for Shaun's surgery, wouldn't tell me who. Obviously. Turns out the donation had been made at the perfect time, because they'd just gotten a call with a match for Shaun, so I'm dropping him off at the hospital. You did it, Bray, he's getting his new heart." A tear slips down my cheek when I hear the catch in his voice, and I unattractively wipe away snot from my nose with the back of my hand while listening to the message over hands free while I drive. "So listen, you've got time. Go home and shower and pack a bag. I'll get Shaun admitted and settled. I have to take off to run a quick errand, but I swear I'll be right back. Can't wait to see you."

Making a quick U-turn, I book it to the bank. I'm not risking anything happening to this SD card, not after everything we've gone through to get this information. After safely locking it in my safety deposit box, I head for home.

I'm both exhausted and giddy - Shaun is getting his surgery. I can't believe it. I was really starting to feel like this day would never come. I swear, it's like the sun *is brighter and the grass is greener and I can't help waving to my grumpy old neighbor with a big ass smile on my face, earning me a confused scowl. "Have a great day, Mrs. Trudy!" I yell, making her scowl even bigger and my smile even wider.*

Nothing could ruin this day. We got answers about Mayra and Shaun is getting his heart. Things are finally going our way.

"Hello, Brailey." The unexpected greeting startles a scream out of me, my purse crashing to the floor and the contents of it scattering all around me. He's hiding in the shadows of my dark living room so I can't see who it is, but it doesn't really matter. The only two people that could possibly be inside my house I know for a fact aren't, which can only mean whoever it is is an intruder.

Dropping to the ground, I frantically start feeling the floor all around me, trying to find the pepper spray I keep in my purse. My eyes stay locked in the direction of the shadow that my intruder is lurking in, too afraid of looking away in case he decides to approach. I want to be ready for him.

My shaky hands finally graze what I can instantly tell is the plastic cylinder containing the spray. My palms are so sweaty it nearly slips right back out when I grip it tightly in my hand.

Before I can stand back up, my intruder appears seemingly out of nowhere, hovering over me and give me my first good look at his face. He looks down at me with evil eyes, wearing a smirk that has me growling at him.

"You."

When I come to I'm lying on Keegan's couch and she's gently shaking my shoulders.

"Are you okay, sweetie? Do you need anything? Something to drink? Maybe a Jack and Coke, hold the Coke?" She's being serious, but I can't help but laugh anyway. Without even trying, Keegan always knows how to make light of even the worst situations.

"I'm okay, really. Where's Wyatt?" I whisper hoarsely, rolling my neck back and forth to try to get rid of some of the stiffness from the position I was laying in on her couch.

"He called the police. After they came and talked to him and took some photos he stayed over there to try and clean up some. Are you really okay?"

"Aside from passing out in the hallway, yeah actually, I'm okay. I don't understand it. Who would do this?" It's a rhetorical question, because obviously Keegan doesn't know who would do something so horrible. I expect reassuring words or clichéd responses, but like always, Keegan surprises me.

"I don't know, but you can bet we'll catch that fucker and then I'm gonna tear him up."

We both burst into laughter, and it doesn't escape me that I'm actually laughing and not freaking out about what's going on.

There's a small knock at the door and Wyatt doesn't

wait for an answer, he just walks in like he lives here. Typical. He looks so timid and unsure at first, but when he sees us laughing his whole body shifts gears and he relaxes. It's obvious he wasn't sure what he was going to be walking into, and considering I passed out for the second time in one day, he most likely was worried I was going to be in bad shape.

"It's all cleared out. Your carpet needs replaced, the drywall needs repaired in a lot of places and pretty much every inch of the apartment is going to need fixed. It's going to take at least a week or so to get it back into shape, but as soon as it's done, we're putting new locks on your door and I'm going to talk to the building manager about putting security cameras up, even if I have to pay for them myself."

"That's just ridiculous, Wyatt. No need to go spending your own money on cameras over this." While I find Wyatt's need to control every situation frustrating, in this case I actually appreciate it. Doesn't mean I'm going to let him use his own money to have cameras installed.

"Nothing about this is ridiculous, it's fucking serious, Brailey," he barks out at me. Even when I wince at his harshness he doesn't back down. "Someone broke in and went to great measures to mess with your head. It's not like this is a random break-in where some meth head was in need of another fix. Whoever did this targeted you specifically and was either looking for something specific or were just trying to terrorize you. Not to mention…"

"Enough!" I cut him off, standing from the couch and ignoring the wave of dizziness that hits me with the sudden movement. "I get it, Wyatt, I do. No one gets it better than me. But if it's all the same to you, maybe just for the rest of the night, I can pretend it's not a big deal. Because when I wake up tomorrow I know shit is going to start hitting the fan, so if tonight is the last night that I get to sleep in blissful ignorance then dammit, I'm going to make the most of it."

All my speech does is poke the bear, and when he lets out a low growl I get that same confused feeling. I want to smack him for being such a controlling prick, then press my body against his and feel his mouth on mine. By the way his pupils dilate I assume he's having the same conflicted emotions, but my eye catches on the bag he's holding.

"Why the hell are you holding my overnight bag?"

"I packed you some stuff while I was over there so you'd have some of your things at my place. It's not much, most of your things were destroyed, but at least this way you don't have to make trips back and forth."

"Oooohhhh, Wyatt's goin' all alpha male on your ass," Keegan teases in a sassy voice.

"I guess I shouldn't expect anything less from you after what happened tonight at the bar, huh?"

"What? What happened!?" Keegan yells from the couch, but we both ignore her.

"We haven't even sorted out all that crap yet, but you've already made the decision to move me into your apartment without my say-so? You are seriously pushing it." I cross my arms and plop back down on the couch, making it clear that I don't plan to go anywhere.

Wyatt drops the bag from his shoulder and marches over to me. I stiffen my spine and brace myself for an angry speech, but he surprises me by dropping to his knees in front of me and uncrossing my arms, taking both my hands in his.

"I'm not trying to control you. I'm very sorry for what happened earlier at the bar. I promise we will talk about that, but I need you to not be stubborn right now. Your safety is non-negotiable and right now it's not safe for you to be in your apartment. So while you may not like it, you're coming to stay with me until we figure out who did this. I'll ask you nicely if it will make you feel better, but just so you know, it won't make a difference if you don't agree. If I have to throw you over my shoulder and handcuff you to my bed to get you to listen to me, then that's what I'll do."

Between the softness in his eyes and the sincerity in his voice, I completely melt during the first half of his little speech. Once he mentions handcuffing me to his bed, I'm no longer melting but rather feeling like I might burst into flames. Keegan is waving her hand back and forth and fanning her face while having a field day with the idea of Wyatt cuffing me.

"And before you suggest staying with Keegan, I can already tell you that idea is out. I'm not endangering anyone else, and I can protect you best if you're close to me. You and I can work out the details of being in such close quarters since I know you've been wanting space, but that's the only part I'm willing to negotiate on."

I rub my temples and try to process what he's saying to me, but it's so late and I'm so exhausted that I figure I can argue in the morning. Right now all I want to do is sleep.

"Fine," I agree reluctantly. Wyatt's triumphant grin makes me want to keep arguing just to spite him, but I don't have the energy for it. "We'll fight about this tomorrow. Right now I just want to go to bed." A wickedness flares in Wyatt's eyes and I quickly correct myself. "To sleep! Nothing else, perv."

Wyatt grins and helps me up from the couch. I zombie walk to the door and Wyatt wraps my arm around his shoulder and pulls me tightly against his side after he picks my overnight bag up off the floor. Once I feel the heat from his body and his calming scent surround me, walking becomes damn near impossible.

I don't even protest when Wyatt scoops me up and walks briskly up the stairs two at a time. I'm already half asleep when I feel him lay me down on a bed. When my face sinks into a pillow I breathe in deeply and without opening my eyes I know he's placed me in his own bed. I'm not even sure if he has a guest bed, and part of my brain tells me to make sure he knows he can't sleep in here with me, but the sleepy part of my brain tells the other part of my brain to shut the hell up.

Sleepy brain, for the win.

CHAPTER
THIRTEEN

"Mark, what the hell are you doing here? How did you even get in?"

I've never seen Mark look so...menacing.

"Is this because I've been avoiding you since we slept together? Look, I know that was super shitty of me, but I was in a bad place that night. I'm sorry if you took that to mean I wanted more or something. I should have-"

"Shut up!" He yells right as the back of his hand connects with my cheek. "Just...stop...talking."

My hands are covering my face, so he can't see the rage boiling inside of me, but he's an idiot if he thinks I'm going to just let him hit me. I had enough shitty foster parents who thought raising their hands to me and Shaun was a way of showing power over us. They only ever got one hit in. After that, I made sure they never hit us again.

I stay crouched, pretending to be in pain while listening to Mark's hurried footsteps pacing back and forth across my hardwood floors.

"Shit, I'm sorry Brailey. I shouldn't have done that. I just...I have a temper. It's the main reason I stay away from people. Sometimes I can't control it. And when you say things that I know you don't mean, like that night not meaning anything, then I can't hold it back any more."

I swear, it's always the damn quiet ones that are truly

batshit. They bottle up all their crazy so much that they just fly right past that grey area and straight into crazy town at the drop of a hat.

"Brailey," he says softly, and when his hand touches my shoulder, I make my move. Covering my eyes with one hand, I reach under my arm to spray his face with the pepper spray. My eyes immediately start burning, but it's nothing compared to the agonizing pain he's suffering from right now. He's screaming in a frequency that probably has every dog in a two-mile radius freaking out.

"You bitch!" He sticks his head under the faucet of my kitchen sink, and I take advantage of his distraction and kick him in the nuts from behind. "Fuck!" He swings wildly, getting lucky and landing a punch to my gut, hard enough to knock me back but not knock the wind out of me. "You don't know who you're messing with. The minute you started looking into Mayra you got put on her radar, and now? After this? You're dead. The only reason you're standing here is because of me, but you just royally fucked yourself."

His threat catches me off guard, giving him the opportunity to lunge for me. The bastard misses, because he's blind from the spray, but I trip over my couch and fall backwards, slamming my head into the corner of my wooden coffee table.

Agonizing pain shoots through my skull, and I know it's bad. I know in that split second before my world goes dark, that if I make it through this, I'm going to kill fucking Mark.

"Brailey!"

My name is being yelled over and over while I shake violently. My throat feels like someone has taken razor blades to it and I hear someone screaming so loudly you would think they were being murdered. Something wet hits my hand and the screaming stops.

"Brailey!"

My eyes pop open, but all I see is blackness. After giving my vision a few seconds to adjust to the dark, I make out the features of Wyatt's face inches away from mine. He presses his forehead to mine and wraps his arms around me tightly, his breathing labored and his shoulders heaving.

"Oh, God, Brailey. Are you okay? Did you have a nightmare?" As my consciousness returns, the details of last night come back to me. "You scared the hell out of me. I've never heard someone scream like that."

I'm not okay. I'm not at all okay. What the hell was that dream? What the hell is even real anymore?

"I'm okay," I lie, my voice hoarse from screaming. "I'm sorry I woke you." I choke on my words, ending up in a coughing fit.

"Let me get you some water," Wyatt says, moving to stand from the bed.

"No! Don't leave," I yell out, yanking on his hand and pulling him back down to sit next to me on the edge of the bed. "Please, will you...will you just stay with me the rest of the night?" I'm not sure what the repercussions of asking Wyatt to sleep in bed with me will end up having, but even despite his mood swings and bossy tendencies, the fact is I truly trust him.

Actually, I more than trust him. As I watch indecision splay across his face, knowing his uncertainty is because he's worried about how this will affect me, forces me to realize I might actually be falling for him.

"Please," I beg, sounding entirely too pathetic but not caring in the slightest. I need him. I need his arms around me, holding me closely. I need it more than I need to breathe.

When Wyatt nods his head I scoot over, giving him room to climb in. I hadn't noticed before that he's only wearing a pair of tight fitting boxers, and even in the pitch black I can make out the hard lines of his torso. At this point I'm not sure if I'm trembling from the lingering adrenaline pumping through me from my nightmare, or from the temptation I feel from being this close to Wyatt.

I watch as he slides under the covers and I give him a small smile when he looks at me uncomfortably, clearly not sure what he's supposed to do now that he's in the bed. Moving to lay down, I put my back to him, trying to hide the ill-timed smile splitting my face. I don't think there will ever be a time where I don't find the shy and unsure side of Wyatt freaking adorable.

He's doing his best to keep a safe distance between us, but that's just not going to work for me, so I reach behind me and grab his arm, draping it over my waist.

That nightmare shook me up, I need comfort, and I'm not afraid to ask for it. Right now is not the time to try and play coy. Being held by Wyatt like this gives me an overwhelming sense of safety, a feeling I only ever seem to experience when he is near.

After several very long minutes, I feel his body finally start to relax behind me. His arm is limp, laying exactly where I left it. He's being cautious not to touch me, and as thankful as I am for his gentlemanly behavior, right now I just need to feel him on me, against me, as close to me as possible. Wyatt seems to let go of his hesitancy entirely when I put my hand over his and twine our fingers together, pulling our clasped hands tightly against my chest.

This is the truly the closest we've been since meeting, and even though it is seriously horrible timing, I can't help but be turned on. No woman in her right mind could be laying in Wyatt's bed, pulled up close against his body, able to feel the evidence of his own arousal against her ass and *not* be on the verge of jumping his bones.

Wyatt seems content to just pretend that erection of his isn't nestled up nicely between my ass cheeks. He's crazy if he thinks I can fall asleep with that monster pressed up against me. Don't ask me what has come over me, because there is no possible way for me to excuse what I do next.

Slowly, and in an incredibly unsubtle way, I arch my back, press my ass further into Wyatt, and rub myself against him. His whole body goes almost as rigid as his dick, but the jerk just sucks in a huge breath and releases it slowly, his body relaxing again as if that little wiggle never happened.

How is that even possible? Not only is he back to pretending there are only two very thin layers of clothing preventing that monster from attacking, but when he exhaled, the heat from his breath sent shivers down my spine. And it has to be intentional that all of a sudden his mouth is right behind my ear, his face practically nestled into my hair, his lips close enough for my skin to imagine phantom kisses all over my neck.

Yeah, when Wyatt's lower lip trails up the side of my neck, leaving a hot, wet trail in its wake, I know for sure he's torturing me intentionally. My breath catches on an inhale when I feel his teeth grazing the outer shell of my ear.

Before I can take my next breath, Wyatt's hand gently untangles from mine, first squeezing my breast lightly before rubbing one finger lightly over my nipple, making it bead to the point of pain. Fire shoots straight from his hand down to my core, taking my lust to unimaginable heights. I don't know if he's still just testing the waters or has turned this into some kind of game, but my patience has run out.

Swinging around and forcing Wyatt on to his back, I make it abundantly clear that the games are over. Climbing on top of him, my head dips, my mouth desperate to taste his. His head lifts to meet me halfway, but before our mouths meet, he flips us back over, once again stealing the upper hand right out from under me. Literally.

I don't need the control; he can freaking have it. When his mouth slants over mine and his hand slips underneath my shirt, slowly and torturously trailing his fingertips up my stomach and over my naked breast, the sensation spreads all over my body like wildfire. All my synapses start firing at once, eliciting a loud and wanton moan to slip from my mouth, and he devours it hungrily.

His tongue effortlessly explores mine, his rhythm never faltering, even when my body jerks violently as his fingers pinch down roughly on my tender nipple. His bare chest rubs over my swollen breasts as he continues his ministrations, driving me past the point of need and all the way into the realm of necessity. I let out an obnoxious whimper when he pulls back, but before I can protest he's ripping my tank top over my head, exposing my overheated skin to the cool air.

He takes only a second to appreciate the view before dipping his head down and pulling my nipple into his mouth. My body bucks off the bed when he bites down hard before flicking it with his tongue, soothing the pain. He cups my other breast with his hand and flicks my nipple, giving it equal attention with his fingers while he lavishes the other with his mouth.

He pushes his lower body against me, and his erection hits me in just the right spot, sending ripples of pleasure into parts of me that I didn't even know existed.

"Now, I need you now." I can't get his boxers off fast enough. I'm tugging and yanking and trying to rip them off in the least sexy way possible, but desperate doesn't even begin to describe what I'm feeling right now.

"Brailey," Wyatt says in a tone that I do *not* like. Sounds too much like hesitation and second guessing, and that kind of attitude has no place in this room right now.

"Now, Wyatt," I growl. This isn't up for discussion. My body needs his, and there is no way in hell he is going to put a stop to this.

After hesitating for one more second, I watch the reluctance drain from his eyes and the lust take over. Soft eyes turn dark, not even blinking as he yanks off my small sleep shorts in one swift motion. When he starts kissing a trail down my neck, I know where he's going, but there's no time for that. The time for foreplay has come and gone, too far behind us to even be seen in the rearview.

"Now." This time it comes out as more of a plea and less of a demand, and Wyatt must sense the need behind that one word, because he moves right back up over my body, entering me in one swift motion.

"So fucking tight," Wyatt grunts out.

I'd love to respond. Doesn't even have to be words; just a moan or a grunt, but I can't. He's filling me up so completely, taking over parts of me that I didn't even know existed.

"Look at me, Brailey." I didn't even realize I had my eyes squeezed shut tightly until his hoarse voice startled them open. Our eyes stay locked, my fingers clutching to his shoulders as he rocks in and out of me.

My lips are tingling, hungry for another kiss, but everything is too intense. I can't look away. I can't move, or speak. I can barely breathe. When he shifts his position, just slightly lifting my bottom, he aligns our bodies at just the right angle. He feels it too; I can tell by the way he squeezes his eyes shut and grunts. Everything about this moment feels right.

The pressure building up in my core, making every muscle in my body contract, every inch of me on edge, just waiting for the impending explosion. Wyatt whispers my name again when I let my eyes drift closed, and right as I reopen them it hits me.

I can feel his hot release inside me as we both hit our climax, and it's the first time I even give any thought to a condom. I'm not on birth control, but there's no room in my brain to worry about that. The only thing I can focus on is the feeling of Wyatt clutching my body to his, our sweaty bodies tangled together, not even caring about the mess we're making on the sheets.

We lay there, panting and struggling to catch our breath, Wyatt's lips firmly planted on the top of my head. Everything about him, his body language and actions, pulls harder at my heart. I'm about five seconds away from becoming that girl that blurts out feelings that are way too soon and totally awkward when said right after sex.

"I um...you should...I just..." Wyatt pulls back enough to look down at me, and I panic. He looks so happy and sated. I can't ruin this moment with crazy-girl talk. I need to steer my thoughts elsewhere, so I blurt out the first thing that comes to mind.

"That was my first orgasm!" I shout a little too loudly. Wyatt's eyes widen in shock and his jaw drops open.

"Say what?"

"I just mean...since losing my memory. I have no memory of having one before, so that was kinda like my first time." The smile he's fighting tells me I'm right, but he's going to make me say the damn words again, I can tell.

"You haven't given yourself one?" He asks incredulously.

The intimacy of what just happened between us gives me a clarity, a truth I've been fighting since meeting Wyatt. My desire to be close to him is only going to get stronger, and it's not because I'm falling for him that I feel he needs to know the truth...it's that I'm pretty sure I already fell.

"Oh, I've been tempted. This super-hot guy moved into the building and he would get me all hot and bothered then leave me high and dry all the time, but I was holding out for the real thing." Wyatt looks so damn proud of himself I can't help but laugh.

"Listen," I say seriously, shifting gears in a way that's probably going to leave him with blue balls. "I know I told you that I lost my memory. What I haven't told you is that it's been coming back to me for a while now." Wyatt sits up, his back ramrod straight and his eyes completely cleared of the foggy lust that was in them moments ago.

"That's great, right?"

"I guess, yeah, I mean of course it is. It's just that...a lot of what I'm remembering doesn't really match up with the few details I've been told about myself and my past. Ever since I stopped taking the sleeping pills Mark prescribed me, I've been dreaming but I'm almost certain they're memories. Now they're coming back to me during the day, and it feels like Deja vu, and sometimes

I think I'm just going crazy because I'm not even sure if the memories are accurate."

Wyatt looks a little forlorn when I stop talking, a confusing expression to be wearing, if you ask me.

"So you haven't told anyone that you've been remembering? Not even Keegan or Mark?"

"No, Mark got mad at the idea of me not taking my pills so I just started avoiding him, and I can't make sense of any of it enough to really explain them to anyone. A lot of it's blurry, just like a dream, so who knows if it's even true."

"Well you need to try, Brailey," Wyatt says as he opens his bedside drawer, pulling out a little notebook and pen. "Just start describing what you can remember, and maybe we can piece things together. I'll help you do it."

I swear I'm getting a migraine when I finally finish telling him everything an hour later. His jaw is clenched and he looks angry, the way it was the entire time I was talking. At this point it's starting to piss me off. He was the one who insisted I do this to begin with, and the longer he just sits there staring down at his notebook and not talking, the more pissed off I get.

He doesn't even bother to look at me when he finally speaks. "I'm sorry."

"Why are you sorry?" I ask, confused. He doesn't answer me, so I yank one of his hands away, getting his attention. He faces me, and I can't even begin to decipher the emotions raging in him right now. I see anguish, regret, pain...none of which I understand.

"For everything. That you're going through all of

this. That I've been acting like a raging asshole since we met. That there's nothing I can say or do to help you in this situation. Mostly, though, I'm sorry that I can't do this."

It takes a second for his last words to register, and when they do, I jerk out of his hold and jump to my feet. "Can't do *what*, exactly." I can see in his eyes that he feels horrible for saying it, but I'm too angry to care. He could have at least waited until tomorrow to tell me he was no longer interested in me, once I'd finally gotten some sleep and had a little caffeine in me or something.

"Brailey, let me explain," Wyatt begs, reaching out for me, but I jerk away from him.

"Don't touch me. I don't want to hear what you have to say." He doesn't try to talk to me as I dress, and I'm not sure if I'm thankful or pissed off that he's not trying harder. Whatever, he's obviously not worth it, which is painfully clear when he doesn't even bother coming after me after I slam his bedroom door behind me.

WYATT

I am such a fucking idiot.

I panicked. I should have stopped things before they got out of control, instead of waiting until I unloaded my dick in her to try and be noble. Now I'm just an asshole. This guilt is eating me alive and it's making me do shit that is going to ruin me. I'm going to give her about thirty seconds, long enough to make it to Keegan's, since there's nowhere else she could possibly go without her purse and phone which is sitting next to me. After that, I'm dragging her ass back up to my apartment so we can talk. Screw this. I'm coming clean.

Hearing about Bryce...I don't know the nature of their relationship, but I was led to believe it went beyond professional. Her memories so far confirm it. I could tell she was holding back when she described him, it was written all over her face. What happens when she gets her full memory back? Will I lose her? Am I a selfish prick for worrying about that?

There's a pretty good chance she's going to hate me once she knows the truth anyway, memories or not.

No matter the consequences, time is up. I need to make a call, and then I'm going after Brailey. I'm going to fight *for* Brailey.

CHAPTER
FOURTEEN

"Brailey!"

How in the actual hell is this really happening right now?

"Mark," I say, spinning on my heel to face the very last person I want to see right now. "It's the middle of the night and you were supposed to be gone already."

He doesn't look the least bit happy to see me. That last dream flashes before my eyes, and I recognize the look in his eyes now. It's the same one he had that day. My instincts kick in and I turn to run away, but he grabs my wrist and yanks me back, putting his hand to my throat and holding me up against the brick wall of the building.

"You think I'm the enemy, and I get that. From your standpoint, it probably seems that way. But you'll find out soon enough that I'm not the one you should be afraid of."

With that he shoves off the wall, squeezing my neck a little as he goes, and I cough and sputter a little as I try to catch my breath. He thrusts a large manila envelope into my hands, my body instinctively gripping it against my stomach, and then he backs away.

"It's just a matter of time now, Brailey," he calls out before disappearing into the shadows.

It would probably be smarter to head back inside

before digging into this envelope, but I can't wait. Immediately I recognize it as the manila envelope that came in the mail the day my apartment was broken into. Not that I can identify every piece of mail that comes through my mailbox every day, but it's not often that one as huge and conspicuous as this one gets mixed in with my pile of bills and junk mail.

The seal is already broken, because of course Mark helped himself to the contents after destroying everything I own.

"Brailey!"

Motherfucker. Can I not catch a break? The answer to that would be *no*, because Keegan is not alone.

"What Keegan?" I snap defensively, aiming my frustration at the wrong person. She's unfazed.

"Come with me," she orders, pulling me towards the building before stopping to face Wyatt. "*You* are not allowed to come with us. I don't care what the hell you do or where the hell you go, but it won't be with us."

The jerk doesn't even put up a fight, just stands there and lets us walk away. As soon as the door to Keegan's apartment closes behind us, I'm tearing into this freaking envelope.

"What the shit, B? Quit yelling, I'm right freaking here. Geez." I crumble onto the couch, my eyes scanning the same lines over and over but not really absorbing anything I read. "What's that?" Keegan asks, yanking the pictures out of my hands.

I cannot believe what's in front of me, it can't be right. There is no possible way this is true. It has to be fabricated. *Has* to be.

"What the hell is this, Brailey?" Keegan asks as her eyes continue to scan the contents in much the same way mine were seconds ago. "Someone's been watching you? What the actual fuck?"

"I...I don't..." I stutter, not able to form a sentence, my mind still reeling. I feel like my skin is crawling, and I feel exposed in a way I've never felt before. How many more pictures are there? How long has this been going on? *Mothershitter!* There are pictures of me taken from INSIDE my apartment!

"Jesus H...Brailey, this is crazy. You need to call the cops. There are pictures with me in them, too. Ones of you the night at the club, of you walking into work...this is...wow..." She trails off as she continues to flip through the photos, but I don't bother responding. What the hell do I say? "Holy shit, Brailey," Keegan's hands are trembling, and I can tell she's as freaked out as I am. Maybe more.

"We should go confront Wyatt," Keegan says, starting to stand.

"No!" I yell, yanking her back down to the couch. "Look at these, Keegan. It's bad enough that Mark has been stalking me, but him catching Wyatt taking stalker pictures of me too is just...this is just too messed up for words. Who the hell *is* Wyatt?" I mutter to myself.

"This is just...Brailey," Keegan trails off. I mean, what is there to say?

Dozens...maybe a hundred pictures of me. Then the pictures change. "Holy shit!" I almost drop the stack, my hands trembling. "These are photos of me and Shaun. I...I remember these. How would someone get these? All this stuff...we...we had it stored…" I know I'm not making sense, but this stuff is coming back to me real time, and it's hard to process and talk about it at the same time.

"This is Shaun?" Keegan's never seen a picture of Shaun. I didn't think I had any. Everything in my house burned in the fire, and of course I didn't remember that we had some of our mementos stored in a little unit until just now either.

"I can't...I just feel like my brain is overloading with information." Rubbing my temples, I try - and fail - to make sense of the flooding of images.

"Why is there a news article in here? Do you know someone named Bryce?"

I grab the cut out news article so quickly it almost tears.

Lawson (left) pictured on duty late last year.

FBI Agent Bryce Lawson Dies in Car Collision

It was reported that FBI Agent Bryce Lawson was driving down South Main when he lost control of his vehicle. The car veered off the road, flipping twice and landing in a ditch before catching fire. We are told the flames spread quickly once they touched the leaking gasoline, and the vehicle went up in flames before emergency personnel were able to arrive on the scene. Mr. Lawson is not from the area, and when inquired the reason to his visit, the FBI declined to respond.

"Brailey, who is Bryce?" Keegan asks softly, but her voice sounds miles away.

"Come back to bed, Bryce!"

I can hear him laugh around his toothbrush. Yes, I sound exceptionally whiny, but those three orgasms he just gave me were exceptionally amazing.

"You know I can't, B-ray," he says with a mouth full of toothpaste. He hocks and spits, then turns to grin at me with toothpaste on his lip, and he's still the sexiest man I've ever laid eyes on.

"You're supposed to be off right now; you shouldn't have to do a stupid video conference with your boss." Yep. Only known each other a couple weeks and only had sex for the first time a few days ago, and I already sound like a stage-five clinger.

Bryce wipes the remaining toothpaste from his face before placing a teasing, torturous kiss on my lips.

"You asshole," I say as I hit him over the head with a pillow when he tries to pull away much too soon.

"You're good for a guy's ego," he teases.

"Whatever. Go do your stupid call then get your ass back here. I actually have a day off and you're going to do that thing with your tongue again that-"

"Ew, c'mon sis, I can hear you!" Shaun shouts from

the hallway. Oops, forgot the door was open.

"Sorry!" I call out just before Shaun sticks his head in the door.

"If this asshole is going to be living here much longer, I think we should start charging him rent."

Bryce puts a mock chokehold on Shaun and gives him a noogie. It always pisses Shaun off when he does that - or at least he acts like it does, but secretly I think he likes it. Other than me, Bryce is the first person to show true affection towards Shaun. It's pretty crazy how quickly they grew on each other. Then again, while I'm working my ass off, they're sitting in my house playing video games all day.

"You better shut up or I'll start charging you rent!"

Laying back in the bed and staring at the ceiling, I let their laughter filter through from the living room and wash over me, bringing me a happiness I'm not sure I've ever really known.

"Brailey," Keegan says less patiently.

"Sorry. Memory," I offer as an explanation. "I...I'm pretty sure I loved him."

"Who?"

My stunned and suddenly very teary eyes meet Keegan's. "Bryce."

WYATT

I'm trying. I'm seriously trying to give her space. Okay, not physically, since I'm standing right outside Keegan's apartment door waiting for...hell, I don't know what I'm waiting for. For me to grow a pair of fucking balls and stop pussy footing around the truth.

I've been given orders to bring Brailey to my boss. He left it up to me to decide whether or not I want to tell her where she's going ahead of time. Fucking thank you for putting that on my shoulders. Either I potentially cause her a lot of confusion and emotional turmoil by telling her now, risking making my life really fucking difficult because it most likely will end up in me dragging her to the car. Or I can wait and let them spring a big ass surprise on her last minute and risk her never talking to me again for keeping something so huge from her.

"What are you going to do, Brailey?"

Keegan's voice travels through the door. I've not been eavesdropping, but sitting right outside means I overheard a little here and there. Not really enough to mean anything, and I've been using the excuse of it being my 'job' to justify spying like an asshole.

"Do about what, Key? He's dead. It doesn't matter if I loved him or not."

Shit. Of all the things to overhear...

"What about Wyatt?" I silently give Keegan an 'atta girl'. *Yeah, what about Wyatt?*

"What about him? It's not like I'm in love with him. After that asshole move he pulled tonight...I don't know,

Keegan. I just need to get my head on straight."

I can't take it anymore. I can't leave, but I can't stand here and listen to this. Pulling Brailey's phone out of my pocket, I knock on Keegan's door and hope they buy my piss poor of an excuse to be bothering them at this hour.

CHAPTER
FIFTEEN

I feel like a bitch. I shouldn't, I know that. Doesn't change anything.

Standing here while Keegan tears into Wyatt, not doing a damn thing to help either one of them, I play spectator to the only two people I have remaining in my life fighting...because of me.

"If you would just let me talk-" Wyatt tries to interject.

"Why? Why would I let you talk? So you can just screw up even worse than you already have? You're lucky I haven't kicked you in the nuts yet, but consider that a warning. I'm about two seconds from making sure you never have children."

Wyatt's hands fly to his crotch, and I wince in sympathetic hypothetical pain for him.

"I know I'm on both of your shit lists, but the fact is that Brailey isn't safe right now. You can hate me if you want, but you should know that I'm going to be parked right outside this apartment if you need me. I just wanted to deliver Brailey her phone and let you guys know that you could sleep easy tonight, okay?"

And just like that, the wall I was trying to build around my heart crumbles all the way back down. I need him. I hate him for making me feel that way, but I do. I need comforting arms and the feel of safety, and as if reading my thoughts, Wyatt marches over and gives me exactly what I need.

"I'm so sorry, Brailey. I never meant to hurt you. There's so much I need to tell you, and I promise I will, but I can't stand the thought of you being angry with me. Of you thinking I meant I didn't want to be with you, because like it or not," Wyatt pulls back to look me in the eye, "I'm falling for you. It wasn't the plan. Nothing about you and this whole situation was part of the plan, but I can't help how I feel. I don't want to lie to you any longer."

Hot tears stream down my cheeks. "Yeah well, you weren't part of my plan either." Wyatt places a chaste kiss on the corner of my mouth before pulling back enough to face Keegan.

"I'll explain everything on the way," he says with an authoritative voice, "but I'm sorry to say you both are going to have to come with me."

"I can't believe I agreed to go along with this," Keegan mutters from the backseat.

She's been less than cooperative since Wyatt stood hovering over her while she packed a bag. It didn't help when he kept making her put stuff back. Apparently wherever we're going doesn't require flat irons or heels.

"Seriously, we've been on the road for a half hour. You said you would explain on the way. We're on the way. Get to explaining," Keegan orders as she leans forward and inserts herself between the two front seats.

"We're on our way to see my boss."

"Okay, Mr. Mysterious, who is your boss? I thought you did websites or some crap?"

Wyatt shifts uncomfortably in his seat. "Well, that was a lie. One of many." He winces, probably expecting me to freak out. Honestly? I figured. I don't think there's a whole lot that could surprise me at this point.

"Well, go on already," Keegan presses.

"I actually work for the FBI."

Okay, well maybe that surprises me a little.

"Shit, this is really hard to explain." It's hard, but I wait patiently while he runs his hand through his hair, trying to gather his thoughts. "I guess I should start from the beginning. Bryce was an agent in my division, though we never worked together. I'm told he came out here to check on someone he'd rescued from a past mission, some kind of hunch she was in trouble. She was a patient at Mayford, but when he got there, he was told she'd been transferred and they wouldn't tell him where.

"He called his boss, who is now my boss, and asked for help. Problem is, without cause, it's not really our jurisdiction to just go looking people up. My boss, always a stickler for the rules, told Bryce there wasn't anything the bureau could do to help. He lucked out and someone from inside Mayford overheard him looking for Mayra - the patient - and offered to help."

"Me," I interject, Wyatt nodding in confirmation.

"Here's where it gets messy. Supposedly Bryce got a call from her - I mean, you - the day he...died." He struggles on the last word, like it's hard for him to get out. "I guess you'd found some information to help, though you didn't say on the message what it was. The problem is that Bryce was in that car accident before you were able to pass along the information. When you lost your memory, whatever information you found was lost along with it."

"Okay," I drag out, trying to figure out where he's going with this. "So far everything you've told me is already stuff I remembered. Which you knew, when I told you and you wrote it all down. Is that why you got weird?"

He winces again. Why is this so uncomfortable for him?

"Yes and no. I've hated keeping stuff from you, Brailey. And I knew once you started to get your memories back, I was going to have to come clean. It's not that I didn't want you to remember, I was just afraid of what the consequences would be once you found out I'd been lying to you."

Reaching my hand over, I snag his and pull it into my lap. His eyes leave the road for a fraction in time to look at me, shock and relief flooding their blue depths.

"So why are you here, Wyatt? What does the FBI want with me? Do they suspect I had something to do with Bryce's death or something?"

"No, nothing like that. After investigating, it turns out Bryce's brake lines were cut. His accident was no accident at all, and attempted murder of a federal agent is serious business. Obviously someone really didn't want you guys looking into Mayra's disappearance, and they were trying to get Bryce out of the picture. I was sent here to look after you and wait to see if your memories came back. Right now, you're our only lead, and it all hinges on you remembering where you put that evidence."

"I actually do remember, I think." Wyatt swerves a little, cursing himself under his breath once he gets the car driving steady again.

"You didn't tell me that part," he says, sounding way more aggravated than I appreciate.

"Well, I didn't know you were digging for information and obviously at the time I felt it wasn't relevant," I snap.

"You're right, I'm sorry. Can you tell me where it is or what you found?" He must sense my hesitancy, because he lets go of my hand and reaches into his back pocket, and pulling out his FBI identification. "I understand you not really trusting me right now. I can also give you the information to contact the bureau if you want to check into my credentials."

I blow out a long breath, realizing that even with all the secrets and lying and hidden identities, I still trust Wyatt. Handing his ID back to him, I explain that I put the SD card in my safety deposit box, but don't remember what was on it. Wyatt looks at the clock on the dashboard and slams his fist down on the steering wheel before pulling out his phone.

"We're going to be delayed. Brailey remembered where the SD card is and it's at a bank. We'll have to stay somewhere overnight and head out first thing after the bank opens. No sir, she doesn't remember what was on it. Yes, sir."

"Hey, how long are we going to be gone?" Keegan chirps as soon as Wyatt ends the call. "I gotta call my work and hope they don't fire my ass for taking an impromptu vacation."

Crap, I hadn't even thought about that.

"I'm not sure how long we'll be gone. Until we figure out who's behind all this, I can't be sure you're safe. We think the reason they didn't come after Brailey again is because she lost her memory, but if they find out she's starting to remember, they might come after her again. And since Brailey refused to go anywhere without you and insisted you come along, then you're stuck with us."

"Wait, you said come after me again," I say as Wyatt pulls into the parking lot of a hotel.

"Yes, we assumed your house burning down wasn't really an accident and the same people targeting Bryce were coming after you."

"It wasn't an accident, you're right."

"You remember that, too?"

"Kinda. I really thought it had to have just been a nightmare or something, but after the way Mark has been acting, I don't know...I'm thinking it really was a memory."

"Tell me after I get us checked in."

Twenty minutes later we're sitting inside a freezing cold, dark hotel room, Keegan on my right with Wyatt perched on the queen size bed across from ours. I relay everything I can remember from that dream, and by the end, Wyatt is so wound up, I'm worried he's going to start throwing punches at the drywall.

"I *knew* that asshole was trouble. Nothing came up when we looked into him, but he *has* to have something to do with this. What the hell was he talking about, saying he's the only reason you were alive? What the actual fuck is going on?"

A knock at the door interrupts Wyatt's rant, and all three of us just stare at it like it might burst open at any second. Finally, Wyatt snaps out of his trance and barks at us to go hide in the bathroom while he checks the door.

"Holy shit, Brailey. It's like we're living out a movie plot right now. How messed up is your life?" She jokes as she drops trou and squats over the toilet.

"Are you seriously going to pee right now?"

"What else are we going to do in here? May as well."

After the toilet finishes flushing we can hear voices talking - two male voices.

"I don't care, Wyatt. You let me see her now. Don't make me hurt you."

"Ha, I'd like to see you try, asshole," Wyatt warns mystery guy number two.

When I hear a loud thud followed by something crashing to the ground, I burst out of the bathroom to find Wyatt rolling around on the ground, losing his hold when the other guy connects his knee with Wyatt's stomach.

His back is to me as he stands, towering over Wyatt who's struggling a little to stand up. Keegan tugs on my sleeve, causing me to bump into the bedside table, and the noise draws both their attention. And that's when I see him. See the face of the man who was insisting on seeing me, and who tried to take down Wyatt just to get to me. It's like staring into the face of a ghost, and his names spills from my lips on a breath.

"Bryce."

Chapter
Sixteen

"Brailey."

Bryce says my name reverently, a mix of relief and awe, but all I feel is nauseous.

"Did you know?" I bite out, putting all my focus on Wyatt's guilty face. He doesn't even have to answer. Another secret. How many more are there?

"Brailey, let me explain," Bryce says reaching out for me, but I jerk back, avoiding his touch.

"I can't. Just...no one touch me," I jerk back again when Wyatt reaches out this time. "I...just give me a minute to process this."

When I back up a little more and the backs of my legs hit the bed, my body automatically sits. Nothing, absolutely *nothing*, makes sense anymore. And the worst part of this situation? I'm literally stuck in this hotel room, because my freaking life is on the line, and who knows what might be waiting outside that door for me.

I can feel myself breaking down. I finally get it - how all those patients I used to take care of must have felt. Hell, who knows? Maybe I'll end up right back at Mayford as a patient again, because I'm on the verge of a mental breakdown that I seriously may never recover from.

"I know this might be a lot to ask, but is there any way you guys could give me some privacy for a little bit?" When neither of them responds, I resort to begging. "Please."

They exchange a look I can't read before walking towards the door. Wyatt turns around just before the door closes, his face so forlorn and vulnerable I have to remind myself I'm angry just so I don't run to him and try to kiss away that worry line that only appears when he furrows his brow.

"We'll be right outside this door. You just yell and we'll be right in, okay?"

Emotion is clogging my throat, but I manage a small nod.

After a couple hours of just sobbing in Keegan's arms, the guys finally come back in. My tears have dried up, but my eyes are swollen and burning. I can't even imagine how awful I look – I am not cute when I cry. I get all splotchy and snotty and it's just not attractive.

Keegan brings me a wet washcloth for my face; the tension in the room growing more awkward by the second.

"I'm sorry, I don't know what's gotten into me. I guess everything just kind of hit me at once. Don't worry I'm all cried out for a while," I say on a laugh. No one even cracks a smile.

"So, uh, I hate to make an already incredibly awkward situation even more awkward, but what's the plan for sleeping arrangements?" Everyone looks at the beds at the same time Keegan asks the question, and she was right – things feel more awkward.

"I can get a second room and stay in there for the night, give you and Bryce a chance to catch up if- "

"No!" I practically throw myself at Wyatt, not liking the idea of him leaving at all. It's not until my face is buried in his chest and his arms are wrapped tightly around me that I feel calm enough to realize just how incredibly insensitive that was to Bryce.

"I-I'm sorry, I didn't," I start to apologize, but Bryce stops me by holding his hand up.

"It's completely fine, Brailey."

"Well, I'm not going to let either of you sleep on the floor since we need you in tip-top shape so you can protect us from the bad guys, and I'm going to assume you aren't going to want to bunk with each other, so Bryce you're with me, Brailey you're with Wyatt."

No one moves for a minute after Keegan gives her orders; not until she claps her hands and yells, "chop chop!"

I silently mouth 'thank you' when Keegan winks at me. The number of my IOUs to Keegan is exponential.

The room stays quiet except for the sounds of us shuffling around each other, taking turns in the bathroom to get changed and ready for bed. By the time I crawl into bed next to Wyatt, my exhaustion goes all the way to my bones.

He's lied to me more times than I can count at this point, and finding out Bryce is alive was definitely a massive one, but we'll have time to talk later. My long cry with Keegan may have blurred my vision with tears, but internally they cleansed me and gave me clarity. This situation isn't easy on anyone, and to focus solely on how it's affecting me and disregard the ramifications to everyone else would be selfish.

Wyatt didn't mean to develop feelings for me as much as I didn't for him. The timing is horrible, but you don't get to choose when you fall for someone. There are aspects of life that are beyond your control, and you can either roll with it or run from it. I'm not a runner.

I snuggle up closer to Wyatt, needing to convey to him without words that everything is okay. *We* are okay. When I nuzzle his chest, he understands and his tentative hold on me tightens.

I may have loved Bryce, but my heart belongs to Wyatt now.

"So what's the plan this morning?" Keegan asks with a mouth full of muffin.

"We need to get to the bank as soon as they open and then head straight back to our headquarters. It's about three hours from here. Once we get there, you two can call your employers and let them know you won't be returning to work for a while."

Keegan's muffin sprays from her mouth to the floor. She's unconcerned with the mess, too busy aiming her wrath at Bryce.

"Hell, no! I have bills to pay and a life to live. It's one thing to ask for a few days off, but I'll lose my job if it's more than that." Bryce shrugs, completely unaware

of the beast he's riling up in Keegan with his nonchalant response. "Hey buddy." Keegan pokes Bryce hard in
the back, seemingly somewhere painful because Bryce
flinches and yells at her for it. "You may not care that I
have bills to pay, but the least you can do is fake it and
not act like a prick."

An argument ensues, and I turn my back to them,
not wanting to get sucked into their early morning bick-
ering.

"Hey Brailey, can I talk to you for a second?"

I hate how unsure Wyatt sounds. It's completely
opposite of the man I met that first day he moved in. It
would be easier to be angry and just put all the blame on
him for my emotional turmoil, but I can see it in his eyes;
he's suffering just like I am. Maybe even worse, since
Bryce is here and he has no idea how I really feel.

"Of course," I assure him quietly. We don't really have a lot of privacy in the cramped hotel room, but
Keegan and Bryce are still arguing so it gives us a few
minutes to talk without voyeurs.

Wyatt awkwardly shoves a long, velvet box at me,
shifting his feet uncomfortably.

Clearly it is a piece of jewelry. No one has ever
given me jewelry before – and yes, I remember that now
– but the box is easily recognizable. Biting back a smile,
I slowly open the box to reveal a simple gold chain, and
on it is a delicate charm.

"It's beautiful," I whisper, fingering the necklace
that holds an antique looking compass and a peach colored jewel.

"I'm about to do something completely out of character for me, so forgive me, but I'm just going to lay it all out there. I'm so sorry for everything I had to keep from you. I hated every second of it. I hated myself for pulling away from you after we had sex, but I never should have let it get that far. Knowing Bryce was alive and there was a chance that after all of this, you would go back to him or hate me for all the secrets…I should have been stronger. A part of me thought it might be the only chance I'd get to be with you…like that…and I don't know, I selfishly wanted the memory."

He cuts me off before I can assure him that I understand.

"I'm not going to ask you to make a choice or to even forgive me right now. Now is not the time and you're still figuring out who you are and what you want. After you're safe, and when you're ready, I want you to know that I'll be here. Even as a friend, though it would kill me, but I'll do it for you. This compass charm…I saw it and thought of you. Of what giving it to you would mean. You've been lost since losing your memory, and I can't even pretend to fathom how hard that must be. This compass symbolizes that you'll never be lost again, Brailey. You are strong and smart and stubborn and capable. You can overcome anything; I truly believe that. What I needed you to know is that if you decide you want me, you have me, and I'll make sure you don't ever have to overcome anything alone."

He shrugs like he didn't just say the sweetest damn thing in the entire world.

Hot tears burn the back of my eyes, and one escapes, slowly sliding down my cheek. "Put it on me?"

His eyes light up just before I turn around and lift up my hair, and his fingers linger a few seconds after he clasps the necklace, sending chills down my spine.

"Thank you for this. You..." I have to take a second to compose myself, not wanting to get too emotional right before we part ways. "You have no idea what this means to me. After I get the SD card from the bank and we're somewhere safe, somewhere we can spend more than five minutes talking privately, then we need to talk about this. Us. Right now, though, I need to ride with Bryce to the bank. Before anything else can happen between us, before I can move forward, I need clarification on some details. Details only Bryce can give me."

Wyatt nods solemnly but doesn't argue, and after placing a kiss to my forehead, he calls out for Keegan. I watch them both leave before turning back to the ghost who just walked back into my life.

"Well, guess it's you and me."

"Brailey, I want you to know that I don't expect anything from you. I know you're still figuring things out, and I know things will probably be very different from how they were before, but I'd like to remain a part of your life."

I feel like a weighted object that's been stuck under the water, until someone finally comes and frees me, letting me rise to the surface at dangerous speeds. Only when I reach the top and try to take my first breath of fresh air, it's not relieving. Instead my lungs feel water-logged, and I can't get rid of the phantom choking that makes me want to cough and spurt up water.

"Why aren't you dead?" I ask once I finally feel like I can speak without throwing up.

"I almost did die. I made it out of the car before it caught fire, and luckily my cell phone was still in my pocket. Instead of dialing 911, I called my boss. I knew something wasn't right, that my brakes had been tampered with. It had to have happened when I was inside the hospital with Shaun, because they were fine before that.

"Anyway, the FBI orchestrated the story of my dying, thinking it would be safer for me if whoever was trying to kill me thought I was dead. I didn't know about you being in the hospital until it was too late for us to get to you. Mayford had already transferred you there for your care, and considering the circumstances of everything, we figured it wasn't safe to go storming in there and yank you out. So instead we sent someone inside to keep an eye on you, make sure nothing happened to you. You have no idea how hard that was for me, not being able to make sure you were safe."

Bryce's hands grip the steering wheel so hard they turn white, his jaw clenched so tightly I wouldn't be surprised if he broke a tooth. Even with only his profile to go off of, I can see the anguish, the truth behind his words.

"He reported back that you lost your memory. The

agency was more concerned with the information you got on Mayra than getting you out of there, and you have to know that everything they did - everything Wyatt did - I had nothing to do with that. I fought them tooth and nail, to the point they had to lock me up for a few days to keep me from coming to you."

"Wait - what? What do you mean what Wyatt did?"

Bryce's eyes go wide, and I realize he's just told me something that apparently I wasn't supposed to know.

"Tell me, Bryce. You want to help me? Then I need the truth. Right now."

"Brailey, I just don't think...this probably isn't the right time. I thought you already knew. This is a lot to take in at once, and I don't want to add-"

"Dammit, Bryce, just fucking tell me!" My hand slams down on the dash hard enough to make my hurt myself, but the seething anger pouring out of me dims the stinging in my palm. "You tell me right now or I'm not giving you that damn SD card. You can get yourself a warrant and deal with all this shit you've gotten me into yourself."

We're parked in front of the bank now, so he's out of time. Reluctantly, he turns to face me, everything about him conveying an apology without words, and it has my gut knotted up tight.

"You weren't remembering fast enough for them. They didn't want to have two men sitting on an assignment that wasn't going anywhere, so they put things in motion."

"Two men?" I ask, but immediately it dawns on me. "Garrett."

"Yeah. He was always around, surveilling from a distance. Trying to catch anyone following you or acting suspiciously, but he wasn't getting anywhere. They needed you to get your memory back."

"Quit stalling," I bite out after a minute of silence.

"Everything that happened to you...that mysterious phone call with the recording of you and Shaun, the fire in your building, the envelope full of pictures and news articles...all of that was planted by Wyatt. In his defense, he was only following orders."

"The break-in? When I was drugged?" I'm practically screeching, but I don't know if that's the reason for Bryce's wince, or if it's just from the anger radiating out of every pore of my skin.

"No, the FBI had nothing to do with either of those things. Most likely whoever broke in to your apartment was looking for that SD card, but we can't be sure yet."

I can't bear to hear any more. This is it. My final breaking point.

I can hear Bryce yelling for me to stop, and though he's only a few feet behind me, he may as well be miles away. I can't hear anything past the blood pounding in my ears. My vision is blurry with unshed tears as I run across the parking lot.

I'm only a few feet away from the bank doors when the tears finally start pouring down my face. Tears flowing at such a rapid pace that my vision is entirely compromised, and I trip on the curb, landing directly on my right elbow before my right hip collides with the hard concrete.

Hands grip my wrists, pulling me up from the

ground, and they pull hard. So hard I yelp out in pain. Those hands shove me into a car, my face slamming into a torn leather seat. My leg is blocking the door, so when it slams shut, it forces my knee to jut upwards and connect with the console of the car. We're moving, and the time to panic has come and gone, so I lay frozen in the backseat, trying to figure out what the hell I do now.

CHAPTER
SEVENTEEN

I'm not sure how I passed out or how long I've been out, but when I come to, my abductor is humming along to the radio like he doesn't have a care in the world.

"Excuse me, um, you mind telling me where you're taking me?" I ask, leaning forward slightly, hoping to get a look at his face. No such luck. He's wearing a hoodie that's covering too much of his face, and apparently I've been out cold for a while, because the sun has already come and gone.

He doesn't respond, but his body shifts and I hear all the locks on the doors clamp down, my natural reaction being to reach for a handle and jiggle it just to make sure. I'm surprisingly pretty clear-headed, given the shitstorm I'm in, so I figure lunging for the door isn't going to do anything but show fear. I can't jump out of a moving vehicle even if it is unlocked, and a stubborn side of me I didn't know I had, keeps me from begging him to let me go.

I mean, if I'm going to die today, I'd rather do it with my dignity still intact. Also, I'm pretty damn sure Bryce caught this jerk's license plate number and probably got a look at his face, so it shouldn't be long before the cavalry finds me. I hope.

Figuring my best bet at staying alive for a while is to behave, I sit back and cross my arms over my chest, doing my best to discreetly watch out the windows for any sign that could tell me where we are or where we're headed.

Twenty minutes later, the driver reaches into the passenger seat and then throws something at me. It flutters down into my lap, and when I pick it up I see it's a piece of fabric. *He wants me to blindfold myself?* Ha. Fat chance. If he wants me blindfolded, he can pull the car over and do it his damn self.

I expect him to get angry or violent when I toss the flimsy fabric right back into the front seat, but he just gives a resigned sigh before throwing it at me again. Like the idiot I am, I lean down to pick it up off the floor, only to come face to face with a gun, the barrel so close it grazes the tip of my nose as I sit back up.

Not wanting to make things any easier on him, I tie the fabric around my eyes with trembling hands while muttering "asshole" under my breath. I'm a bizarre mix of scared out of my mind and pissed off. I want to cry and run away, but at the same time I want to punch this guy in the nuts.

Only a few minutes pass before the car comes to a stop. I know it was a few minutes because I've been counting in my head. All my other senses are heightened, so when the driver's side door opens and slams shut, it feels so loud that I flinch. A second later, someone, I'm assuming the driver, is reaching into the backseat and yanking me out so hard my shoulder almost dislocates. When I make no effort to right myself or walk on my own, he pistol whips me and I feel blood spray out of my mouth. I try to put my hand to my lip and feel how badly it's cut, but he yanks on my arm again, dragging me behind him.

It freaking hurts, and I would be wise to try and stand, but I want to feel what's beneath me. Anything to give me a clue as to where I might be. At first the ground is just loose dirt and rocks, but after a few feet my hands graze tall blades of grass. The angle he's using to drag me contorts my arm in a way that makes me yell out in pain, and suddenly I'm being dragged up what feels like wooden steps. They must be old because I feel splinters digging into my bare torso, my shirt having slipped up while being dragged.

I bite down on my lip hard enough to draw blood, refusing to show him how much pain he's causing me. After what I count to be five steps, he comes to a stop and based on his grunt, opens a fairly heavy door. He's yanking on my arm again, pulling me over a concrete ledge that tears the skin off my already splintered waist, then drags me across a cold, smooth floor. Not tile, because there is no consistent pattern, but based on the pits and grooves I feel beneath my hand, I'd guess it to be an old concrete floor. Maybe an industrial building? A basement of some sort?

Tired of being tugged around like a rag doll, I dig my nails into his arm as hard as I can, and I feel the blood rise to the surface underneath my nails. He lets go and my arm falls limply to my side, my shoulder too strained, rendering my arm completely useless.

Suddenly, I'm being hoisted off the ground and into a chair, my hands yanked around the back of it, then being tied together with something. I consider trying to yank out of his hold or kick my legs, but his movements are too quick for me to react. Despite my lack of resistance, he backhands me hard, and my head snaps to the side. Searing pain travels from my jaw down my neck, and I hear him snickering to himself as his footsteps get further and further away.

Total silence encompasses the room, and it's maddening. My wrists are aching, my back is killing me, and I'm pretty sure my lip is busted, but it's not until I feel like I have to pee that I start yelling. Quick, quiet footsteps approach me, then my blindfold is yanked off.

"Shut up!" A female voice yells at me. *Female?* My eyes are trying to adjust to the lighting, so it takes a second before I can actually see her face.

"Mayra?" I blink hard a few times, wondering if my mind is just playing tricks on me. But sure enough, there is Mayra standing right in front of me. "What are you doing here?" I ask dumbly. A more pertinent question would be to ask her why *I* am here, because she's obviously here due to some kind of involvement in my kidnapping.

"I'm here because *you* ruined everything," she responds in the creepiest, coldest voice I've ever heard. I shudder so hard the movement rocks my chair a little. She takes that to mean I'm trying to escape, resulting in her slapping her hand across my face.

"Dammit, that hurt, My!"

"*Don't* call me that! We aren't friends. Only my friends call me My," she says with a pout. Mayra is so twitchy and spastic that I seriously think she might be on some kind of drug. Really looking at her, I notice she's wearing the standard issue clothing Mayford gives all their patients, only hers are so filthy you can hardly tell what color they are. Dirt and grime are crammed underneath broken fingernails, and her wrists and ankles are covered in bruises.

"What have they done to you Mayra?"

Despite how hard I try to make my voice soothing and sympathetic, Mayra only seems angrier. "Oh, so now suddenly someone gives a shit about me?"

The reality of what's right in front of me hits me so hard I swear my chair rocks a little. "Mayra, have you been down here this whole time? Mayra, Bryce has been looking for you. He came here to find you right after you tried to call him. Mayford told him you'd been transferred, but he didn't believe them. He kept looking-"

"Shut up!" She screams in my face, her eyes empty and hollow. Mayra is just a shell of the person she was before. I don't even know this person. "You're lying. They told me. They told me no one cared and no one even asked about me. They said-"

"Who, Mayra? Who said those things?"

The anger seeps out of her, and I watch her visibly retreat inside herself. On one hand, I guess it's good she's no longer screaming or hitting me, but on the other hand, I can't stand seeing her so broken. No matter how many times I call out to her now, she doesn't answer. I'm fairly certain she doesn't even hear me. Her back is to me, but she's only a few feet away, her knees pulled into her chest as she rocks back and forth on the floor.

From the dark recesses, a tall figure emerges and starts to approach Mayra and I with slow, deliberate steps. The only light in the room is from a low hanging bulb directly above my head, so it's not until he's only a few steps away that I see his face.

"Mark," I seethe.

"Mayra," he says in an oddly sweet tone before turning his attention back to me.

"What am I doing here, Mark? Are you the one who grabbed me at the bank?"

Mark throws his head back and laughs, and my fingers clench behind my back, my arms itching to break free of their restraints so I can claw his eyes out.

"I'm not stupid, Brailey, of course it wasn't me who took you in broad daylight in front of an FBI agent."

"How did you even know where I'd be?"

"Your little agent friends are too busy fighting over you to do their jobs properly. I took advantage of their distraction. It's amazing what you can learn online about how to trail someone without getting caught, among other things."

Of all things, the only thought I have right now is that if Mark's smug face is the last thing I see before I die, then that is seriously one shitty way to go.

"Why," I bite out through gritted teeth.

"I saw you coming out of Director Mayford's office the day you lost your memory. I knew what you were doing; I'd been watching you for a while. I couldn't let you and that agent find out where Mayra was, I had to stop you. I didn't want to hurt you Brailey, but you didn't give me a choice. I came to your house to find out what you did with the information you stole on Mayra, but you attacked me. I thought you were dead when you fell, there was blood everywhere and I panicked. I swear I couldn't find a pulse, and I couldn't risk getting caught. My fingerprints were in your house, probably on your body, so I set the fire. Your neighbors spotted the flames early and the emergency responders were nearby and they were able to get you out in time. When I watched them carry you out with an oxygen mask on your face, I knew I'd screwed up. I had to make it right."

"So why haven't you hurt me yet? Once you knew I didn't remember, why not go ahead and kill me then?"

"I couldn't risk it. They declared your injury and the fire an accident, and if something happened to you under my care then they might start looking into things further. I needed to let you put some distance between yourself and Mayford before anything else happened. You were supposed to keep in touch, Brailey. You were supposed to buy the story of our relationship so that I could keep you close, but you started pulling away and cutting me out. You became a liability I couldn't afford. It certainly complicated things when I figured out who Wyatt was, but it's amazing what you can accomplish when so much is on the line."

"So I assume that means I'm here because you plan to kill me?" My heart is pounding out of my chest, my hands have gone completely numb from the zip ties holding them to the chair, and breathing has become a laborious task, yet somehow I manage to put a little sarcasm in my question.

"If you would have just let it go then I wouldn't have to take such extreme measures," he responds with a mix of anger and resignation.

"What about that information I stole? Don't you need me so you can figure out where it is? Whatever it is you're trying to hide, Mark, they will find it with or without me. There's no way to keep your secrets anymore, especially since you took me while I was under the supervision of federal agents. You're either delusional or naïve if you think you can actually pull this off without getting caught."

When his hand slices across my face, busting my lip open, I'm not the least bit regretful for antagonizing him. If he's going to kill me anyway, then he's not going to get the satisfaction of making me beg for my life.

"Mark," Mayra interjects softly, and he turns his anger on her, though I swear even with the dim lighting, I can see his face soften just a little when he looks at her.

"Go to your room and lock the door. Do *not* come out until I say you can," he orders, and Mayra silently obeys his orders, never once making eye contact with me again before she leaves.

After the door closes behind her, Mark crouches in front of me, so close our noses are almost touching. "You need to watch who you talk to like that," he grinds out. Drops of his spittle land on my face, and I instinctively spit the mouth full of blood I have from my busted lip directly into his eye. This time when he backhands me, he hits me hard enough to send me and the metal chair I'm attached to flying sideways. My left shoulder connects with the ground with a loud crack, breaking my fall just enough to keep my head from taking a blow. I'm certain at least one bone is broken, but at least I'm conscious.

From my vulnerable state, all I can do is watch as

his foot comes swinging forward, connecting with my rib cage. On the third kick I hear another crack, and the fourth knocks the wind out of me. I know at the very least he's bruised a lung when I start coughing up blood. My chances of defending myself, even if I weren't still strapped to a chair, would be pretty much nil at this point.

He's yelling something over and over again, and it sounds like he's blaming me, saying with each kick that it's my fault he's hurting me.

Through my blurry vision, I see Mark being tackled from the side, then I feel tugging at my wrists for a few seconds before the zip ties are pulled away. I still feel like I can't catch a breath, and each inhalation sends agonizing pain shooting through every inch of my body.

"Brailey, you're okay. You're going to be okay." I choke on a sob when I hear his voice. He came for me. I knew he would.

CHAPTER
EIGHTEEN

"Bryce!"

I only meant to help when I called out his name, wanting to warn him that Mark was about to slam a copper pipe against the back of his head, but instead it distracted him. Have you ever heard the sound of a heavy pipe colliding with bone? It's sickening, and yet somehow, Bryce manages to get back up. He's wobbly and doesn't look like he'll be able to stay upright for very long, but he stubbornly makes it all the way back up to his feet.

Wyatt is cradling my head while I continue to cough up blood every time I try to breathe. Yelling for Bryce was a mistake, and it put undue pressure on my already straining lungs.

Bryce stumbles and hits the wall hard, using it to hold himself up. Mark is holding a gun, pointing it directly at Bryce, and from my vantage point, I can see blood dripping down the back of Bryce's head. Though he's holding his hands up in surrender, Mark doesn't look at all like he's going to just let us walk out of here.

After placing my head down gently onto the floor, Wyatt slowly stands while pulling his own gun from its holster on his side. Carefully, he points it at Mark before calling out his name, pulling Mark's attention away from Bryce and onto himself. As soon as the gun isn't pointed at him, Bryce's legs give out and he slides to the floor, leaving a trail of blood on the wall behind him.

"Think about what you're doing, Mark. You're aiming a gun at federal agents. The chances of you getting away with all of this are slim. We already have backup on the way, there's no escaping. If you put the gun down now and surrender, then things will go a lot smoother for you. If you pull that trigger though and end up killing someone? That's a much harsher sentence. Just put the gun down and I'll make sure to let them know you cooperated."

Wyatt has been walking slowly towards the other side of the room while trying to calm Mark down. Mark doesn't seem to notice that Wyatt's just distracting him, and as soon as Mark's back is to us, I make my way over to Bryce. I need to make sure he's alive. I'm slow moving, and I have to practically bite a hole through my lip to keep from screaming out every time I drag my body another inch, but eventually I make it the few feet it takes to get to Bryce.

His breathing is shallow and he's barely conscious, but his eyes are open and he's hanging on by a thread. I want to talk to him, tell him to stay with me, to fight to stay awake, but I don't want to pull Mark's attention again. Me causing a distraction is the reason Bryce is in such terrible shape to begin with.

Careful not to jostle him too much, I manage to get Bryce's button up shirt off of him. Wyatt is struggling to keep all of Mark's attention, which he currently has. Mark is practically screaming at him, and I have to force myself not to worry about Wyatt and focus on

Bryce, who needs me more right now. I have to wedge the sleeve between my thighs so I can tear with my good arm. On the first tug, there's no give and my mouth falls open, a silent scream escaping.

I'm not strong enough to tear the material, especially in my condition. Seeing a loose thread in the seam of the arm hole, I tug at it until it creates a small hole. Putting the other sleeve in my mouth to have something to bite down on so I don't almost scream again, I hook my finger in the hole and pull as hard as I can, ripping the sleeve completely away from the rest of the shirt.

After taking a second to try and catch my breath again, I pull at the thread down the seam of the arm, and once it's completely undone, I continue biting down on the shirt while struggling to sit up. I need to get higher if I'm going to wrap this makeshift tourniquet around Bryce's head.

Trying to do it with one arm is pointless. I have no choice but try and use my injured arm, which is at the very least fractured at the shoulder joint. This time I'm not able to muffle the scream entirely, but Wyatt notices and makes noise to cover me until I've got the material knotted as tightly as possible around Bryce's head.

I finish just in time, because as soon as I fall back, completely exhausted, Mark's attention swings back to us. In reality, the whole ordeal only took maybe five minutes, but I feel like I've just tried to run a marathon after staying awake for three days straight. My body has never felt this fatigued. My heavy eyelids beg for rest, but I know if I close my eyes for even a second, then I'm done for.

Wyatt takes advantage of Mark's distraction and rams into him like a linebacker, sending Mark flying backwards. On his way down, Mark manages to get off a shot, but it goes wild, missing Wyatt entirely. As if in slow motion, I watch Wyatt's finger tightening on the trigger, but Mark gets off another shot, this time hitting Wyatt.

I don't know where he was shot or if he's okay, there's no time to check. Reacting on instinct, I reach around Bryce and feel his gun holster is empty. Dammit. That must be the gun Mark is using. I frantically start grappling at Bryce's jeans, a buried and forgotten memory coming back to me and I yank the gun off the holster he keeps on his ankle. Four, maybe five rounds go off before flames come out of nowhere and engulf the entire room.

Before my head ducks down, I see the wall collapse on top of Mark and Wyatt get thrown backwards from the blow of the explosion. I toss my body over Bryce's to shield him, and after a few seconds, once I feel it's safe, I slowly lift my head and see the flames already dying down. I don't know what caused the explosion, but there's nothing flammable in the room, so the flames appear to be snuffing themselves out.

Aside from being covered in dirt and soot, the only injuries I appear to have sustained from the explosion are a few cuts from the debris. The air in the room is thick with smoke and dirt, burning my eyes and putting more strain on my injured lungs.

When I hear Wyatt call out my name, I start clawing at the ground, using my good arm to drag myself over to him, the sounds of his coughing guiding me through the foggy room.

"I'm so sorry, Wyatt. I'm so sorry." My apologies come out of nowhere the instant I see his face, a hot stream of tears falling down my face. "Where are you hit? Are you okay? Wyatt, talk to me!"

Despite the insane amount of pain he must be in, he still gives me that damn cocky smirk of his, and I've never been happier to see it.

"I'm okay, the bullet went through my shoulder. I'm more worried about you. How did-"

I cut him off with kisses, peppering them all over his face. "I love you, Wyatt," I say suddenly, pulling back to look in his eyes. "I should have said it sooner. I don't know what I would have done if you died today and I never got to tell you, so I'm telling you now. I love you. I love you, okay?"

I keep repeating those three words in between each kiss until I'm practically smothering him, not letting up until he lets out a pained laugh.

"I love you too, Brailey."

Sirens wail in the distance and I send up a silent prayer of thanks that help is on the way. We're going to make it.

"Brailey listen, they're going to have to separate us to get us to a hospital, but there's one more thing I need to come clean about before they do."

"It can wait, Wyatt. Whatever it is, it doesn't matter. All that matters is that we're okay."

He stops me when I move to kiss him again. "Brailey...Shaun is alive."

My head rears back in shock. Surely I heard him wrong.

"As soon as Bryce knew his accident wasn't really an accident, he had Shaun transferred into protective custody where he recovered in a private hospital. They faked his death along with Bryce's to keep him safe."

I turn back to see medics running over to Bryce who lays unconscious on the floor, and watch as they lift him - the man I owe everything to - onto a stretcher. Clinging to life, they carry him out, and all I can think is that he better damn well live, because there is no way he's going to have saved everyone's life but his own.

CHAPTER
NINETEEN

D o you have any idea what it feels like to be trapped inside your own body?
I'll tell you how it feels. It fucking sucks.

I haven't led a perfect life, and I'm not a saint, but how in the hell did I wind up going from being a hero in love to being the guy in a coma who has nothing to show for months of misery other than a big gash in the head as a souvenir. It's not even going to leave a scar that makes me look badass. Instead I'll probably just have a big bald spot that with my luck, won't even be able to be covered up with a hat.

Still, despite the total fucked-upness of the situation, I don't regret a minute of it. Brailey and Shaun don't know it yet, but they're the ones who saved me. When I wake up from this damn coma and finally get the chance, I'm going to make sure they know it.

Truthfully, the minute I heard Brailey lost her memory, I pretty much knew our time was done. Sure, a small part of me held out hope that maybe one day she would remember and we could find a way to get back to where we were, but it was a very small part. The bigger part of me knew she was going to be moving on and making a life for herself, and that even if she remembered, she would have changed. Memories can evoke emotions, but time changes everything.

Preparing for the loss of her didn't lessen the blow any. It didn't prepare me for the punch to the gut I took the minute I saw her in that hotel room. I've never felt like a bigger asshole than when she looked at me with wide eyes, clearly stunned beyond words to find out that I was, in fact, very alive. When she wouldn't let me touch her? That was the final blow that did me in. She wasn't mine anymore. My Brailey was gone.

In that moment I accepted it, resolved to start moving on without her as soon as we got ourselves out of that mess. Turned out what I considered to be 'closure' really wasn't, because later when Wyatt and I were standing guard outside the hotel room and he confessed that he loved Brailey? Let's just say that I deserve some sort of medal or a goddamn peace prize or... *something* for not taking a swing at his face.

Honestly? The only reason I didn't is because he was expecting it, and I really didn't feel like getting my ass kicked over a girl that wasn't mine to fight over anymore. Things certainly didn't get any better when I got stuck with that crazy chick, Keegan, all night. She hogged the bed, stole the covers more than once, and wouldn't quit rubbing her ass all over me. It was like being sandwiched between two different kinds of torture.

Now? Now I get to endure further torture by having to listen while not being able to move, or speak or open my freaking eyes.

Brailey's reunion with Shaun was fucking painful. Especially when he told her that I was the one who made the anonymous donation for his surgery. She was never supposed to know that. Over two months I'd been waiting for that reunion; spending almost every damn day with Shaun while we waited for the time when we'd get to see Brailey again. Even in foster care those two had never been separated, and while Brailey didn't remember for a while, Shaun did. I spent so much time with the kid while Brailey and I were looking for Mayra so we were already close; those extra months only brought us closer. My heart broke a little more hearing them both cry and hug each other, hating that I couldn't see what I'd waited so long to be a part of.

Guess I better get used to it. I don't know how much of a role I'll have in either of their lives now. Even though it sucks to admit, Wyatt is good for Brailey. When she found out that the life insurance money wasn't actually life insurance money, because, well, Shaun isn't really dead, she tried to give it back. Wyatt talked her off that stupid ledge. After everything she went through, she deserves that little payout from the FBI.

To make matters worse, apparently fucking Mark got away and apparently no one has been able to track him. The security cameras outside the bank got a partial plate, but I already know the person who took her wasn't Mark. I got a good look at his face. Too bad I can't talk to a sketch artist – or *anyone*, for that matter. Mayra was missing from the scene, so he either took her with him or killed her and dumped the body. I prefer to assume it was the former, because there is no way in hell I'm letting that girl die after all I've gone through to find her.

Thank God Wyatt had the good sense to put a tracker in that necklace he gave Brailey the morning before she was abducted. Even though I could have lived a thousand lifetimes without needing to know the reason he calls her peaches is because the first time they met she was wearing a peach colored dress and used peach scented shampoo and peaches, peaches, peaches. I'll never eat a damn peach again. Don't care if I sound like a petulant child, no one can hear me anyway.

If it hadn't been for that stupid explosion, we probably would have gotten Mark. By 'we' I mean the FBI, because I was barely conscious at that point. The way Wyatt explained the explosion to Brailey and Keegan was that apparently the furnace room was right next door to us, and Mayford was unaware that they had a gas leak. When Brailey fired off shots, one of them hit a copper pipe inside the wall, which created a spark. The fire died down almost instantly once all the gases burnt up, but the pressure buildup was enough to blow through the sheetrock, sending Wyatt flying back and while the wall came down on Mark, since he was standing right next to it.

He may have escaped, but there's no way in hell he got out of there without being seriously injured.

If listening to the happy couple and a very whiney Keegan wasn't bad enough, my parents just showed up. My mom won't leave me alone. She's a mess, crying over me all the time, and though my dad rarely talks, I can smell the faint tobacco from his pipe so I know he's near.

Worst part so far? Keegan giving me a sponge bath. Yeah I heard her talking the nurse into letting her, going so far as to claim to be my fiancé. Based on the giggling she did when she got to my junk, I'm assuming it was just a ruse to see me naked. Does she have some kind of necrophilia or something? I mean, I've got a pulse but I'm like a living corpse here. Plus, she's a nurse. Nurses shouldn't giggle when they see the male anatomy. Trust me - she has *no* reason to giggle at my anatomy, and when I finally get out of this bed, I'll make sure she pays for that.

Yeah, a lot of crazy shit has gone through my mind for however long I've been out. With no way to keep track of time, I have no clue how long it's been, but I know it's been long enough for Brailey to do some serious healing. She had two fractured ribs, a bruised lung, a broken arm and dislocated shoulder and other various injuries. Oh, and she also missed her period.

So much shit I wish I could un-hear. It's amazing what people will say when they think you can't hear them.

Wyatt resigned. Got to overhear that conversation, too. They wanted to send him out on assignment to try and track Mark, and he was unwilling to leave Brailey while she's recovering. Plus, he's still pretty pissed about all the messed up shit they did to her. Can't say I blame him there, but that means they could have idiots working the case and the longer it takes to find Mark's trail, the colder it gets.

I don't know when I'll wake up or what waits for me when I do, but I know one thing for sure...

Mark better be ready for me.

ACKNOWLEDGEMENTS

This is by far the most important part of publishing, and the part I seriously hate the most. It is impossible for me to not leave someone out or forget something important when I write these. I can already see myself offering profuse apologies to someone vital in my life because I was too forgetful to remember and acknowledge their importance.

These will be in no particular order - but I'm going to start with my group of crazies because I know they will be the ones to ream me a new one if I put them too far down.

Michelle Haines Thank you for fangirling me. If you hadn't, we might not be friends, and if we hadn't met, my life would be missing something. You have put up with so much from me in the short amount of time we've known each other, and though you're all the way across the country and we've never met, I feel like I've known you forever. I already owe you so much - for being there for me personally, dealing with my insecurities and crazy tangents, supporting my career and letting me bounce millions of different ideas off of you. Someday I swear, I'll find a way to repay you.

The Crazy Train You guys were an unexpected addition to my life and you have already made this journey a hundred times more enjoyable. When I got added to your little group, I had no idea that I was about to find amazing new best friends.

Jo Lopez I knew from the first message I got from you that you and I would be great friends. It was insta-love. You have become an integral part of my life and my author career. Your loyalty and dedication to helping the authors you love is just one of the awesome things about you. P.S. - I promise to let you out of the basement soon. Maybe.

Jessica Davey You always manage to make me smile. I could be having a horrible day, but your off-topic rants and emphatic messages always cheer me up. Your support and feedback have been vital in the making of Farewell. Not to mention the penis-shaped gummies that I've yet to taste. Just feels wrong to bite into them….

Kerry Louiseh I only exist as a part of the crazy train because of you. You and your friends adopted me and put up with my lurking and erratic behavior. And let it always be known that YOU impacted Farewell in a HUGE way. If you hadn't hated on the book, I wouldn't have made the changes that I believe made it a helluva lot better. You also get credit for the new gray hairs that popped up during that time of last minute editing.

Alice Ballinger I wish I could bottle up my emotions from when I read your messages after you read Farewell. Your reaction ruined me for any other reviewers. It was so over the top and emotionally batshit

- AKA exactly what I wanted to hear. I'm not a hugger, but I wanted to hug you so bad. Is that weird? It sounded weird... oh well. Nothing I say will be any weirder than your obsession with sloths.

Brandi Zelenka Ah, Brandi. I miss you. As I write this, you've been fairly absent from my world and I don't like that. I often recall upon our conversations and creepily call upon memories of you. Thank you for reading and re-reading and re-reading Farewell and not cussing me out for the constant changes.

Stephanie Mugnano Thank you for riding my ass about the details where it comes to injuries and all those other aspects I would have had no clue about. You made me nuts, forcing me to do research and tweak things so they would be correct, and it's exactly what I needed.

Renae Ayers I owe you an extra amount of gratitude for not calling the police or CPS on me when I started asking you questions like: Where would a bullet have to hit someone to cause a lot of blood loss but not kill them? If someone was going to try and kill someone in the hospital using a drug, but the dosage was too small and it didn't kill them, what would they use? And where would they get it? And so on...

Beta Readers Lindsay Johnston, Valerie Roeseler and Amanda Gillespie:
I don't have an editor, and this book is the first time

I've used BETA readers. I, personally, can tell a HUGE difference. Especially since I'm my own worst enemy when it comes to keeping track of my own damn story. If it hadn't been for all of you putting up with my typos and mismatching information and constant changes (yeah - they all had to read several drafts because I kept changing stuff) then I know this book wouldn't be half as good. You all ROCK.

Samanthe **Beck** I'm sure you never thought responding to that first tweet would land you in the role of unofficial mentor to a newbie author, but I stuck you in that role anyway. I blame it on your genuinely sweet and caring personality. If you would just be rude to me, I'd go away, but I don't think you have it in you. Your advice, encouragement, and friendship in general are so special to me. I hope you know I don't take for granted that you take the time to befriend some random fangirl, and I will forever be grateful for all you've done.

Bloggers Where would indie authors be without the bloggers? Thank you for taking a chance on my books and then taking the time to promote them. Every single time I receive a good review, it feels like the first time. The kindness and generosity that comes out of our little community never ceases to amaze me. Specifically: Bloggers From Down Under, LucyLicious Reads, Amanda's Book Nook for Adults, Nerdy Dirty & Flirty, and sooo many more.

Stacey Davies at Ab Fab Book Blog and S.A.S.S. - I've already told you several times, but I don't think

I can say it enough. You deserve SO much more credit than I can even give you. The insight and advice I gained from you and S.A.S.S. is invaluable. I literally knew NOTHING about the underground community that is for indie authors.

To the authors who inspire me and don't report me or block me for stalking them:

Meghan Quinn You are so sweet, so funny, and so pretty. It's really not fair, but instead of being bitter about all the gifts you have, I'm just thankful for your kindness, generosity and all the amazing books you continue to write.

Tara Sivec Your dramatics make life worth living. You're so damn witty it doesn't seem natural, and your personality is so energetic it's contagious. I hadn't read enough of your books to truly appreciate you the first time we met, but that didn't keep it from being memorable. Can I come live with you? Because I can't imagine there being a dull moment in your presence.

Brooke Blaine I've been stalking you from afar for a while and just now came out of the woodwork. It might seem sudden to you, but it's been a longstanding friendship in my eyes. But I know how easily you get creeped out, so I'll dial it back a little. Thank you for writing shit-your-pants funny books and for teaching me Basic White Girl lingo. I always learn something new with you.

Mom Thank you for always believing in me and supporting my writing, even if you don't particularly care for the content. It just shows that you truly have unconditional love, and I have never had to worry about disappointing or letting you down.

Monica Buettner AKA my future sister-in-law - thank you for helping me brainstorm, for helping watch the kids and for putting up with my disappearances when I was writing. You have been a huge help with all my storylines.

Last but not least, my husband I can't even put into words just how vital my husband is to my publishing. Not only does he offer unwavering support, but he helps with all the technical aspects of self-publishing. This time around especially, he's put up with melt downs and mood swings and panic attacks because of my complicated storyline. He spent hours looking for software, reading articles and helping me come up with the best way for me to brainstorm productively. At this point, he's done pretty much everything but write the actual book. So he is the one and only reason I actually get to write.

To anyone I may have missed, I'm so sorry - make sure and scream at me so I won't forget next time.

Xoxo